SIOBHAN'S
SECRET

A CELTIC FANTASY

NIKKI BROADWELL

AIRMID PUBLISHING
TUCSON, ARIZONA

Siobhan's Secret

This is a work of fiction. All names, places, characters, and events presented here are products of the author's imagination.

Formatting by: Polgarus Studio
Cover design by: Daniela Colleo—www.stunningbookcovers.com

"The Goddess does not rule the world; She is the world."
-Starhawk-

PROLOGUE

The raven's wings were the black of night, his eyes bright with knowing. He watched everything from his perch high up in the tree. The sun curved slowly across the sky and disappeared, leaving streaks of orange and rose, and still he didn't move. And when the moon rose his dark shape stood out against the cool light, his bill clacking as he rubbed it along the branch. Under the tree that marked the intersection between this realm and that, the goddesses paraded, filmy dresses flowing around their shapely legs, their voices lifting in the sacred song of Otherworld. The night air thickened around them, the song drifting into the breeze and carried far and wide and into a separate domain that held secrets that would soon be revealed. The raven observed and planned, his thoughts hazy but sure. Ravens were the link between the worlds, and his future was as clear as the night air gathering around him.

Kat's fingers tightened on the door handle, her stomach churning as she pulled it closed behind her. Inside that house her life lay like shards of broken glass, a scatter of bright fragments that could never be put back together. Glancing upward she saw her stepfather peering down at her from the second story bedroom window, his rough features dark with anger. They had argued, and for the first time Kat had said her piece. "My mother didn't die by natural means!" she'd shrieked, watching his skin turn a mottled magenta. "And I'm going to prove it."

"Just try it, little girl," he'd replied, his eyes narrowing.

He hadn't even denied it, only threatening her with his stance and tone. He would use whatever it took to grind her down and disprove what she knew to be true.

Darkness was spreading across the city, the idea of a meal or a place to lay her head fading with the light. She stumbled down a street of row houses, watching lights clicking on, the sound of laughter reaching her ears. Her head ached, her legs weak from traversing the city streets— in search of what? She had no place to go.

The splash of water, ever widening circles as leaves pulled away in the gentle breeze to land delicately, bright spots of color on an otherwise dark expanse. The girl wore only a pale shift, her thick brown hair loosely piled on her head and secured with a stick. Her skin was as pale as the tunic she wore, small breasts visible beneath the now transparent fabric. She bent to cup water into her hands, using it to wash her face before moving deeper into the pond until she could no longer touch the sandy bottom. And there she floated, her eyes closed, her body suspended as though held by invisible hands.

The woodland behind the pond was alive with summer sounds— the chatter of birds, the chirp of frogs and crickets, the snuffle of skunks and other small creatures rooting on the forest floor. Turquoise dragonflies flitted across the still water, their iridescent wings catching the light. Symbolizing change, self-realization and the deeper meaning of life, the whir of their wings was another source of solace, the girl's eyes opening for a moment to watch them.

The day lengthened and stretched, the sun hovering in a cerulean sky. No clouds marred the slow trajectory, shadows growing longer as the bright orb moved steadily toward the west. The girl roused herself, wondering how long she'd been here. Some memory or thought touched her mind, as though she'd forgotten something important. The water rippled as she shifted her body, allowing the place and the water to cradle her once again. The forest felt her contented sigh, the animals perking up to listen. But a moment later a terrible screeching filled the air, the woodland, the pond and the flight of dragonflies disappearing.

Kat woke in a doorway, her body stiff with cold. The dream had taken her away from the grim reality of her current life, giving her a much needed respite, but waking to it again felt worse than ever, her face still swollen from crying the day before. Cars honked, sirens screeched, the

3

cacophony of people, traffic, and the progression of life moving by too fast for her to take in. She put her hands over her eyes and gave in to the desperation, tears tracking down her already chapped cheeks. She had nothing with her but a satchel and a small bag of clothes, her connection to everything she loved held hostage by Jack.

The sidewalk was clogged with people, Kat's progress interrupted as she tried to avoid being mowed down. Every so often she let out a heavy sniff, attempting to stop the flow of tears. She felt invisible as men and women skirted around her. Where was she going? She had no idea where her feet had taken her until she noticed the line of people in front of the soup kitchen and the sign hanging over the door next to it that read, 'women's shelter'. Before she could question her decision she had swung the heavy glass door open and entered the dark space filled with cots.

"Of course dear, I understand," the middle-aged gray-haired matron said sympathetically. "You need a place to lay your head for a moment until you can move forward again." Her watery eyes scanned across Kat's dress and overnight bag, "Do you have a job?"

Kat shook her head. Yes. She'd *had* a job, but since her mother's death she'd been unable to focus on much of anything. "I'm looking," she muttered, knowing that the woman saw through the lie.

The woman straightened as another bedraggled soul entered the room. "Your bed is right over there," she told Kat, pointing into the shadows. "We've been besieged lately; it's lucky you came when you did. There's a church right across the street and the soup kitchen is next door.

Say your prayers and you'll be out of here before you know it." She gave Kat a little push, turning to greet the hollow-eyed woman who had now reached the desk. Kat headed toward the shadowy space where the empty cot waited, a sense of impending doom lodged in the middle of her belly.

How in the world had she ended up here with all these down and out women? Not so long ago she'd been happy, had a job to go to and hopes for a bright future. Now she was lost in a sea that churned and took her under, her brain filled with flotsam. She placed her things under the bed and tried not to feel the lethargy that permeated the room. There were a few screens placed here and there that broke up the space and added the illusion of privacy, but there was nothing by her cot, only the dismal gray painted wall that led upward to an equally dismal filthy window too high to see out.

This building had been some sort of warehouse before it was turned into the shelter, and the cobwebs still remained. But when she glanced around at the other residents the self-pity turned into compassion; many looked way worse off than she did. She lay flat on the bed and closed her eyes, trying to block out the whimpering, the coughing and sneezing and the smell of musty clothes and stale cigarette smoke.

2

irmid's eyes welled as she turned away from the balcony that hung over the world. Her brown hair was filled with bits of twig and hung in tangles around her sharp-boned face, her hazel eyes troubled. She was the earth goddess, the one who healed the sick and brought the dead back to life in her special spring. She lived in Otherworld in the woods with the animals and birds, collecting herbs for her potions. In the day she wandered the narrow animal trails and watched spiders spinning their webs, examined the drops of dew on the jack-in-the-pulpits and studied the mosses that clung to rocks. At night she made her fire and slept out under the stars, eating the nuts and berries she'd collected. If it hadn't been for the summons she'd be there still, not here staring down on a world gone dark and dreary.

The moon goddess, Arianrhod, joined her, her green eyes wide with distress. Pale hair hung down her back in a loose plait, her jade velvet gown in sharp contrast to the simple belted tunic Airmid wore. Her gaze was fixated on the brown cloud of pollution, the empty swaths where there should have been waterways and grassland and thousands upon thousands of trees. No animals traversed the empty landscape; nothing remained but dust and rock.

Arianrhod had travelled here from her turreted castle of ice close to the shore of Caer Sidi where she had an atrium filled with birds, trees covered with fruit of every description, as well as roses and lavender flowers, their scents lifting into the moisture laden air. In Otherworld she reigned over the northern climes and wove time and fate on her silver wheel. At night she became an owl, gliding across the dark skies. Fertility and rebirth were her special talents. But like Airmid, she'd been drawn away from her life, summoned here with her sister goddesses, for what she didn't know. She finally collected herself, swallowing down her sadness and despair. "We have been called upon to take pity on these beings who beseech us for help. But how can we possibly help them? Earth is already destroyed."

A wispy ethereal shape joined them from the wide archway leading into the castle, a feathery dress clinging to her willowy frame. "I have prophesized this for a century now, have even visited and whispered in their ears. But money has taken over any sense they once had." Corra was the goddess of prophecy, her realm the whole of Otherworld. She was the crane goddess, shape shifting to fly far on wide wings. At this moment her hair held the red crown of the crane, her eyes still changing from the orange of the bird to her normal amber.

Airmid gazed at her helplessly. "Money? Money means nothing—don't they know that by now? What can we do? If they call we must answer—isn't that the rule?"

Arianrhod turned away to avoid seeing the devastation

that lay below. "They had everything they needed," she murmured, her eyes welling.

"Are we expected to save a species that has hastened its own demise?" Corra asked, suddenly angry. "Why do they not learn?"

Airmid shook her head, sending bits of leaf and twig flying. "I cannot fathom how we can help. I prefer my forests and my creatures to this marble monstrosity in which we are housed," she added, turning to gaze on the turreted castle behind them. The interior was filled with birds of every color and size, their calls like wind chimes moving in a breeze. The ceiling disappeared into mist, the domed roof gold on the outside and dazzling pale blue glass on the inside. A garden filled with flowers and trees surrounded the enormous structure, vanishing into the distance. The sky domed above it all, billowy, sun-tinged clouds surrounding the island where the magnificent palace floated.

The moon goddess grimaced, winding her long pale braid around her hand. "And I my castle of ice. But here we are."

"Are you sure this isn't some cruel trick perpetrated by an imp or a fairy?" the crane goddess asked. "Humans have been working hard to destroy themselves for centuries. If we paid attention to every sad plea that reached our ears we'd have no time for our own noble pursuits."

Arianrhod glared at her. "Their world intersects with ours, Corra. The destruction they have wrought will soon affect Otherworld. I weave time and fate, braiding it all together to make manifest what is not. As the goddess of the moon I see into the human soul. And what I see there breaks my heart. I am perfectly willing to use my skills to recover what has been lost."

Corra shrugged her narrow shoulders, and shook out her feathery gray dress. "I have seen the future, and it does not bode well for this particular world. I say we let it die out." When she leaned over the edge of the balustrade two gray feathers came loose from her dress and drifted downward, floating on the breeze.

"What are you three hatching up now?" a commanding voice asked. An equally commanding woman appeared in the doorway into the castle. The edifice loomed behind her, golden spires and silvery luminescence rising up to blot out the sky. Inside the castle, shafts of golden light filtered downward from the skylights to puddle on the marble floors.

Morrighan was the goddess of war, and her stance and the fire in her eyes was testament to her strength. Her hair was the color of raven feathers, lustrous in the bright sunlight as the orb slipped ever so slowly toward the west. One second her eyes looked dark as the darkest night and in the next they seemed to glow. Her skin was as pale as milk, and her inky gown hung in lacy folds that barely covered her ample breasts. "Well? Is no one to answer me?"

Arianrhod frowned, marring the porcelain smoothness of her forehead, green eyes flashing. "It is nothing *you* would be interested in."

"Now, I shall ask again," Morrighan said, her haughty gaze going from one goddess to the other. "I received a summons from our beloved Dagda, who does not call without good reason."

"Dagda ordered this?" Airmid asked. "Why would he be interested in this one young woman down there?"

As she pointed, the distant scene seemed to rise up, either that or the goddesses dwelling place amongst the clouds lowered, because soon what lay below loomed larger and larger, as though a camera lens had zoomed in to bring it all into focus. Now the view was of streets filled with potholes, and cars and houses, the unspoiled beauty of the past replaced with garbage cans and scattered trash, the homeless huddled in rags, and the screech of car horns and the babble of people.

A young woman stood on a sidewalk, her gaze raised, her hands in prayer position. People skirted around her with frowns of annoyance, one man even going so far as to shove her aside when she got in his way. His voice echoed, the words rising to where the goddesses watched. "What the hell is wrong with you?" he yelled.

The young woman either didn't hear him or chose to ignore his angry tone. It was a cold day and she was dressed for summer, a filmy yellow dress clinging to her thin frame. Her eyes were large in her triangular face, the look in them beseeching. "Please," she whispered. "Please help me." When two gray feathers drifted down, she bent to pick them up, a hopeful expression replacing the one of despair. She gazed at the soft feathers in her hands before lifting her eyes to the heavens once more.

Morrighan made a derisive sound. "She thinks we're angels. And we are far from it."

"We are not that dissimilar."

Morrighan turned her dark stare on the healing goddess. "We could not be more unalike, Airmid. For one thing angels have wings, and for another they are associated with the religious nonsense humans have conjured up to explain everything from deja-vu to what they refer to as miracles. And now that poor woman down there is holding two feathers and thinking goddess knows what about where they came from. Really, Corra—couldn't you have been a tiny bit more careful? That dress is *shedding*."

Corra backed away from the railing, her bird eyes fastening on the goddess of war. "When you are in the shape of the raven, you shed as well."

Morrighan laughed, running her fingers through her glossy hair. "But mine are black. No human would bother picking *them* up." A moment later a dark bird could be seen circling the castle. "One of my friends is here now," she murmured, looking up.

"If you are so anxious to leave, why not fly away and leave us in peace?" Corra asked, her harried movements sending feathers flying in all directions. "And why you're at it, ask the Dagda what is so special about this girl."

"I think I shall—there is nothing better than a flight through the clouds." Morrighan gave a laugh just before she shifted to raven, her beady bird eyes just as haughty as her human ones. Her wings extended as though testing for a second, before she lifted off. She joined the other bird, their dark shapes gliding upward on the thermals before tumbling downward together and swiftly flying out of sight.

"Oh, I find her so annoying," Corra hissed. "I'm sure that was Dagda in his raven shape. I hope she finds out why he's given us this assignment. Since when is he interested in the human realm?"

Arianrhod made a dismissive gesture. "The reason does

not matter. What matters is that we focus on our charge and stop arguing about the details. As far as Morrighan's sexual nonsense, that's her business.'"

"But her entire reason for being is alien to what the rest of us believe," Corra continued.

"She represents death," Airmid added.

"No, Airmid, that is not true," Arianrhod said. "She may be the goddess of war but she does not court death, nor does she symbolize it. She is one of us, and we must see all sides of her. She is a necessary part of who we are."

A clatter of hooves announced the arrival of Rhiannon, the horse goddess, her white mare coming to a halt at the doorway. Birds fluttered around her tangled mass of red hair, intelligent emerald eyes peering at the other goddesses as she slid off the horse's back. Her name meant white witch or great queen, her magic lay in the healing birds that flew around her that could put people to sleep or bring the dead back to life. A gown of crimson flowed around her legs as she marched to where the other goddesses stood by the railing. "Is that our charge?" she asked, leaning over to peer downward.

Airmid nodded.

"I would have been here sooner but I had an errand to run first."

"Let me guess. Pwyll?"

Rhiannon turned to face the moon goddess. "Are you jealous of my consort?" she asked sweetly.

Arianrhod smiled for the first time. Rhiannon was a favorite of hers. "Not all all. How are he and your son, Pryderi?"

"It is Pryderi who has troubled us of late. If I had known

how hard being a mother would be I might not have succumbed to Pwyll's charms."

"Likely story," Corra said, smoothing her dress with tapered fingers.

Rhiannon laughed. "Yes, he is a mighty lover, my mortal prince. I will mourn him when he is gone."

"Now that we are all assembled," the moon goddess said, turning back to look down, "what shall we do about this poor underdressed woman who the mighty, all father, *Dagda*, has placed in our care?"

Kat was dreaming again, but when the screech of
sirens broke through she awakened. She was
not in a sylvan glade floating in a pond; she was
lying on an uncomfortable cot, a threadbare blanket barely
covering her. The dream was a recurring one and she
wished more than anything that it would simply come true.
A heavy feeling settled into her. This was her real life. But
as soon as she rose to dress the past burst into her mind,
hurtling her back to her mom's death.

Her mother had been perfectly fine the day Kat set out on
a weeklong trip for work. "Have a wonderful trip, sweetie,"
were the last words her mother said to her, the hug afterward
one that she would hang onto forever. Kat's eyes filled with
tears, her thoughts clouded and full of despair. There was no
way her mother could have sickened and died that quickly. No
autopsy had been performed. And since Jack refused to
discuss it, she had no idea what had been listed as cause of
death. Without the support of her mom she felt untethered;
she had no idea what to do or where to go.

Outside the shelter Kat glanced up from the shadowy darkness cast by the row of high-rises, her gaze caught by the cumulus clouds limned with golden light. When she squinted she could imagine a castle within them, beautiful goddesses dressed in pale gossamer gowns wandering barefoot through the hallowed halls. In her hands she held two soft grey feathers that had fallen right at her feet. When they drifted down she'd been asking for help; actually the more apt word was *begging*. She'd been begging for help. She would have been on her knees except she knew someone in a hurry would have trampled her. What did it mean that the feathers appeared at that exact moment? They were small, not from a pigeon, more like the undercoat of some exotic bird. Had an angel sent her a message? But if they were feathers from angel wings wouldn't they be white and larger? She shook the thought from her head. She didn't believe in angels—didn't believe in much of anything right now. As always when her mood turned dark she thought of her mother who had always managed to bring her out of herself. But her mother was gone.

The church across the street caught her eye, the stone façade dark and forbidding. Going to a church to make a plea to something greater was out of the question—she didn't believe in organized religion, the thought of her mother's recent funeral reminding her of why. She hadn't been there for it; Jack had arranged it all before she got back from her trip. But she knew for certain that her mom would have hated being stuck in an airtight box and buried in the ground. Siobhan loved the light, had always professed a desire to be cremated, her ashes to be scattered in the forest or the ocean.

The death was hard to swallow, especially her stepfather's version of events. "Your mother was ill for a long time, Katel. I know you think her death was sudden, but it wasn't at all." Not even two months had gone by and already Jack had put the house on the market and had another woman on his arm.

Her mind twisted with pain, sending her back in time to relive the gurgle of the coffeemaker, the thump as Siobhan chopped up vegetables on the butcher block, her sweet voice lifted in song. For just a second Kat completely forgot where she lived now. And then she remembered—it was at a shelter for those who had no place to go. She was homeless.

She wrapped her arms around her shivering body, realizing suddenly that she had left the shelter wearing a thin cotton sundress. People hustled by her wearing coats and heavy sweaters, hats on their heads. It was as though her dream of summer had permeated into this reality—in other words she was losing her mind. And then she remembered that the last time she'd worn this dress was the last time she'd spent any quality time with her mom. *Before Jack.*

When Kat re-entered the shelter the first thing she did was pull a pair of heavy pants and a sweater out of her suitcase she had stashed under her cot. Her worn boots were in there too, not new and stylish, but at least they would keep her feet warm. After that she borrowed the phone to call the police and report her suspicions about her mom's death. The person she spoke with at the local station was dismissive and curt, taking down her information, but telling her that making an accusation of this nature without proof was tantamount to libel. "Hire a lawyer," was the woman's final say on the issue. Kat hung up feeling worse than she already did. She was homeless and penniless, with no way of proving what she knew to be true.

Her suitcase held everything she owned, including a sterling silver Celtic knot pendant her mother had given her. "It belonged to your father," Siobhan had told her. "He gave it to me in place of a ring, I suppose," she'd added, laughing. "He told me it held the magic of the old ways."

"He wasn't the kind to settle down," her mom had explained when Kat questioned her further. "I hate to admit it, Kat, but I didn't even know his last name! He came into my life when I needed him, stayed for a year, and then left. But he made sure I had everything I needed to provide for you, and stuck around long enough to see his daughter born. I loved him, and I know he loved me. I always hoped he'd show up again, but he never has."

"Was he the love of your life?" Kat had asked, wishing her father was there instead of the dreaded Jack.

Her mother had stared into the distance, her eyes going misty. "Yes, I suppose he was."

His name was Dag. He must have been of Norwegian descent or from one of the Scandinavian countries. Her mom had described him as a big strapping hunk of a man with dark curly hair and eyes like cut sapphires. The fanciful description always made Kat smile. Her eyes were her mother's color, kind of hazel with gold flecks, but her mother's hair was reddish gold and hers was much darker. Her mother had given Kat her own name of Davies since Dag had never revealed his.

Kat pulled the leather cord over her head, her fingers wrapping around it. "If what Mom said about the magic of the old ways is true, please help me find it." But when the silver responded, vibrating in her hand, she let go, afraid for an instant. *It's just an old piece of jewelry*, she told herself nervously.

A new woman had arrived since this morning, her violet eyes trained on Kat. White hair hung down her back in undulating waves, a simple belted brown wool dress covering her from neck to mid calf. Black tights and high leather boots completed her simple outfit. There was an unusual brightness in her eyes that belied her age. When their gaze met the woman smiled and then turned away to pull a book out of her cloth bag. She opened it and began to read.

Most of the women at the shelter were far older than Kat, and looked like life had just knocked them down. Evidence of alcohol abuse and drug use was evidenced in the sunken eyes, unhealthy skin, and bad teeth; the stink of cigarette smoke clung to hair and clothes. There were also a few mothers with young children who were thin and exhausted, most of them sick. Compared with the others, Kat had no excuse for being here, other than her brain seemed unable to focus; if she were unable to follow through, there was no point in trying to get a job.

The one book Kat owned lay open in her lap, the goddess Cerridwen staring up from the page. '*The crone of wisdom and the underworld*', she read, '*the goddess of inspiration, rebirth, transformation and prophecy*'. Being reborn sounded good and so did transformation. When she leaned closer she had the strangest sensation that the woman peering up from the book could see her. She quickly closed it and stowed it under her bed.

When she glanced up again the old woman was watching her with an expression that seemed more than idle curiosity. Her hair was now braided and hung over one shoulder. When Kat tried a tentative smile, she smiled back.

It was sometime later that a drunken man burst into the shelter, his glazed eyes fixed on nothing. Kat stood to shoo him out, but instead he pushed against her, mumbling some nonsense that she couldn't understand.

"Please stop!" Kat shouted, attempting to keep him from moving further inside the room. Bedlam ensued behind her, the gasp and shriek of children and scared mothers loud in her ears.

Several women rushed over to help, one of them the older one two beds over. Her violet eyes lit on Kat before pinning the man with her gaze. "Stop," she said in a perfectly normal voice.

The man dropped his arms to his side, looking bewildered. "Where am I?"

"You are in the women's shelter," she told him, taking hold of his upper arm. "You need to find your way back to where you live."

"I don't live anywhere," he muttered, slurring.

"Well then, let's ask these nice ladies where the men's shelter is." She turned to the two women who stood wide-eyed, watching.

"It's just down the end of the block," the older one

answered. "You can't miss it."

"What's your name?" she asked him as they left the shelter arm in arm.

"Tom," he muttered. "Don't rightly know what I'm doin' these days."

"Well, Tom, I'll walk you down the street. Perhaps not drinking for a few days might help?" Their voices faded as she led him, stumbling, away.

"Are you all right, dear?" a brown-haired woman with kind eyes asked Kat worriedly.

"I'm fine. He didn't hurt me, just seemed confused more than anything."

She nodded. "They see the sign that reads shelter and forget to read the rest of it. So many homeless now," she muttered.

Kat glanced out the door at the people walking by staring at their cell phones. It was a miracle they didn't all run into each other. When she looked at the bed where the woman had left her book face down, she noticed the title. *What you need to know about the twenty-first century.* The chapter title was: *Electronic devices and their uses.* She didn't know about electronic devices? Everyone knew about that, even five-year-old kids. Maybe she was one of those old people who had let time pass by without embracing the new technologies.

When the woman returned she stopped by Kat's cot. "He was harmless, you know."

"I did feel that, but he scared me anyway."

"Of course he did—he was out of his mind and a big man. He's settling in nicely at the other shelter. I'm just glad he was willing to stay there—so many are not."

"They don't want a bed and a meal?"

She shook her head, her violet eyes narrowing. "Many are simply not of this world anymore. The idea of being confined is terrifying to them. And why are you here?"

Kat started, her cheeks suddenly hot. "I...I..."

"If you'd rather not say, that's fine. The reason I'm here is because I am no longer considered hireable." She chuckled. "I look ancient to you, I'm sure, but I have a lot to offer—there are benefits to being around for so long. Unfortunately this time and culture do not value the wisdom of the aged. Older women are not revered here like they are in so many other cultures; we might not have the physical stamina of a twenty-year-old, but our inner energy is much more pronounced—do you understand?"

Kat shook her head. Energy to her was what she either had or didn't have in order to get her through the day. And the lack of it was why she was living here and not trying to find a job. She suddenly felt very tired.

"My name is Cerridwen, like the Welsh goddess of the underworld. Do you know of her?"

Kat began to shake her head no until she remembered Cerridwen in her book. "It's a pretty name," Kat offered. "Do you have a nickname?"

Cerridwen laughed. "If you'd like you may call me Gwen."

Gwen's eyes were deep set, the violet color shifting and changing. Kat fell into them, thoughts disappearing as she floated on a calm sea. It was only when Gwen spoke again that she resurfaced, the reality of where she was like a punch in the stomach. "What did you say?" she asked.

"You may call on me whenever you want."

"Call on you…how can you help me? I'm stuck here until I can find a way out."

"You are not stuck anywhere, Kat. It is only your mind that tells you so."

Kat didn't answer, turning away to stare out the door at the clouds racing across the sky. The weather perfectly matched her mood, the uncertainty of what was coming just like the anxiety she felt every day regarding her future. She wanted her life back, but without her mom in it, life didn't seem very appealing. She glanced at the older woman who had just called her by name. She had no memory of introducing herself.

Birds sang, the distinct green smell of things growing permeating the mist laden air. Insects buzzed by her ears, tiny wings whirring. The aroma of lavender wafted by on the breeze, the flowers alive with bees collecting nectar. Instead of floating on her back in the pond, Kat was sitting on a mossy bank watching bluebottle dragonflies skimming the opaque green water. She felt lazy, soporific, the sun warming her shoulders through her thin dress. Her bare toes curling into mud, the feel of it pleasant. What a beautiful day it was.

"Yes, it is a lovely day."

Her head whipped around to see Gwen behind her, the old woman dressed in a similar gauzy garment, a long braid of white hair hanging down her back. Her wrinkled face was rosy; smile lines fanned out around her deep-set eyes. "How did you get here?" Kat asked.

She laughed, a warbling trill that sounded like one of the birds calling in the trees behind the pond. "You mean in your dream?"

"Well, yes, I guess that is what I mean."

"It is not only your dream, Kat. Others are here as well."

"But…I've never seen anyone."

"Until now. There are many here who you are meant to meet."

Kat frowned, gazing at the forest of trees and the wildflowers waving in the meadow. "I don't want other people here. This is my happy place."

"Anyone you come upon here will be a friend. Am I not welcome?"

Kat stared at the old woman. Was she unhappy with her presence? Actually her being here seemed right somehow. "No, I mean...yes. Now that you're here it seems like you've always been here."

Gwen smiled. "I have always been here, I just haven't shown myself. You weren't quite ready for me."

"This is a dream, right? I always wake up. But it seems different this time."

The old woman nodded. "You have crossed the threshold."

"Threshold—what does that mean?"

"Into Otherworld. Into the magic."

Kat was just about to ask another question when she heard the screech of tires followed by the sound of glass splintering. The dream faded bit by bit until there was nothing left.

Kat woke from her nap feeling drugged. Sirens split the air, the sound growing closer by the second. The view outside the shelter revealed a car half way into the sidewalk and wrapped around a parking meter, steam rising from the hood. A man and a woman had managed to crawl out the crumpled door and stood hunched together, arms crossed tight across their chests. A taxi was stopped in front of them, a man waving his arms and yelling.

She glanced around the room where several women lay asleep or dealing with small children. Her gaze came to rest on Gwen, who was sitting cross-legged on her bed, a shawl around her shoulders. The old woman had been in her dream and acted like she owned it. Kat felt miffed for a moment—it was *her* dream, the one she'd been having ever since…ever since her mother died. It was her escape dream. And now another person had invaded it, a person she didn't know and didn't really want to know.

She turned away abruptly, her mind going in circles. Gwen hadn't *really* been there…it was only a dream. But why had she dreamed it? What did Gwen have to do with Kat's life?

After the fog cleared from her brain she rose and pulled a sweater over her head, one that her mother had knitted for her. It was soft wool, a Celtic design in gray and white and brown, and very warm. A second later she was out the door and hurrying away from the police cars and the ambulance, moving along a sidewalk filled with anxious pedestrians. Maybe she should have spoken to the old woman before she left. Gwen seemed friendly enough—it wasn't her fault Kat had dreamed about her.

And yet this dream she'd been having was all about a place of solace where she could finally relax. Guess that was gone now, what with 'others' invading it. She shook her head, stepping aside as a man came barrelling toward her, his eyes glued to his phone like it was some sort of homing beacon. He narrowly missed colliding with her, his gaze never leaving whatever fascinating thing he was staring at. What was wrong with everyone?

Or maybe there was something wrong with her for not being part of this world. She'd never owned a phone and probably never would—especially since they cost hundreds of dollars, not to mention the money she would need to pay every month for the privilege of owning one. Would she ever have a place of her own or anything resembling a life?

When she arrived at the used bookstore on the corner she stepped inside, hoping to find a job listed on their bulletin board—one that she could do in her current state of utter depression. The corkboard was filled with bits of paper and numbers pinned haphazardly across it, job offers and things for sale listed in no particular order.

"What kinda work you lookin' for?" a man asked. He ran dirty hands through his straggly blonde hair, his bloodshot eyes meeting hers.

"I…I don't know. Something that doesn't require a lot of expertise?"

He laughed, showing straight white teeth. "You could be a mule," he whispered.

"What's a mule?"

He stared at her, leaning close. "Someone who carries packages from one place to another?"

"That doesn't sound bad. How much does it pay?"

"Depends on what the package is."

Kat realized suddenly that he was talking about drugs. "No. I don't think so," she said, moving away to peruse the job listings. Two of them caught her eye. One was for a baby-sitter and the other was for a dog walker. Certainly she could manage those. She tore off the slips of paper listing the phone numbers and walked away, hoping to dissuade the overly friendly guy who seemed glued to her.

At the counter when she asked if they had a pay phone the clerk burst into peals of laughter. "Where'd you come from? We haven't had a pay phone for twenty years."

Kat looked around the store, noticing that the man who'd told her about the mule job was still close by and appeared to be listening. She stuffed the numbers in her satchel and hurried toward the door, not even stopping to browse through the used fantasies. Once outside she hurried toward the shelter without looking back. But when she had to pause at a red light she noticed him jogging after her.

Once he reached her he smiled and tipped his non-existent hat. "My name's Bran. Did you find a job opening you liked?"

Kat glared at him, wishing him away, but he didn't move. When the light changed and she started across she was right beside her.

"Where do you live, anyway?" he continued, matching her lengthening stride. "The only place up this way is the women's shelter and that expensive apartment building five blocks up."

Kat tried to ignore him, but between avoiding the mass of pedestrians and bumping into him every few seconds she finally gave up. "I'm staying at the shelter," she finally admitted.

"You live at the shelter? I would have pegged you for a trust fund kid who lived in that place up there." He pointed into the distance at a fancy high rise with ironwork balconies.

"What gave you that idea?" she asked, glancing down at her worn jeans and handmade sweater, the scuffed boots she was wearing.

He lifted one shoulder. "Maybe it's how you carry

yourself—I don't know. What happened that you're at the shelter?"

Kat stopped and turned, trying to maintain her cool. "What's it to you?"

He shrugged again, running his fingers through the sparse beard he seemed to be attempting to grow. "You're really pretty," he finally blurted, turning beet red a second later.

Kat pulled her gaze from his and continued walking, trying not to get caught up in his aura. Even with his unkempt appearance there was something compelling about him...

"I have a small apartment a mile or so that way," he said, pointing down a side street that meandered between several tall buildings. "I share it with four guys or I'd invite you to stay."

Kat stopped dead, turning to face him. "And you think I'd jump at the chance? I can't imagine how desperate I'd have to be to take you up on an offer like that."

"Sorreee," he said, raising both hands in the air. "For someone living at the shelter you certainly have an attitude. See ya around...um...what's your name, anyway?"

"It's Katel...Kat," she said before she could stop herself.

"Well, Katel, it was nice chatting with you." Bran bowed low before turning to follow the road intersecting the one they were on. He didn't look back, his loping stride disappearing into an alley.

Just a drugee, Kat thought, hurrying on. And yet something about him twined around inside her like a fast growing vine. By the time she reached the shelter she'd imagined at least three scenarios that featured Bran as a main character. In all of them he had a wide smile on his face, and even though he was still dressed like a bum, his hair was clean and his fingernails didn't have dirt under them. *What is wrong with me? Am I so lonely that any weirdo can crawl inside my mind?* She pulled open the heavy glass door and entered the shelter, but her thoughts had taken a very different route.

"**C**erridwen is down there!" Arianrhod cried out, pointing.

The other goddesses joined her at the edge of the balcony to gaze downward, their eyes going wide. "I wondered why she hadn't arrived," Airmid murmured. "But why didn't she mention what she was planning?"

"She's usurped us, gone behind our backs," Corra muttered darkly. "I've never trusted her."

"But she's the wisdom keeper, Corra!" Airmid cried. "She's the one we go to when we need advice."

"I do not need advice,"Corra grumped. "*I* am the goddess of prophecy."

Arianrhod pressed her thin lips together. "That's all well and good, Corra, but you cannot predict for yourself, now can you?"

"Maybe I can," Corra mumbled, turning away. "Aren't we supposed to be helping this young woman? How can we help her if Cerridwen is already in residence?"

"Perhaps this unfortunate waif needs all our help,"

Morrighan said, arriving from inside the castle. "Looks to me like she's a lost soul with no idea how to save herself."

"And look who she's just met," Rhiannon said, peering downward. The healing birds circled her, gossamer wings glistening in the light. They made an ever-changing halo around her head.

Airmid squinted in the brightness. "Is that Bran? He looks like a bum."

"Yes," Rhiannon answered. "I would know him anywhere, although I cannot fathom why he's using that disguise."

"But why would the god of protection be...?"

Morrighan laughed, staring at her sister goddess. "Do you hear yourself? He's been sent to protect her."

"But why him?" Corra asked, frowning. Bran was also a god of ravens and prophecy, a fact that the goddess of prophecy resented. "You should be upset too," she continued, turning to Morrighan.

"Why should I be upset—because his name means raven? I am long past such egocentric meanderings. He is also the god of regeneration. We all share similarities of one kind or another."

"But who sent him?" Arianrhod asked. "The Dagda called us together to assist this young woman and now she has nearly every deity we know at her disposal."

"Perhaps Bran has taken this upon himself without the Dagda's approval. He is sometimes a hothead," Morrighan murmured. "He's obviously decided for himself how to dress. The Dagda would never allow one of us to appear like that."

"Dagda didn't say anything about Bran the last time you were together?"

Morrighan shrugged and tossed her dark hair back. "The Dagda is not one for talking. We have other things on our minds when we're together."

"Really, Morrighan. Don't you ever think of anything else?" Arianrhod muttered.

"Come, girls, let's not bicker," Rhiannon said, glancing from one to the other. "Bran is down there dressed like a drugged out bum, odd, even for him. It does seem as though he's acting on his own."

"Dagda is not as fond of Bran as the rest of us," Morrighan offered, staring downward. "But Bran serves those who need protection and goddess knows this woman fits that description. It is quite likely he's gone rogue."

"But appearing to her as a drug addict does not exactly engender confidence," Corra said.

Airmid leaned across the railing, trying to locate the god. "Perhaps he has taken this guise because it allows him to fit in with those who need protecting. Dressed like that he resembles the street people."

"After seeing what we've seen today I refuse to step foot in that cesspool," Morrighan hissed, moving away from the railing. "If I meet with her it will be in Otherworld only."

"Fine, Morrighan. You can meet her in her dreams. I prefer a more hands on approach."

"Go for it, Airmid. You've always been a do-gooder. If you want to befriend her in that hellhole, fine. Maybe you can also dress like a street person and pretend to be hooked on drugs."

When Airmid stuck out her tongue and made a face, Morrighan let out a cackle, breaking the sudden tension.

The goddesses spent the next hour trying to decide who would go where and how to present themselves. "We cannot appear as we are," Arianrhod argued. "Just gazing upon us could cause blindness!"

Airmid laughed. "We do have a brightness about us, but I'm sure we can blend in if need be. I suggest human dress and a glamour to disguise our identity."

"Who among us, aside from Airmid, wishes to be seen down there?" Corra asked, shuddering. "I find it most daunting."

"I will not mind it," Rhiannon responded. "I am more attuned to the human world after being married to my prince. I look forward to it."

"So Arianrhod, Morrighan and Corra will meet with her in the dream world, and Rhiannon and I will befriend her on earth. Are we decided?"

"But what shall we wear—how shall we appear?" Arianrhod asked anxiously.

"In her dreams we can show ourselves as we are. If Cerridwen wants to appear in sackcloth and ashes, that's her business, but I don't feel like dressing down," Morrighan answered, plucking at her gorgeous black lace dress.

"Will we seek out Bran?" Rhiannon asked Airmid.

"I have the sense that he will find us," she answered.

"And once he does we can coordinate our efforts." Rhiannon glanced at Morrighan who seemed to know more about their assignment than anyone else. "What exactly is our mission?"

"From the little the Dagda has divulged it is to help this young woman rediscover her destiny. At the moment she is a lost soul with no way to move forward."

Corra's eyes glazed over, a gasp coming from her a few seconds later. "Her destiny is utterly dark to me!" she cried out. "Why is it not clear?"

But the other goddesses were caught up in discussing their plans and did not hear her.

Kat walked along a leaf-strewn path, her gaze on the dappled light and shadows shifting on the trail before her. Her thoughts were calm, the serenity of where she was making her happy. This time she knew she was dreaming, knew that this beautiful and magical landscape was her mind's way of providing respite. Her feet were bare, a gauzy dress clinging to her slim body as she came out of the forest into a meadow filled with wildflowers. But as she breathed deeply to take in the various scents she heard a rustle behind her, turning to see Bran walking toward her. "What are **you** doing here?" she asked him, anger undoing the calm from a moment before.

His head cocked to one side, a perplexed expression on his features. "Why? Am I not allowed?"

His eyes were the color of the shadows, his hair cleaner than she remembered it, shoulder-length strands glinting gold in the sunlight. His feet were bare, and a loose-fitting pair of drawstring pants hung on his slim hips, an indigo V-necked tunic revealing his tanned chest. A leather cord hung around his neck, a pendant hidden beneath the fabric of his shirt. She had to admit he was handsome, but…"This is my dream and I didn't invite you!" she shouted before she could stop herself.

"Really? It seems it's my dream as well," he answered calmly.

"It can't be!"

"Well, if it isn't, then you're the one who brought me here."

Kat thought about that for a second. He was right. "But…"

"But what? It's beautiful here and there are lots of areas to explore. Wouldn't you like some company?"

"Not really," she muttered, examining the wildflowers around her bare feet. She turned away from him, her gaze going to the woods looming in the distance, and the mountain of greenery and rocks rising up on her right. Suddenly everything had changed, an anxious feeling in the pit of her stomach. "I come here to…"

"The same reason I come here," he finished for her, "to escape reality."

"I was going to say calm myself, but I guess it's the same thing." When she looked up he was standing very close—too close. She backed up a step, but in the process his gaze caught hers. The color of his eyes shifted and changed, an energy passing between them. She was suddenly dizzy, disoriented. When she swayed he caught her elbow and steadied her.

"Careful," he said, concerned.

She jerked away and tried to ignore the tingle his touch had produced. "I need to wake up now," she mumbled.

Kat's eyes opened, the darkness scaring her for an instant. The dream had been so real this time, almost as though…she shifted on the cot, attempting to get comfortable. Around her the snores of the women permeated her consciousness, the reality of her life sending a knot of dread into her belly.

"Are you all right, Kat?"

Gwen stood next to her cot, the white of her hair glowing in the darkness. "I'm fine—I just had a dream."

Gwen sat down next to her, reaching out to push the damp hair off her forehead. "Bad or good?"

The feel of Gwen's touch reminded Kat of her mother. Tears sprang into her eyes as she let the feeling penetrate into her psyche. "Neither. It was just…so real."

Gwen smiled and let her hand drop into her lap. "Otherworld *is* real, Kat. I've already told you that, haven't I?"

Kat flinched away, trying to determine how to react. Yes, she'd seen a woman who looked like Gwen in one of her dreams, but…

"Don't worry. Things will seem better in the morning," the old woman said in a singsong voice.

Gwen stroked Kat's hair, her low hum sending waves of calm into her body and her mind. Kat's eyes closed, something deep inside her going quiet as she drifted off to sleep.

Kat was standing in front of the bookstore when she saw Bran behind her reflected in the window. Instead of turning to greet him she hurried inside, heading to the corkboard to look at job offers. The two phone numbers she'd collected two weeks back had disappeared before she had the chance to call on them. Was it possible they were still available? But when she searched, there was no more mention of the dog walker job, or the babysitter. Of course they would have been snapped up quickly.

She was still standing there perusing the job lists when she felt a presence next to her, turning to look straight into Bran's eyes. He seemed more normal today, aside from the bloodshot eyes from what she figured was smoking pot. He looked like a pothead with his dreadlocks and blue jeans; his T-shirt had a picture of Jerry Garcia on the front, The Grateful Dead under it in gothic lettering.

"Hey, Kat," he said, his lips curling into a smile.

"Hi Bran, long time no see."

He frowned, watching her carefully. "Two weeks, right?"

"If you say so," she answered, turning back to the board. Was she seriously thinking that they'd met in her dream?

"I've been hoping to run into you again. I know someone who needs a dog walker. Doesn't pay much, but maybe if you added another small job or two you could get out of the shelter. I also have a friend who has an apartment with an extra room."

She whirled on him. "Sharing an apartment with a drugged out loser? That sounds just great, Bran—is it a guy? Of course it is, you pervert."

Bran's eyes went wide and he backed away. "What is your problem? And no, it isn't a *guy*—it's an old girlfriend of mine. She's really nice and she doesn't do drugs."

Kat was suddenly ashamed, unsure why she'd reacted that way. Her face heated up as she tried to find words to excuse her behavior. "I...I'm sorry. I'm just..."

"On edge, overwhelmed? Yeah, I get it, but don't take your nasty mood out on me. I'm only trying to help."

When tears threatened, Kat whirled around and ran for the door, hurtling through it and barely missing an incoming customer. She took off down the street at a run. Why had she behaved that way? She had no explanation.

"You've had a lot of trauma in your life recently, Kat," Gwen said later after she'd spilled her guts. "Your trust for others is at an all time low. From what you've described, though, I'd say this Bran person could be a decent man. Perhaps if you see him again you could at least check out the situation he mentioned? Does he seem drugged out or dangerous?" Gwen sat on the edge of the cot, a concerned expression on her face.

Kat gazed into the dark eyes, visualizing Bran in her mind. There were two of them now—the guy here and the one she met in her dream. She decided not to mention that for fear of Gwen's response. "No, not really. I thought he was a stalker at first but he seemed nice enough this last time. But what if I'm wrong?"

Gwen nodded. "You don't trust yourself to know. I understand. If you see him again try and stay focused on your internal radar system. We all have one. See if your reactions are valid."

Kat pulled her knees up and wrapped her arms around them, her gaze on the girl across the room breastfeeding a tiny infant. She seemed younger than Kat, a bewildered expression on her thin face. At least Kat didn't have a baby to take care of. When she glanced back to where Gwen had been a moment before the old woman was gone. And when she looked around the room she didn't see her anywhere.

eeks had gone by since Kat's last encounter with Bran. Gwen had seemingly disappeared from the shelter, her bed now occupied by a middle-aged woman who had a terrible cold. Kat had developed a sore throat since her arrival, and blamed it on her. And she had no money to buy throat lozenges or any over the counter remedies.

The weather was warming up, the days lengthening. Imbolc, the festival on February first that marked the beginning of spring, had come and gone; she was learning all about the Celtic festivals from reading the book on Celtic gods and goddesses. The fire festival of Beltane, marking the beginning of summer, was coming on the first of May, and her goal was to be out of the shelter by then. But how that would happen was a gray area that she tried not to dwell on.

She had gone by the bookstore several times to look for job opportunities but so far hadn't found one she could manage. And worse than that she hadn't run into Bran. He was probably avoiding her after their last encounter when she acted like such a bitch. The strangest thing that had happened recently was her lack of dreams—she hadn't been back to her place of solace for a long time, which made her life even more unbearable.

And she couldn't stop thinking about her mother and how she knew beyond a shadow of a doubt that Jack had killed her. But how had he done it? And more importantly, how in the world could she prove it? She had no money to hire a PI, and if she went to the police they'd laugh in her face. It was coming up on the six-month mark, but time didn't seem to diminish the pain she felt. If anything it was getting worse.

She missed Gwen's counsel, her absence made worse by the lack of dreaming. When she'd asked the matrons who ran the shelter about her, they had no idea who she was talking about. How could they not remember the woman who'd subdued the intruder? In her estimation Gwen had a presence that stuck with a person; her piercing lilac/blue eyes and masses of waist length white hair were unforgettable.

Every day she dragged herself out of bed and made her way to the soup kitchen, but whenever she caught a glimpse of herself in a mirror it was as though she was wasting away. It wasn't exactly weight loss, it was more like she was becoming see-through—or at least that's how it felt. If she didn't take care she'd disappear all together.

She threw on a threadbare sweater someone had left behind and pulled on her jeans and boots. Time to get outside and think her way through the situation she was in. May was only two months away—

Kat was sitting on a bench in the park when she saw Bran. For a moment she considered taking off before he saw her, but then she remembered what Gwen had suggested. Most of her reluctance had to do with how she'd treated him the last time they'd been together. She was already blushing with the memory. She breathed in deeply and focused on her internal radar, willing him to see her. It was less than a minute later that he headed toward her.

"How've you been?" he asked, sitting next to her.

"Not too great. Sorry about what a bitch I was last time I saw you."

He shook his head dismissively. "I forgot about that a long time ago. Any interest in the room I mentioned? If you're willing you could pay the rent by helping out my friend."

Kat barely heard him as she concentrated on her radar. His proximity was doing strange things to her breathing and she was afraid to meet his eyes. "What kind of help does she need?" she finally asked, her gaze on the ground.

"You'd have to ask her."

Before she could stop herself she had lifted her gaze to his, a shiver making its way up her spine when their eyes met. His had changed color to match the sage green shirt he was wearing. They reminded her of moss. His jeans were clean, his hair too. For a second she saw him as he'd been in the dream, his eyes sparkling and bright, and wearing the indigo tunic that showed off his tanned chest.

"What do you think?" he finally asked.

She realized she had no idea how long she'd been staring. "Um…I'm willing to meet her for sure. I'm really sick of the shelter, especially now that my one friend there is gone. But I have no money for food or anything."

"If you help with cooking and cleaning I'm sure you could work something out. Why aren't you in college?"

The sudden change of topic startled her. "I…I'm twenty years old. Did you think I was younger?"

"No. I didn't know how old you were, but I've noticed since being down here…I mean living here…that a lot of people that seem close to your age are studying at one of the colleges around the city."

"How old are *you*?"

"I…I'm, um, around…I mean… twenty-five?"

Kat laughed. "You aren't sure?"

"I'm twenty-five, but sometimes I feel a lot older."

"Tell me about it—right now I feel positively *ancient*."

"What are you interested in? For school, I mean."

Kat contemplated the question, her gaze on his mouth. *I'm interested in you right now.* "Honestly, I don't even know. I used to like to draw and paint but I stopped when I got the job at the box factory." When she looked at him he was watching her with his eyebrows pulled together, as though he was actually interested. "I guess when my mom died I kind of gave up on life," she continued.

"Yeah, I get that. My dad died a few years ago and it took me an entire year to get my shit together."

"What did you do?"

"I bummed around and slept on friend's couches and smoked a lot of weed."

"Isn't that what you do now?"

Bran laughed, the first time she'd heard him. It was a full throaty sound that she hoped to hear again.

"I have a job, but it's mostly at night."

"What is it?"

"Night watchman at a warehouse downtown. There's been a bunch of break-ins around there."

"Do you carry a gun?"

"No." There was a pause before he added, "I have a black belt in karate. And I have a beeper if something goes down."

When he slid his arm along the back of the bench behind her the smell of him enveloped her for a second—spice and sunlight. "That sounds scary to me."

He shrugged. "Temporary job until I can find a better one."

An itch to move closer to him stirred in her, but instead of acting on it she rose from the bench. "Can we go see your friend now?"

"Sure, unless she's out doing her thing."

"What's her thing?"

"She collects mushrooms and herbs and roots in the woods."

"What woods? Besides this park all I can see is cement and apartment buildings."

He smiled. "She knows where they all are—there's at least a few green spaces left in the city, if you know where to look."

"What does she do with the stuff she finds?"

"She makes herbal remedies. I think you'll like her."

When his fingers reached for hers to lead her toward the street she had a vision of her dreamscape, the two of them locked in an embrace. A flush rose into her cheeks. She pulled her hand away and followed him out of the park toward the noise and traffic, realizing that for the time they'd been together she'd hadn't noticed the honking, yelling and general mayhem only twenty or so feet away from the bench where they'd been sitting.

The apartment building where Bran's friend lived was weathered brick, built in the early part of the twentieth century. It had seen better days, but in some ways its elegant touches made up for the missing bricks and the framing around the windows that needed repainting.

The elevator no longer worked so they took the stairs, Kat hurrying after Bran's fast paced ascent. He waited at the third floor until she reached him, and then waited some more while she caught her breath. "It's 333," he said, heading off.

The door into the woman's apartment had been painted grass green, a brass knocker in the shape of an owl staring out from its middle. Bran lifted it and let it fall. "She likes nature," he explained, winking.

Less than a minute later the door opened, revealing a slim woman with tangled brown hair wearing what resembled a woven sack. A wide leather belt cinched tight hugged her waist, her feet bare. "Bran!" she exclaimed, moving forward to kiss him on both cheeks in the European way. "Come in," she invited, glancing at Kat with a wide smile. "I was expecting you."

Kat wondered how she'd known they were coming, but all thought was taken from her mind when she saw what lay before her. Birds flew around the high-ceilinged living room, their calls echoing off the walls. The floor was covered in moss and rocks, and there was even a tree, the branches spreading from one side of the room to the other. "Make yourself comfortable," the woman said, gesturing to a couple of flat rocks. "I'll make us some herbal tea."

"Airmid, this is Kat!" Bran called as she disappeared into the kitchen.

"Hi Kat," she called back. "Pleased to meet you."

Kat lowered to a rock and surveyed the room, marvelling. "How did you manage all this?" she asked when Airmid returned with a tray. It felt exactly as if she was sitting in a forest.

Airmid laughed. "I lived in a woodland before I came here. I had to make the apartment feel like home. Don't worry, your bedroom is perfectly normal," she added.

"My…" Kat glanced at Bran who had his eyebrows raised, staring at her expectantly.

"You will stay, won't you?" Airmid asked. "I'll pay you to help me with my remedies."

Kat gazed into the gray-green eyes, completely bewitched by the woman's smile. "Well, I…"

"Yes," Bran answered for her. "She'll take your extra room. Now how much will you pay her for helping you?"

"Let the poor woman speak for herself," Airmid scolded, turning to Kat.

"Can I see the room?" Kat asked.

Airmid left the tea tray on a stump and hurried down a hallway, Kat in close pursuit. When Airmid opened the door into the room, golden light spilled across the threshold. A canopy bed covered with a pale blue lacy spread sat against one wall, a fireplace with an ornate marble mantel directly opposite. Tall mullioned windows were open and looked out on sky and clouds, the glass free of dust and grime. It wasn't huge, but the room had a spacious feeling with the high ceiling, the large windows adding to it. An antique highboy dresser sat by the fireplace, a chair and a secretary occupying the wall beside the door leading into the adjoining bathroom; Kat let out a gasp when she saw the tiny hexagonal tiles in black and white and the claw foot tub. "I love it!" she gushed.

Airmid clapped her hands. "Oh good! I've needed an apprentice for some time—hope you don't mind mess."

Before Kat could respond, Airmid was off again, heading down the dark hall to where Bran sat cross-legged under the tree sipping from an earthenware mug.

As Kat entered the forested room she wondered again how Airmid had managed to move a real tree and all the dirt, stones and moss up the stairs. It must have taken several burly men hours to accomplish. And what did her landlord think of the changes she'd made—or did he even know? Was it a real tree? And if so, where did the roots go? She moved close to touch the bark, feeling the life that bubbled beneath her fingers. "How did you get this up here?"

Airmid laughed. "I have friends in high places."

"But the roots—where do they go?"

"This kind of tree has shallow roots," Bran said, glancing quickly at Airmid.

"Yes, that's right," she agreed. "It did take a while to hoist the dirt up three flights of stairs."

"And the landlord?"

"Good brew," Bran interrupted, handing Kat a full mug. "What's this one got in it?"

Airmid settled on the moss next to Kat. "A bit of chamomile, a few rosehips and some peppermint," she answered, breathing in deeply. "The rose comes through nicely, doesn't it?" She turned to Kat. "Do you like tea?"

"I like this one. I usually drink coffee, that is when I have money to…"

Her voice trailed off and she looked down.

"You'll have money soon enough. I hope you like tramping through the woods."

"I do," Kat said, meeting Airmid's clear gaze. "But I don't know anything about herbs."

Airmid smiled. "You'll learn."

Kat glanced at Airmid, excitement building inside her. She had the sense that her life was about to take a turn for the better.

8

"**W**hy are so many of us needed for one girl?" Arianrhod asked peevishly.

Airmid turned from the double boiler on the stove. "Why are you here? I thought your duties in this regard lay in Otherworld."

Arianrhod frowned. "I thought you might like to see one of your sister goddesses after being stuck in this hellish place for a fortnight."

"Have you seen how I decorated? It is hardly a hellhole, Arianrhod."

Airmid had grown used to the busyness and the noise. And now that she knew where to hunt for her herbs she'd become almost happy.

It wasn't like Otherworld, where everything was abundant, but something inside her enjoyed the challenge of hunting for what she needed and knowing that nature, no matter how bad the pollution or lack of nutrients, would find a way. In the process she'd had random conversations with many different people, seeing their eyes light up when she told them what she was doing. The encounters gave her hope and made her smile.

"You shouldn't have come," she hissed, turning to Arianrhod. "If Kat sees you dressed like that she'll wonder what's going on."

The moon goddess laughed, looking down at the gold brocade gown trimmed in forest green. Her flaxen hair was braided and twisted in ropes around her exquisitely shaped skull. "I can tell her I'm an actress."

Airmid cocked her head, listening. "She's on her way now, so I suggest you disappear before she arrives. She's quite astute and intuitive."

"For a poor waif who can't make it in the world?" Arianrhod scoffed. She turned when she heard the click of the front door, vanishing into the living room a moment later.

"Kat? Is that you?"

Kat appeared in the kitchen doorway, her cheeks rosy from the cold. "What are you making?"

Airmid moved aside to show her the melting coconut oil and mango butter. "Face cream," she said. "I've noticed there's quite a demand for products of this sort in this world."

"In this world?"

"I meant to say in the city," she corrected, hiding her blush.

"Where will you sell it?"

"I'll start a pop-up. There's a studio apartment on the first floor facing the street. I've already spoken with the landlord."

"And your name is perfect," Kat said excitedly. "Airmid is the Celtic goddess of healing."

"Oh, right,"Airmid said, smiling. "I had to buy a few ingredientsthis time, but if we take a trip later on today I can gather some mosses and chamomile flowers, maybe even some leaves and bark from the witch hazel. I noticed a few bushes the last time I was foraging. Are you free to tag along?"

Kat nodded, shrugging off her sweater. "Bran took me out to breakfast."

Airmid glanced at her. "You like him, don't you?"

"I don't know—he's nice enough," she said noncommittally.

Kat was obviously infatuated with Bran and terrified to admit it, even to herself. Did Bran know? Both gods and men were so lacking when it came to insights of this sort. Bran was well aware that intimate relationships with humans were strictly forbidden. Hopefully he wouldn't encourage her.

"Tell me about your family, Kat. You've hardly spoken a word about them, other than your mother's death."

"My stepfather killed her," Kat muttered.

Airmid widened her eyes. "Are you sure?"

"I'm sure," Kat replied.

"How did he do it?"

Kat whirled on her. "I don't want to talk about it!" She ran from the kitchen, the bedroom door slamming a moment later.

Airmid sighed. This was the third time she'd attempted to talk with Kat about this issue. Expressing the pain and anger she harbored was the first step to her healing. If she couldn't get her to open up, all of this would be for naught. But then she remembered Otherworld and her sister goddesses who were waiting to do their part. Kat wasn't dreaming much lately, but with the special brew Airmid had in mind she was sure she could get her back to where this world and Otherworld intersected. She wondered again about Dagda's enigmatic instructions. What was it about this particular young woman that made her special? It wasn't like the Dagda to engage in the human world, especially like this.

She turned off the stove and moved to the window where she'd placed her pots of lavender and calendula, plucking off a few stems of each. In the kitchen again she placed the woody stems and flowers in the mortar and pestle and began to work them into a pulp. Once that was done she would simmer them in rosehip oil and then strain them to remove the stemmy parts before mixing them in with argan oil and the coconut oil and mango butter.

To open a pop-up she would need quite a few jars of product to sell, as well as some labels done up—she'd scanned the boutiques and stores to get ideas. She began to hum, her mood lifting as she thought of the people she would meet and the satisfaction that came from hard work. She intended to include Kat in her plans and hoped the girl would be open to working with the public. If she could involve her in the process, it might improve the girl's mood and lower her reluctance to talk. And there were those in this world who had healing abilities—perhaps Kat was one of them. But her first order of business was to gain Kat's trust.

Kat sat cross-legged on the bed trying hard not to cry. Why did she feel like this? Airmid was nice and had given her a place to live and was paying for her help. Maybe it was Airmid's constant good mood that irritated her, as though there was something wrong with Kat for not feeling the same way. The woman's cheerfulness was almost worse than the sadness emanating from the women at the shelter—at least she was on the same page with them and felt a connection.

Part of her bad mood had to be because she wasn't dreaming. That landscape of calm had somehow buoyed her spirits and given her hope. Even her friendship with Bran hadn't helped. She had to admit she felt attracted to him, but after they spent time together she was right back where she'd been before they got together. Her good moods were as fleeting as the clouds scattering across the sky.

A gentle knock brought her out of her musings. "Kat?" Her voice was soft and caring, another trait of hers that drove Kat crazy. She knew it was illogical, but for some reason she couldn't bear to hear the sympathy in Airmid's tone.

"I'm here," she called back.

"Can I come in?"

"Door's open."

Airmid appeared, her face a mask of worry. "You've been in here for hours. You didn't even come with me to look for herbs today. What is wrong?"

Kat turned away and shook her head. "I don't know. I'm just tired I guess."

Airmid sat down next to her on the edge of the bed. "I can see the suffering you're going through. I only want to help—why won't you let me in?"

Kat flinched away from her. "I don't need any help."

A moment went by and another, the air thickening in the room. When Kat glanced at Airmid, she was scowling, her normally soft eyes hard with rage. A second later her voice reverberated as she spat out what she had to say.

"If you don't want to be here go back to the shelter. I'm tired of worrying about you and I'm tired of caring when you won't care for yourself. If you don't snap out of this and make some effort I want you out of here."

Kat was unable to speak as she watched Airmid turn and stalk from the room. For a moment she just sat there dazed until something inside her seemed to spring alive. She *did* want to be here and she liked helping with the herbs. She'd been excited about her new reality. Airmid was right—she was hanging on to her grief like a lifebuoy and refusing to let go and swim.

She hurried from the room to find Airmid in the kitchen stirring something on the stove. "I'm sorry."

Airmid turned. "There is no need to be sorry, Kat. But I meant what I said. I'd hoped we'd become friends, but so far you act like I'm part of your problem. Did you treat your mother this way?"

"Of course not!" Kat shouted. "But you aren't my mother."

"No, but I'd hoped to be a friend, someone you could trust. Why don't you trust me?"

Kat's stomach clenched. "I…I don't trust anyone."

"Well, it's time that changed," Airmid said in a voice reserved for children, turning back to the stove.

Kat stood there for several moments trying to think what to say. Finally she moved closer to look in the pot. "What's that?"

"My wrinkle cream recipe. If you have any interest in helping I would appreciate it if you could fill out the labels I bought. Each one needs to have the words **Airmid's Healing Potions** printed on it and the name of the particular cream. I have a list there on the table with what I've made and the ingredients." She pointed to the clean jars waiting, the lids beside them. "If you want to help, fill out the labels and stick them on the lids—ten of each please."

Kat let out a sigh and headed to the table to collect a pen and the contact sheets of round labels. "When does the pop-up open?"

Airmid turned, her eyes dark with something Kat couldn't identify. "On Saturn's day."

"Saturday?"

"Yes, on Saturday. That gives us only a couple of days to get everything ready. Are you in?"

Kat nodded. "I'm in."

"Good," Airmid said, turning back to the stove.

Kat worked quietly, taking her time with the lettering to make it look professional. She was actually good at this. The sound of the gas flame and the rhythmic plunk of the wooden spoon soothed her over active mind, settling whatever had been plaguing her. They didn't speak again, but something had shifted. Airmid had broken through her defences, and they both knew it.

Before bed that night Airmid made tea, handing her a cup. "This will help you sleep," she said.

"How'd you know?"

"That you have insomnia? I hear you at night muttering and getting up and down."

"Do you sleep?"

Airmid laughed. "Not much. But I don't need much. You, on the other hand, need a lot of sleep right now."

"Do I?"

"Yes, Kat. Your mind is healing, your body too. You need rest to heal."

"Maybe my mind needs to heal, but my body's fine."

Airmid shook her head. "You've only just begun to eat properly. You're still too thin. You have little energy when we hunt for herbs. I am not saying this as a criticism, only to let you know what I've observed. You will regain your strength, but being able to sleep is certainly a necessary part of it."

Kat stared into space as she sipped. Was Airmid a seer or a witch? There was something odd about her, as though she knew what Kat was thinking and feeling before she knew it herself. The tea was different, pungent and bitter, without the usual peppermint flavor. "What's in this?"

"It's a sleeping potion. I'm having it too."

Kat watched Airmid sip with her eyes downcast. There was something the woman wasn't saying. But Kat decided to let it go—sleeping through the night sounded good. She hoped the tea worked.

Kat saw the pond shimmering in the distance, the light turning it into molten silver. Cattails swung back and forth in the warm breeze, bits of fluff breaking off and whirling about in the moisture-laden air. She was hurrying toward it when she saw the two women basking in the water wearing gossamer dresses; their long hair was twisted and held up with smooth twigs. One was fair-haired the other dark. She heard them laughing as they splashed. It was one thing to have Bran show up, even Cerridwen had been tolerable, but what were these two strange women doing in her dream?

Before she could turn away they'd spied her, calling out in dulcet tones for her to join them. Her mind told her to run in the other direction, but she couldn't seem to get her feet to obey, and found herself walking toward them.

"Kat!" the bright-haired woman said, hurrying close. "We've been expecting you!" Her eyes were the green of emeralds, her skin pale and flawless. Her thin form and small breasts showed clearly though the wet fabric clinging to her body.

Before Kat could answer, the other woman approached, her eyes and hair both as dark as charcoal. Full breasts pressed against the see-through fabric, her hips wide and her voice commanding as she called out a greeting.

Just a few moments before she'd been happy and calm, and now she was faced with two strangers who seemed to know her and were ruining her peace. "Why are you here?" she asked. "This is my dream, my pond."

"I am Arianrhod, the goddess of the moon," the flaxen-haired woman said with a tinkling laugh. "We have been called upon to help you."

"And I am Morrighan," the dark-haired one added, "the goddess of war, among other things. This is not only your dream—'tis Otherworld, where it intersects with your world. We have heard you call to us."

"I didn't—I wouldn't," Kat said, backing away. "I come here to find peace."

"We are here to help you find that peace," Arianrhod said softly, reaching out a hand.

Before she could stop herself Kat had grabbed hold of the long fingers and was letting the woman tug her toward the pond. When they reached the cattails the two goddesses helped Kat off with her dress and pulled her with them into the water. She felt a sort of helplessness and lassitude as she allowed them to handle her body, as though her ability to say no had been stripped away with her clothes. Her mind told her to resist them, but her body had other things in mind, relaxing as they dunked her under the water to wet her hair and then washed it, their fingers working against her scalp making her sigh with pleasure.

When they were finished with her hair they washed her body, using rushes they'd collected to massage away aches and pains as they cradled her in their arms. Her body released completely, letting go of deep tensions as they worked her over. Her eyes closed, her mind barely aware of their lilting whispers, the feel of their strong fingers and the warmth of the water like the best massage she would ever have. She floated somewhere in a place she'd never been, her mind and body unwinding for the first time since her mother's death.

Kat woke sometime later on the grass by the pond. She was naked, the sun's last rays casting rosy light across her tingling skin. When she sat up and looked around there was no sign of the two goddesses. She hugged her arms around her chest, a shiver of unease moving through her. She had the strangest sense that she'd gone through some goddess initiation process, washed clean to prepare her for something greater. And that's when the fear set in. Her mouth opened in a scream that echoed...

The scream woke her, Kat's heart beating fast in her chest. She was in bed and wearing her nightgown, her hair dry. She tried to put it all aside, to tell herself it was only a dream, but it didn't feel that way. Her body felt different, her limbs loose and relaxed.

She dressed hurriedly and went to the kitchen, wanting to tell Airmid about the dream before she forgot.

"Now tell me their names again?" Airmid asked, following Kat into the living room.

Kat settled under the tree and placed her mug of tea next to her. Was it her imagination or had the room expanded in the past few days? Birds chirped and sang, their wings glinting in the sunlight that spilled through the windows. "Arianrhod and Morrighan. They said they were goddesses. Who are they?"

"I suppose they're who they said they were—didn't you believe them?"

Kat stared into the middle distance remembering her goddess book. "I've read about them," she muttered, "but I didn't think they were real...what am I saying?" She let out an uneasy laugh. "It was only a dream."

"A dream that seems to have had a profound effect on you," Airmid reminded her. "Didn't you tell me you met

Cerridwen in a dream? And from what I remember of that conversation she said the same thing—that your pond is where Otherworld and this world intersect."

Kat swiveled to stare at her. "You believe this? All it does is scare me half to death. How can there even be a place called Otherworld? What *is* Otherworld?"

"It's where the light usurps the dark, where everything lives together in harmony, where the gods and goddesses dwell. It is a wondrous and..." she stopped speaking to wipe tears from her eyes. "I guess I'm not as happy here as I thought," she muttered.

"Please tell me you aren't saying you live there."

Airmid shook her head. "No, of course not. But I have read of its beauty."

"It's a myth," Kat said. "It says so in my goddess book. It's only Celtic mythology."

"Mythology is written down from stories that have been repeated over time," Airmid said. "Even the Arthur and Merlin myth holds a kernel of truth." She frowned and shook herself as if to dispel the mood. "Today is the day we must prepare the pop-up. Will you help me?"

Kat nodded, glad to be getting on with real life. The memory of the goddesses faded as she followed Airmid into the kitchen and picked up a few jars of skin cream and placed them in a box. "Shall I take these down?"

Airmid nodded, but Kat could tell her mood had darkened, a shadow coming across her features as she bent to pick up another box. Kat wondered about Airmid's sudden tears, the look on her face when she described Otherworld. It was as though the woman had actually been there. But that was impossible.

10

At Airmid's behest the goddesses convened in the castle for a meeting. It was her contention that they were working at cross-purposes. "What did you two do to Kat?" she asked, staring hard at Arianrhod and Morrighan.

"We initiated her into the world of the goddess—what do you think?" Morrighan answered. "She has to believe in us now."

"Meeting you has confused her even further. And because of her confusion I gave myself away, bursting into tears when I spoke of Otherworld. I thought I was happy down there, and now I realize I've been fooling myself."

Morrighan's eyes narrowed. "So this is all about you. The girl is better, is she not?"

"No, she is not. She told me she's afraid to dream for fear of what else might happen. She keeps herself awake by drinking coffee and refuses my tea. I am very worried about her."

"Ah yes, humans require sleep...how tiresome," Morrighan muttered. "We soothed away every bit of pain that young woman carried. She must have felt some relief."

"It isn't that easy, Morrighan. Humans need time to process. I know you meant well, but what you did added to her list of problems, taking away the one place where she's always felt safe."

"She felt safe in Otherworld?" Arianrhod asked. "How is that for irony?"

"She doesn't know it's Otherworld—she thought it was her happy place."

Morrighan scowled. "She will have to get used to the truth."

Airmid let out a mirthless laugh. "She has a dead mother and a murder to unravel as well as a life to discover. Now is hardly the time to add a parallel world to her uncertainty. We must wait until she's strong enough to deal with this."

"So you want us to stay away—is that it?" Arianrhod asked.

"Yes. I want you to stay out of her dreams until she's stronger."

Morrighan turned to gaze longingly up at the sky where a dark raven rode the thermals.

Airmid nudged her. "Go and fly with him and tell him what I've told you. We cannot overwhelm this poor girl."

"He's being patient but he's missed me these past weeks."

"Give him our best," Arianrhod said sarcastically.

Morrighan gave her a sharp look before she changed into a bird, wings wide as she flew to her lover, the god Dagda.

Arianrhod and Airmid were on the balcony later when they heard the moans coming from the room behind them. The goddess of the moon made a face. "They've been rutting in there for hours."

Airmid laughed. "You're jealous."

Arianrhod shook her head, a disgusted expression on her pale features. "Maybe I am, but why must they be so noisy about it? It's like she wants the entire world to know what they're up to in there."

"I doubt she's thinking at all right now."

"And Dagda—what is he doing?" Arianrhod continued as though Airmid hadn't spoken. "Isn't he supposed to be above such things?"

"Above such things?" Airmid let out a snort. "Goddesses have babies. And as far as I know there's only one way to make one."

"Will Morrighan have one?" Arianrhod asked in shock.

"If the myths are true, yes, she will. And Dagda will be the father."

"Why don't I remember the myths? And more importantly, why aren't they happening right now?"

"Because our world has now intersected with the human world and we are forgetting who we are."

"Not completely."

"No, not completely, but if it keeps encroaching, our myths will die out as well as all of us. I can only assume that this is why we're being tasked with this young woman—she must be some kind of link between us and the human realm."

"I hope so," Arianrhod said, her eyes wide. "I don't want to disappear."

"None of us do."

Morrighan joined them a short time later, a silk robe tied loosely around her body. She looked utterly relaxed. "The Dagda has spoken," she murmured, running fingers through her tangled hair.

Arianrhod made a sound in the back of her throat. "That isn't all he's done."

Morrighan chuckled. "We had some time to talk in between…well…you know." She waved her hand in the air.

"You made it loud and clear what you two were doing in there. So what did the great Dagda have to say, *in between*, as you called it?"

"He told me that this girl has a special future that includes Otherworld. As you know, things have turned very dark down there, what with over-population, pollution, climate change and so on. Apparently this Kat has a role to play, which means she's more important than ever."

"And what specifically is that role?" Airmid asked. "She's only one person."

Morrighan gazed into the darkness. "He wouldn't tell me."

"Oh, come on, Morrighan," Arianrhod said peevishly. "You can't tell me that the god you just had sex with decided to withhold information from you. How are we supposed to know what to do if he won't tell us the rest of it?"

"He said it's dangerous for us to know—that it could affect the future."

Airmid scoffed. "Sometimes these elder gods are too full of themselves to believe. I am well aware that Kat needs to discover her path, but fate? Is she fated to do something to save her world? Or is it ours she's supposed to save? They are both up for grabs."

Morrighan shrugged, pulling her robe closed. "That is all he would say."

"Where is he now?" Airmid asked, moving toward the opening into the castle.

"He's gone. He left before moonrise."

Airmid let out an irritated sigh. "He didn't reveal one new thing. We already knew she had a role to play. But what is it, and why her?"

Morrighan lifted one shoulder. "Since you've relieved me of my duties down there, I don't really care."

11

Kat explained the ingredients in the jar of face cream, extolling the virtues of no preservatives or alcohol. "It will keep for a year," she told the middle-aged woman standing in front of her.

"But, no preservatives? Isn't that against some regulation?"

Airmid joined Kat, her eyes seeming to swim with light. "This is my special recipe," she told the woman in a quiet voice. "If you use it those wrinkles next to your mouth will disappear. I guarantee it."

The woman smiled and opened the jar, putting her nose close. "It smells like lavender." She glanced up. "Do I get my money back if it doesn't work?"

Airmid laughed. "Of course you will, but in order to know if it works we need a before and after picture. Are you willing to let Kat take your picture with her phone so that we have a record?"

Kat reached into her pocket for the cell phone Bran had recently bestowed upon her. She hadn't used it much, but she was familiar with the camera option after taking a couple of selfies with Bran. She held it up and pointed it at the woman, focusing on her face. "Ready?"

The woman smiled and nodded. Kat clicked the red button and showed the woman the picture before handing her the jar of cream.

"How long will it take?" she asked dubiously, handing over a wad of cash.

"It you haven't seen results in a month please come back and I'll refund your money."

"A month? That seems extreme. I will have run out by then."

Airmid smiled. "That's the point, isn't it? If it works you'll need another jar."

When the woman left Airmid stuffed the bills into the cash box, a frown on her face.

"What's the matter?" Kat asked, glancing at the nearly full cash box. "We've almost sold out."

"I don't like it when people distrust me," she said. "I would never cheat them."

Kat laughed. "But you're the exception to the rule. Most of these wrinkle products don't work."

"Really? But why would people say they do if they don't?"

Kat just stared at her. "Where have *you* been? That's how the world works."

Airmid's expression clouded for a moment, but when another customer arrived, she plastered a smile on her face and hurried to help her.

Kat was cleaning up when Bran arrived wearing a ratty sweatshirt and the same torn jeans. "I have something to show you," he said, glancing sideways at Airmid.

"Go," Airmid said. "I can finish cleaning up."

"Are you sure?"

"Of course—just go."

Once they were outside Bran took hold of her arm to lead her across the busy street. "How'd you do?"

They dodged cars as she tried to find her voice, finally able to speak once they safely reached the other side. "Made a ton of money. And I used your phone to take a picture of one of our customers—before and after pictures," she explained when she saw the look of confusion on his face.

"That phone is yours, Kat."

"But you're the one paying the bill. How can it be mine?"

"It's in your name, and once you get established you can pay your own bill. You're like a babe in the woods when it comes to the modern world. Didn't your parents teach you anything? Have you ever used a computer?"

"Only at school. Mom didn't have one, and Jack…well, Jack had an office where he did his business."

"And your mom never got one? No cell phone either?"

"Jack didn't want to pay for it and he never wanted her to work. She was a stay at home mom, so why would she need a computer?"

Bran shook his head. "And then he killed her."

"How'd you know that?" Kat cried out, stopping to stare at him.

Bran frowned. "You told me—don't you remember?"

Kat continued walking with no idea of where they were going. "I don't know for sure that he did it," she muttered.

"Yes, you do. And you will prove it one of these days."

She glanced up at him beside her, surprised by the determined expression on his face. "Are you the god of prophecy or something? I wish I was as confident as you are. Where do I even start?"

Bran took hold of her hand and tugged her down the sidewalk. "Right now I have other things on my mind."

They crossed another small street, ending up at a nondescript painted brick building. There was no sign outside, only an open door and the sound of music wafting out. She glanced at him, afraid for a second. "Where are we?" she whispered.

"You'll see," he smiled, leading the way inside.

There were groups of people standing here and there, a bunch of easels set up with artwork on each one. A bearded man played guitar, another man accompanying him on a bass guitar while a blonde woman sang. It was rock music from the nineties, music Kat remembered from when she lived on the commune. She was immediately transported back to that time—the last time she'd been truly happy. "What is this place?" she whispered, looking around at the women and men dressed in paint spattered jeans and overalls.

"It's a drop in studio for artists who want to work from a model."

And then she saw the woman drinking a cup of tea and padding barefoot from one easel to the next to examine the images of her done in pastels, colored pencils, charcoal and tubes of watercolors. "Why did you bring me here?"

"Because you told me you were once interested in art. This is a community of artists and it costs very little to join them." He turned to look at her. "Even you can afford the nominal fee."

"But I don't have supplies, or…" At that point she was cut off as the model approached. "Bran!" she exclaimed, kissing him on the mouth. "What in the world are you doing here?"

Bran glanced quickly at Kat, his face turning red. "I could ask you the same thing, Rhiannon," he muttered, looking her up and down.

She let out a throaty laugh. "This is the perfect gig for me."

Bran motioned to where Kat stood mesmerized by the woman's lack of modesty, her breasts completely exposed where the robe gapped. "This is Kat. She's an artist."

"No, no, I'm not," Kat protested. "I used to like to draw, that's all."

Rhiannon's wondrous eyes landed on Kat, an appraising gaze running across her. "You have the look of an artist," she said, her hand going to her chin.

"Interest is the first step." She gestured to indicate the people, the easels and the band. "Today is the last day of this session. It is why we're having a party. We do this every six weeks. Many of these folks have never done art before—and just look at what they've produced!"

Kat walked around the room, examining the drawings and paintings. Some looked primitive, others had taken off in a completely different direction, turning Rhiannon's body into a sort of landscape. Each one was individual and had its own beauty. "What do you think?" Bran asked, joining her.

"It's fun for sure, but I'd be…"

"You'll fit right in," Bran assured her. "And you'll meet some like-minded people. It's time for you to find something for yourself that's separate from Airmid. There's an entire world out here waiting for you."

Kat thought about Airmid and the trust that was beginning to build between them. It had taken over two months. Could she be comfortable here with a bunch of strangers? And she had no idea where to go for supplies or whether she had enough money to afford them. Airmid was generous, but helping her with the herbs and the skin creams didn't bring in much.

"I've already talked to Airmid about it. She thinks it's a great idea," he continued as though reading her mind.

"But I don't make enough to spend it on art supplies."

"What else are you spending it on? Your rent is taken care of, and from what I've seen you don't ever buy clothes. Come on, Kat. Just give it a try."

Kat glanced down at her worn boots, the jeans she'd had since she was in high school. The light sweater she wore had been left behind at the shelter, abandoned by someone. "Will you come with me?"

He laughed. "Me draw? Maybe stick figures."

"If you come with me I'll do it. Otherwise, no."

Bran turned to where Rhiannon stood talking with a young blonde woman.

"You'll be close to Rhiannon," Kat added, misreading the expression on his face.

His gaze met hers. "Rhiannon is an old friend, that's all."

"That kiss didn't register *friend* in my mind."

Bran chuckled. "Rhiannon kisses every man she meets—it's just her way."

Kat turned to gaze at the statuesque woman. "She's gorgeous."

Bran shrugged. "Not my type."

"And what is your type?"

His mossy eyes met hers. "I prefer skinny women with long brown hair and a waiflike way about them," he said, deadpan.

Kat let out a loud laugh before she could stop herself. A few people glanced her way and then continued with their conversations. "You are so full of crap," she hissed.

"Am I?" he asked, his eyebrows rising.

When a tingle of sensation went through her body she quickly turned her gaze away. He wasn't attracted to her—he couldn't be. But when she glanced back at him he was still watching her, an expectant look on his face.

"What?"

"You're just as beautiful as Rhiannon, you know."

"I am not!"

"You don't see yourself as others do, Kat." When the music started up again he grabbed her hand and made her jitterbug with him.

Good thing Mom taught me to dance, she thought as he swung her around and twirled her. She saw Rhiannon watching them, a thoughtful expression on her features.

On the way home an hour later Bran continued to badger her about joining the studio. He walked backward facing her, his hands gesturing as he talked about what supplies she would need to begin.

"Why are you so determined to get me involved?"

He turned to walk beside her again. "Because I know

you'll love it. And if you really want me to, I'll come along the first few times."

"Are you still working nights?"

He nodded, running a hand over his recently shaved chin. "Another week and I'll be ready to move on."

"And what then?"

"It depends on you."

Kat stared at him in surprise. "On me? Why?"

He let out a long sigh. "I feel protective of you, Kat. I can't move away from here until you…"

"Until I what? It's not like I'm going to suddenly become an artist, or even make a bunch of friends. That's not who I am."

"And who are you, exactly?" he asked, stopping in the middle of the sidewalk.

She tugged him into an alley to let people by. "I don't know what I want or who I am right now. I have to solve Mom's murder, but I don't have the means to do it. If I go to the police again they'll laugh in my face. I don't have a proper job and my living situation is temporary. You don't need to hang around to protect me, Bran." She stared at him sadly, wishing he had another motive for the time he spent with her.

His gaze fastened on hers, a zing of raw energy passing between them. A moment later he leaned down and kissed her. Their tongues met before she pulled abruptly away. Her heart had begun to beat erratically and her knees had gone weak. If she hadn't pulled away when she did she was sure she would have collapsed.

He held her steady, his hands on her arms. "Are you okay?"

She tried to keep him from noticing how undone she really was, her body still trembling with the intensity of what she'd felt. "I've had boyfriends before. It's not like you're the first man to kiss me," she said. When she pulled away and walked toward the street he hurried after her.

"I'm sorry—I shouldn't have done that," he muttered when he caught up. "It's not part of my job description." This last was said in a whisper that she could barely hear.

"What did you just say? What job description? Did someone tell you to befriend me and gain my trust?"

Bran looked disturbed for a second, his brows pulling together. Instead of answering he took her arm to steer her across the street, letting go once they were on the other side. Once they reached her apartment building he shoved his hands in his pockets. "Say hello to Airmid for me." Before she could answer he was loping away.

Airmid greeted her with hands on hips like an anxious mother. "Where have you been?"

"Bran took me to some art studio in another part of town where he knew the model—Rhiannon."

Airmid's eyes went wide. "Rhiannon? Red hair, buxom?"

"She's gorgeous and voluptuous and she kissed him full on the mouth."

Airmid smiled. "That's Rhiannon, all right. Did you join in?"

"Join in the kissing?"

"No. In the artwork—the drawing or painting or whatever it was they were doing."

"I don't have any supplies for that," she stated flatly, heading by Airmid toward the bedroom.

"I have supplies," Airmid called after her. "Check in the closet in your room. They're yours if you want them—I have no use for them."

But Kat was still too shaken by Bran's unexpected kiss and the weird statement about job description to pay much attention to her.

After her shower when she was searching through her closet for something clean to wear, she noticed the oblong box on the floor labelled art supplies; she was positive it hadn't been there the last time she looked. Inside it was a box of pastels, a box of watercolors, brushes of various sizes and bristle types, some charcoal and a large tablet of pristine paper that could be used for pretty much anything except oil paint. She pulled them out and thought about it. After what happened with Bran she felt uncomfortable and unsure what to think. Could she work up the courage to go by herself? And where was the place, anyway? She hadn't been paying attention to the route, more interested in the conversation between them. And that's when the feeling returned, the out of control tingling that indicated her body's response to his kiss. No kiss she'd ever engaged in had felt like that.

It was after dinner before she opened up about Bran and the kiss. "I don't know what to think—he kissed Rhiannon too. Is he just that way or does it mean something?"

Airmid picked up the dishes and carried them to the sink. "What does it mean to you?"

"He mentioned protecting me. I don't want him kissing

me because he feels sorry for me and thinks I'm some waif who can't survive without him."

Airmid didn't say anything for a moment. When she did speak her eyebrows had looped into a frown. "I'm not sure you should think about Bran as boyfriend material."

Kat let out a sigh. "I doubt I'll see him again."

Airmid nodded. "That's probably for the best. He may not be who you think he is."

Bran had referred to Airmid as an old girlfriend. Did she still have feelings for him? "When did you date him?"

"When...*what?*"

"Do you have feelings for him? Is that why you don't want me going out with him?"

Airmid stared at her wide-eyed. "We...we were only together a short time."

"You know something about him that you're not saying."

"I...he's a decent sort, Kat. I just don't think he's for you. Best to steer clear for the time being."

"Is he into drugs? I thought he was at first, but lately he..."

"No."

"Then what?"

"He...he doesn't come from here. He lives in another realm...I mean city. He has family obligations that he needs to attend to."

The conversation ended there, Kat's confusion mounting even further. That kiss had rocked her world. And now Airmid was telling her he had family somewhere else. Did that include a wife? She was suddenly hot and cold all over.

12

"I'm telling you that he's crossed a sacred boundary!" Airmid insisted, watching Corra's skeptical expression. She'd met the crane goddess in the castle, unable to keep the news to herself while they waited for the rest of the goddesses.

"Maybe it's just a part of his plan—you know, to get her over her fear of men."

"What fear of men? She told me she's had several intimate relationships, starting the year she turned seventeen. If you're talking about her stepfather, I don't think that counts."

Corra turned as the other three goddesses arrived.

"What's with the rush to meet again?" Morrighan asked. "Dagda and I…"

"You and Dagda," Arianrhod grumbled. "Don't even talk about it."

Morrighan swivelled to glare at the moon goddess. "You only wish you had a god devoted to you the way he is to me."

Rhiannon held up her hand. "Enough! Why are we here?"

"Bran has crossed the line."

"What has he done?"

"He's 'making the moves', I guess is the current expression, on Kat."

Rhiannon let out a belly laugh. "Our Bran? That doesn't seem likely—I just saw him with Kat the other day and they seemed to be friends, not lovers."

"I didn't say they were lovers—not yet."

"What did Kat tell you?"

"Only that he kissed her. But I can tell she feels his power and she's succumbing."

"Feels his power…"

"She said she tingles when he touches her and she's dreamed about him. And now she thinks he's dumped her because of how she reacted when they kissed."

"And?" Morrighan prompted. "How *did* she react?"

"She pulled away. And he said something about protecting her, which set her off. Not only shouldn't he have kissed her, but revealing his mission is totally against the rules."

Morrighan scoffed. "A god kissed her and she pulled away? He must not have kissed her properly. When Dagda kisses me, I…"

"You think kissing her is less problematic than telling her he's protecting her?" Arianrhod interrupted.

"Well…" Airmid began. "It's the protection that is his duty as a god. As far as the kissing goes, I think he lost control of himself. But Kat doesn't like the idea of him thinking she needs protection."

"One of us needs to talk with him," Rhiannon said. She frowned when they all stared at her without speaking. "Me? Why me?"

"Because you've established a presence down there and you and Bran are close," Airmid said.

Rhiannon let out a huff of annoyance. "You have a presence as well, Airmid, and you and Bran go way back."

"We all go way back, Rhiannon, but with the art studio connection you're in a better position to have a private moment with him. I'm living with Kat."

"I'll do it, but you owe me," she finally agreed, glaring at the other goddesses.

"While you're at it, ask him exactly what his intentions are with this young woman. According to her she scared him away. Perhaps he's decided to protect her from the shadows? If he takes this thing with Kat any further it could cause all sorts of problems."

Rhiannon eyes narrowed in concentration. "Bran has always held himself back in these sorts of circumstances. I cannot see him breaking the rules."

"Not one to get involved with a human girl?" Arianrhod asked. "I would certainly hope not!"

"Don't knock it if you haven't tried it," Rhiannon murmured.

"If you see a raven hanging around the apartment you'll know he's protecting her 'from the shadows'," Morrighan pointed out, using air quotes.

Arianrhod eyes grew wide. "Have you flown with him too? How many sex partners do you need?"

Morrighan's expression darkened. "I have never lain with Bran. My fealty is with Dagda. Just because Bran can turn into a raven doesn't mean we're lovers."

"Likely story," Arianrhod muttered.

"Really, Arianrhod, get over yourself! I'm telling you the

truth. I suggest you find a lover, sooner rather than later. Your attitude is beginning to grate."

Rhiannon unbuttoned her gown, pulling one arm out of the sleeve. "How about we wrap this up? I have a modeling job to get to and I'm sure the rest of you have duties to perform."

"Let me know after you speak with Bran,"Airmid whispered as the other goddesses readied to leave.

Rhiannon nodded as she stepped out of her gown and pulled a loose fitting tunic over her head. She wrapped a leather belt around her waist and pulled on a pair of knee high boots, an outfit more suited to the human world. "I do hope he comes around the studio again. If he doesn't I won't have an opportunity to talk with him."

"I've given Kat art supplies—my hope is that she will attend the class with or without him."

"That won't help me, though, will it?"

Airmid shrugged. "If Bran is enamored he'll find a way to be around her."

Rhiannon smiled. "I still can't see our Bran with this waif-like girl."

Airmid raised her brows. "I hate to say it, but they look right together. Let's hope Kat is correct in thinking she scared him off."

Rhiannon whistled for her mare and when the horse appeared she vaulted onto her back. "I'll do what I can."

Airmid watched her gallop away before she moved under the trees, holding branches aside to find her way back to the apartment.

The castle emptied, the golden light dimming as they all dispersed in various directions. The birds continued their song until the goddesses were gone, and then they quieted, retreating into the thick branches to nest until the light returned.

13

Kat gathered the supplies together, using her satchel for the smaller items and carrying the pad of paper under her arm. She'd let two weeks go by since Bran had taken her to the studio, her indecision finally broken by Airmid's insistence that she at least try it out. "You told me you love to draw and paint. It's time you had a day off from working with me. Next weekend we'll have another pop-up site, but for today I can manage on my own."

Nerves gathered in her stomach when she left the apartment, the pad slipping from under her arm and landing on the sidewalk when an enormous black bird flew by and landed on top of a telephone pole. When she glanced up she had the strangest impression that the bird was staring directly at her.

Kat hadn't gone one hundred yards when the rain began. She hurried under a portico to wait it out, wondering why it picked this exact moment to rain. Above her the dark bird let out a hideous cackle, his wings wide as he flew in agitated circles. A second later the rain abruptly stopped.

Just in time, she thought, hurrying to where the crosswalk had turned green.

Her head was bent to her phone when she realized she was doing the very thing that irritated her about all the people she passed—looking at her phone to follow the map on Google. Every time she paused, whether to wait for a light or because she needed to adjust her load or check her phone, she noticed a dark bird on a pole or in the air just above her. It couldn't be the same one, could it? She tried to ignore it and hurried on.

When Kat entered the studio Rhiannon was there, a bright smile on her face. "I was hoping you'd come back. Is Bran with you?"

"No. I haven't seen him since the last time I was here." Kat gazed around the room. "I...I'm nervous," she confided, watching people setting up their easels and whatever materials they brought along.

Rhiannon scoffed. "No one pays attention to anyone else—they're far too focused on me and their work. It's very meditative."

Kat relaxed, confidence flowing into her from the woman's encouraging expression. "Meditative sounds good."

Two hours later Kat emerged from her second drawing. The first was done in charcoal and seemed amateurish and forced, but the second one showed some promise, she thought, the pastels blending nicely to bring out the cream and peach tones of Rhiannon's skin next to the vivid red of her hair. Rhiannon had done short poses for twenty minutes before she took the longer pose, her back to where Kat had set up her easel. In Kat's rendition the masses of red hair dominated the white paper, Rhiannon's shoulders and part of one cheek in shadow. It was arty, she thought, moving from one side to the other to assess the work.

"That turned out nicely," a man's voice said at her shoulder. She glanced over her shoulder to see one of her fellow artists standing there, squinting as he examined the portrait.

All at once she was filled with nerves, her hands trembling where she held the stick of color. "It needs something," she said, looking it over.

"Maybe a background color, here and here?" he suggested, touching the white spaces she'd left.

She nodded, agreeing. "Needs a contrast between her skin tones and the background."

"Maybe a blue gray."

Kat looked down at her pastels, picking out two or three colors to blend. She didn't start in until the man left her to talk with other artists around the room.

Meanwhile Bran had arrived and was across the room talking to Rhiannon, his head inclined to hers. She watched them out of the corner of her eye as she worked, feeling a little twinge of jealousy when Rhiannon tugged him into the changing room in back. She glanced around the room, watching the other artists working. Her being here seemed perfectly right and natural—that is until Bran appeared. Twenty minutes later the artists began to pack up their gear, Kat along with them. Neither Rhiannon nor Bran had re-emerged.

When Kat reached the apartment building another black bird was sitting on top of an old fashioned light fixture outside the main entrance. It was preening its feathers and stopped to stare at her as she crossed the threshold. She gazed up at it, trying not to be alarmed by its seeming interest in her. The popup notice on the front apartment was gone, the door propped open and obvious signs of a tenant moving in. Kat hurried upstairs.

As soon as she opened the door into 333 the scent of rosehips and coconut oil assailed her nostrils. In the kitchen she found Airmid bent over an old book, her eyebrows pulled together in a frown of concentration. She turned as soon as she heard Kat. "Looking up some more recipes," she said, closing the leather bound book and returning it to the shelf above the table. "How did it go?"

Kat shrugged and put her supplies down. "Okay until Bran arrived."

Airmid looked mildly interested "Bran was there?"

"Yeah, but he didn't talk to me—he and Rhiannon went to have sex or something."

Airmid frowned. "Sex? Are they an item?"

"I didn't think so, but they went into the back and didn't come out again."

"Hmm," Airmid said, moving to the stove where her concoction bubbled.

"Rhiannon is gorgeous," Kat continued, grabbing an apple out of the basket on the kitchen table. "I guess I can't blame him."

Airmid stirred for a moment and turned the heat off. "Bran's never mentioned any special fondness for her. Maybe they were just talking."

Kat took a bite of apple, thinking about the curtain hanging between the back room and the studio. It did seem kind of foolhardy to have sex back there with all the students present, any one of whom could surprise them in the act. "You might be right."

"Seems like you're a bit miffed with him?"

Kat shrugged again and opened the window over the sink to throw her apple core out. "I noticed that our pop-up downstairs is gone."

Airmid nodded, grabbing the hand mixer from the drawer next to the stove. "Can you beat this for me?" she asked, handing Kat the electrical device and the beaters. "Next weekend we have a new location—I've already put flyers up."

"Where is it?"

"A couple of blocks over in an abandoned warehouse."

Kat thought about the art studio—it was closed on Saturday and Sunday— wondering it that was the location. Improbable. She hooked the beaters on and began to beat the hardening mixture, her mind on Rhiannon's robe and the amazing body under it that the woman didn't feel it necessary to hide. She mentally chastised herself. Rhiannon was a model and had been naked for most of the day. Why did she have to cover herself up when everyone there had already seen her? But she knew it was Bran being there that bothered her. She'd barely been covered when they were talking, her breasts fully exposed for him to see. How could he not be interested in her?

Kat wished she had even an ounce of the confidence the woman exuded. She could never take off her clothes in front of a room full of people. But then again she didn't look like Rhiannon. Bran's quip about her being as beautiful as Rhiannon was laughable. But it didn't make her want to laugh.

Kat was returning to the apartment from a visit to the bookstore when she thought she saw Airmid disappearing behind the tree in the living room. When she went to take a closer look there was nothing there but the back wall. She pushed aside the branches, looking for a door, but there wasn't one.

Airmid definitely wasn't at home, her latest skin cream scooped into jars and neatly lined up on the kitchen counter. The labels were there, waiting for Kat to fill them in. All she'd seen was part of her leg and a flash of movement—she had to have imagined it. Her mind must be unraveling.

She stared out the window over the sink, going over all the strange events of the past weeks. And that's when her attention was taken by a dark shadow, her gaze lifting to see an enormous bird flying past. What was with these damn crows?

It was a few minutes later that she heard a knock on the door. When she opened it Bran was standing there, a sheepish grin on his face.

"Sorry I didn't get a chance to talk to you yesterday. Rhiannon wanted to go over some business with me."

"Business? You mean her modeling job?"

"That and other things."

"What other things, Bran?"

He frowned. "Just stuff, you know."

"Stuff? I thought you two were probably having sex back there."

His eyebrows rose. "What? I'm not interested in her in that way. I told you that already."

"But she was barely clothed, and…"

"So what? She doesn't turn me on."

Kat just stared at him, trying to decide whether to believe him. He certainly seemed sincere enough, but how could he not be interested? "Are you good with business?"

He nodded. "I have an MBA," he admitted, looking embarrassed. "I'm the one who suggested the pop-up—didn't Airmid tell you?"

"No—she says she has another spot for it this coming weekend."

"Yeah—the studio." He removed the leather satchel hanging over his shoulder, opening it to pull out a laptop computer. "Thought you could use one of these to spread the word." He handed it over.

She stared at it. "How can you afford this?"

He frowned. "I make good money."

"You don't dress like it," she said, examining his jeans, dirty tennis shoes and stained Grateful Dead T-shirt. His hair was lank, a scruffy two-day growth covering his chin.

"I guess I'm a hippy at heart," he admitted. "Can I borrow your shower?"

"Sure, but what about clean clothes? Do you have any?"

"Can you wash these?" He looked pathetic for a moment, like a lost puppy.

"The apartment does have a laundry room," she offered dubiously. "But it'll take a while."

"I have time if you do. Can I borrow a robe?"

Kat smiled, imagining him wearing her pink fluffy robe. "I'll do it. Just throw your clothes out and I'll take them down while you shower. Don't you have a shower where you live?"

"Roommates use up all the hot water."

Kat knew this was a lie by how he glanced away and the blush that spread across his cheeks. "Whatever. Go!" she urged, gesturing toward her room.

She waited for a while before she entered the bedroom. She heard the sound of the shower before she picked up the clothes he'd left in a heap on the floor. "My robe's hanging on the hook on the door!" she called out before adding her pile of dirty clothes to his and heading downstairs to do a load.

By the time Kat returned, Airmid was back and singing a song in some foreign language that mingled with the trill of the birds. "Where did you go?" Kat asked. "I swear I thought I saw you walk through the wall under the tree."

Airmid looked startled before she let out a nervous laugh. "Um...I had to check out the pop-up location. Who's in the shower?"

"Bran—he told me some bull about his roommates hogging all the hot water. He desperately needed a shower."

Airmid looked amused. "He's never been the cleanest of men."

"Were you ever lovers?"

Airmid scoffed. "No. Just friends."

"He said girlfriend."

"Yes. I'm a girl and I'm his friend." She glanced at the jars. "I hoped you'd have the labels done by now. I wanted to take a box or two over this evening."

"The pop-up location is where I go for drawing. Did you know?"

"How'd you figure that out?"

"Bran…" Kat turned as Bran appeared in the kitchen wearing her robe. Both she and Airmid burst into laughter.

His cheeks reddened. "Is this color wrong for my skin tone?"

Kat doubled over, unable to control herself for several moments.

An hour later she was down in the laundry room folding clothes, her attention on the fact that Bran had no underwear in his pile. Did a lot of men go without underwear? From there her mind turned to more salacious imagery that she quickly put a stop to.

14

"She saw me," Airmid told the other goddesses.

Morrighan frowned. "You need to be more careful."

"Thanks, *mom*—don't you think I know that? I didn't expect her to walk into the apartment at that exact moment."

"Maybe you should come through from another location," Arianrhod suggested.

"But it's so simple to step from one forest to this one—so direct." Airmid sighed, staring into the branches of the forest of hardwoods and conifers she'd created. It had spread since her last visit, the castle expanding with it; where it ended was no longer discernible. "She's beginning to ask questions."

"About what?"

"Why a huge black bird keeps following her and how in the world a man who dresses like a bum living on the street has an MBA. Stuff like that."

Morrighan laughed. "You're talking about Bran I take it."

Arianrhod left the balcony and moved inside to join the conversation. "And what do you say?"

"I told her that ravens sometimes migrate and that Bran is a unique individual."

"But she's not satisfied, is she?" Morrighan asked.

"No, not really. And this computer thing is driving me crazy. Now I'm supposed to understand the twenty-first century? Can someone *please* ask Dagda what he expects from us—first these horrible dangerous and noisy tools that are supposed to make life easy, and now this contraption that whirs and does strange things before I can figure out what I'm doing."

"I'll speak with him," the war goddess answered. "He still hasn't revealed why he's given us this assignment."

"Us? What exactly are you doing to further our task?"

The goddess of war frowned, her eyes turning the color of red-hot embers. "I'm the liaison between the rest of you and Dagda. Isn't that enough?"

"Seems to me you're more like the liaison between yourself and Dagda," Arianrhod muttered.

When a fawn raced by, chased by a mountain lion, Airmid let out a shriek and took off, vanishing into the trees.

Arianrhod's lips pressed together in annoyance. "I told her having a forest inside the castle was a bad idea—why doesn't she ever listen to me?"

Corra huffed, plucking a gray feather off her arm. "Same reason no one will listen to me—and *I'm* the goddess of prophecy."

The dreamscape was dull and gloomy, mist rolling through the trees like lumbering gray beasts. Kat squinted ahead wondering why things were so different this time. She'd never been in her recurring dream without sunlight and warmth, a soft breeze on her skin. This time her arms were hugged tightly around her shivering body, her hair dank and clinging to her neck from the cold fog, her mood growing darker with every step she took. And this forest didn't look right either. The trees were huddled too tightly together, so thick she could barely make her way around them. There was no path to follow. Where was the lovely pond, the berry bushes filled with the chirp of birds? She could hear the groan of the trees as they closed in around her.

A low growl made the hair on her arms stand up, adrenaline racing through her veins. Shadows gathered in clumps, their shapes shifting and changing. When another growl came she took off at a run, branches and thorny bushes catching in her hair, in her clothes and scratching up her arms and bare legs. She heard something crashing behind her, the sounds growing closer no matter how fast she ran. She pinched herself, telling herself to wake up, but the dream refused to end. Was it possible to die in a dream?

A backlit figure stood in the distance at the edge of the forest, the only part visible the cloud of white hair surrounding her shadowed face. Was that Gwen? Kat hurtled toward her.

"My dear girl, what on earth is wrong?" she asked when Kat threw herself into her arms.

"Something..." she gasped, "something chasing me."

Cerridwen peered into the forest. "I see nothing. Perhaps you imagined it."

Kat shook her head, still struggling for breath. "I'm dreaming, but I know what I heard..." But when she turned to look back, the forest was completely benign, fog replaced with sunlight sifting through the dark branches and illuminating the shadows. The path that had dwindled into nothing was now wide and free of the tree roots she'd stumbled over.

"And you want to wake up but you can't," Gwen said.

Kat stared at her. "Who are you? You look just like the woman I met at the shelter, but then she..."

"Disappeared," the woman finished for her. "I left because you no longer needed me, Katel."

"How do you know my full name?"

"Didn't you tell me?"

"I don't think so." Kat glanced into the forest again. "And what happened back there? The forest is totally different now—what did you do?"

Cerridwen's eyes widened slightly. "I did nothing. Your mind created whatever it was that scared you."

"But why would I do that? This has always been my laughing place."

She smiled, putting an arm around Kat's shaking shoulders. "I think it's time to reveal a bit more about why you're here. Are you ready to hear it?"

Kat gazed into her dark eyes, fear closing around her throat like a noose. "This is a dream—it's always been a dream. I will wake up."

Cerridwen watched her for a moment before bending to pick up a dark feather off the ground. "You have seen me here, you have seen Bran here. You've met Arianrhod and Morrighan here. Why are you so afraid?"

She held the feather out and Kat took it, wondering why the old woman felt it necessary to hand it over. It was black and glossy like the feathers of the dark birds...Kat let out a gasp and a moment later the scene began to fade. At the same time she heard a voice calling insistently. The last thing she saw was Cerridwen smiling at her before she woke up in her bed.

"Kat! Are you awake?" Airmid sounded frantic.

"I just woke up!" she called back, glancing at the clock. This was the day of the new pop-up and she'd overslept! She jumped out of bed and hurried to dress.

She found Airmid in the kitchen packing up boxes. "Carry these down, would you? Bran managed to borrow a car to transport our product. And when you come back up can you grab the computer? With Bran's help I'm trying to be a bit more organized this time."

Feeling Airmid's urgency, Kat picked up a box of jars and hurried out the open door.

Bran was at the bottom of the stairs and grabbed the box out of her hands. "You look like you just woke up," he said, his untroubled gaze on her uncombed hair, un-tucked shirt and the sleep still in her eyes.

"I overslept," she muttered, turning away to run back

upstairs. Today of all days Bran's hair was clean and he was dressed in a collared shirt and jeans that didn't have holes. He'd even shaved. Meanwhile he'd seen her at her absolute worst.

Two more trips and everything had been loaded, including Airmid and Kat. Bran drove, his jerky weaving and sudden braking throwing Kat forward to smack her head. "Don't you know how to drive?" she shouted, rubbing her forehead.

He glanced at her sheepishly. "There's a first time for everything."

"Are you serious?" She turned to Airmid in the back. "Did you know?"

Airmid shrugged and smiled.

Kat shook her head, her knuckles white where they clutched the sides of the seat as they rounded another corner going too fast. "Do you have a license?"

Bran didn't respond as he swerved to miss a car.

Kat sighed with relief once they arrived at the studio. "I'll drive on the way home," she told him, grabbing a box of jars and hurrying inside. Behind her Rhiannon greeted Bran by kissing him on both cheeks before whispering something in his ear.

The day went by quickly, all the skin products sold out by mid afternoon. Kat was too busy filling orders to pay any attention to Bran and Rhiannon, but before she left she noticed the two of them watching her and whispering. She turned away to help Airmid pack up the empty boxes and register the sales on the computer.

"Wonderful day!" Airmid said brightly, handing over the cash she owed Kat. "I only hope next week goes as well."

"And where will we be next week?"

Airmid showed her the ad she'd put up on Facebook with a picture of the small storefront. "This looks familiar," Kat said, studying it.

Airmid glanced at her. "It's in your neighborhood, just down the street from where you lived."

"How do you know where I lived?"

Airmid looked like a deer in the headlights for a moment before she regained her composure. "Someone told me—maybe Bran?"

"He doesn't know."

"Well, someone I talked to knew, Kat. Maybe you told more people than you realized."

Kat shook her head, scanning back to her first days and the people she'd met in the shelter. She'd told no one. When her gaze met Airmid's she was drawn into her gray-green eyes, a misty haze taking away her doubts. She must have told someone and just forgotten about it. Yes—she was certain she'd spoken to Airmid about her stepfather. In one of those conversations she must have revealed her former home—the one she shared with her mother. She didn't want to be anywhere near it ever again, but after today it was obvious that Airmid needed her help.

Once they'd packed up Kat and Bran argued about who would drive back. "You don't have a license," she told him, trying to push past him to the driver's side.

"Do you?"

"Well, no. But I know how to drive."

He shook his head and slipped past her to hop in the car. "Not fair!" she yelled with hands on hips.

"Will you two stop fooling around?" Airmid called out. "I'd like to get home sometime before midnight."

On the way back to the apartment Kat grilled Bran about what he and Rhiannon had talked about. "You two were whispering and looking at me."

When he glanced at her and swerved, she grabbed the wheel, her thigh pressing against his. A shock of energy moved between them, their eyes locking for a split second before she slid away.

"I don't remember," he finally answered. "She was probably telling me what a good artist you are. You never showed me what you did the other day."

"That's because you and Rhiannon disappeared into the back room," she snapped. "And never came out again."

"I was helping her with her finances—I already told you that."

Kat stared out the window, trying to let go of her confusion regarding this man. She was restless, expecting something she couldn't identify. Ever since their one kiss he'd been standoffish and remote with her—aside from the day of the shower, she thought, smiling. Seeing him standing there in her pink robe had brought tears of mirth to her eyes. If only he let his guard down more often.

She remembered Airmid's warning—did he have some complicated family life miles away from here? She wanted to ask him, but not with Airmid in the back seat. It was bad enough having Airmid bear witness to her jealous questioning regarding Rhiannon.

When they reached the apartment she wanted Bran to come upstairs, but before she could even broach the subject he was driving away in the vintage Ford, the car weaving in and out of traffic to the honks and yells of other drivers.

"I hope he doesn't get stopped for driving without a license," she muttered as she followed Airmid up the stairs.

"Oh, he won't—he's lucky that way." Airmid stacked the empty boxes and slid them under the table in the kitchen. "I forgot to ask how you slept last night. Any better?"

Kat paused with a box in her hands, remembering. "I had a terrible dream. Something was chasing me—some sort of big animal, but when I came out of the forest, Gwen was there—you know, the white haired woman I met at the shelter? She told me it was my dream and I made up all the bad stuff. Why would I do that?"

Airmid straightened from where she was arranging more boxes. "Dreams are often metaphors for what's troubling us. Perhaps you feel plagued by something? And Gwen must represent a mother or grandmother figure to you. I can think of a number of interpretations of the imagery you described." She took the box out of Kat's hands and stowed it under the table.

"I wish my dreams would give me answers instead of more questions."

"Not too long ago you were afraid to dream. At least you're over that."

Kat nodded. "But I wish the dreams were like they used to be when I was floating in a pond and felt like all my troubles were gone. Now it's like reality is intruding into my dream world."

"Perhaps you're getting closer to discovering something important, Kat."

In her bedroom later Kat found a black feather on the floor next to the bed. She picked it up and stared at it. It looked like the one Gwen had handed her in her dream, but...that just wasn't possible. Must have blown in from outside.

16

Kat heard the knock on the door while she was in the kitchen making coffee. When she opened it a man was standing there wearing a uniform, his peach fuzz cheeks and slicked back blonde hair revealing his youth. "Are you Katel Davies?"

"Yes, that's my name."

"A person has come forward to make a complaint about the circumstances of Siobhan Davies death," he told her, shifting from one foot to the other. "That is the name of your mother, correct?"

Kat nodded. "Who made the complaint?"

"I'm not at liberty to say."

Kat stared past him at the dust motes gathering in the hallway. "Would you like to come in?" she asked.

"Yes, ma'am, I would. The chief sent me here to relay this information."

Kat smiled at his use of ma'am. She'd never been called that before. As soon as he was inside and the door closed she realized the folly of letting him in. He was a cop, and what Airmid had done to the apartment was way beyond legal. She quickly pulled the door into the living room closed and led the way to the kitchen. "I've always thought my stepfather murdered my mother, but I have no way of proving it. And I have no money to hire a lawyer. How'd you even find me?"

"Did you at any time contact the police about this issue?"

"Well, yes, I did. But they were less than interested."

"Yes, ma'am, I understand. And you're right. If you came into the precinct and accused your stepfather without the means to prove it, no one would take you seriously. But your information and name were taken down and we tracked you to this address."

"This person who made the complaint—a man? And one who has credentials, I'd guess."

He smiled. "You're correct. He must have standing in the community or the chief wouldn't have given him the time of day."

"Mom's been dead for nearly a year now. Would it be too late to have her exhumed and tested for poison?"

He looked slightly shocked for a second before he answered. "I'd have to ask the medical examiner."

"What did this guy say, exactly? Did he mention poison?"

"He didn't mention any method, only that he felt she'd died from something other than natural causes."

Kat racked her memory for anyone she knew who might have an opinion about her mother's death. Jack had many friends, but from what she'd seen of them, they were all just as despicable as he was. "I can't for the life of me think who this person is. Won't you give me a hint?"

"Can't, ma'am. But if you want to come down to the precinct you can talk with a detective and give your version of events."

"I can?"

He nodded. "There's been one complaint already and you're an eye witness to what went on in that house."

Unfortunately she had not seen any evidence of poisoning, but what other means could it be? And she'd been absent for the week before her mother died. He could have used some kind of lethal injection that didn't show up in the blood, but if that were the case they'd never be able to prove it. "What if he used something that disappears?"

He shrugged. "Can't speak to that. All I can tell you is there's a credible witness who is saying foul play."

"When should I come down and talk to a detective?"

"Do you have the time now?"

Airmid was out shopping for supplies and not due back for several hours. Kat had nothing to do. "Can you bring me home afterward?"

The young officer nodded. "Part of my job, ma'am."

A half hour later she was sitting in a room at the precinct facing a police officer who was holding a pen and paper.

The detective wrote something down and glanced up at her out of his vivid blue eyes. "And what else can you tell me?"

"Only that my mom was fine when I left and a week later she was dead."

"Heart attack?"

"No. He told me she'd been sick for a long time—but it was a lie."

"You're talking about Jack Turner, correct?"

"Yes, my stepfather."

"And no autopsy performed."

"I wasn't here for the burial, but there would be no reason for an autopsy."

"And the coroner's report?"

"I certainly don't have it. I guess Jack does, but I have no idea where he is now."

"Easy enough to find it. He sold the house?"

Kat nodded, a lump creeping up her throat. "He threw me out and gave me nothing that belonged to her."

The detective didn't respond, continuing to take notes with his head down.

"I accused him of killing her."

The detective lifted his gaze. "You did what?"

"I told him I knew he killed her."

"And what did he say?"

"He said, 'Prove it, little girl.'"

"Didn't deny it?"

"Nope."

The detective closed his pad and stood up. "That's all for now. Leave your cell phone number with the desk sergeant. I'll be in touch once I locate the coroner's report."

"But what about the person who reported this—can you tell me his name?"

He shook his head. "He was promised complete anonymity, but he does know we've contacted you."

Kat stood and went ahead of him out the door, turning before heading down the hall. "Thanks," she said.

He nodded.

The other cop gave her a ride home, listening patiently as she described what had gone on with the blue-eyed detective. "He didn't tell me who lodged the complaint. How can I find out?"

The cop, who's name was Joe, smiled. "It's privileged information until it goes to court."

"Court? It could go to court?"

Joe nodded. "If you're making accusations of murder, the case will more than likely end up in the courts."

"But what if we dig her up and do an autopsy?"

"Can't do that without sufficient reason."

"But I don't have money for a lawyer, so unless this mystery man has evidence to prove what he's saying we're screwed!"

Joe nodded. "It's the way the law works."

"Crap."

"Let Detective Johansson do his job. He's very good at what he does."

Airmid seemed surprised when Kat relayed what had happened. "And no idea who this man might be?"

Kat shook her head. "I've been trying to remember anyone who came around who wasn't close friends with Jack. Jack made sure that Mom was always under his thumb. As far as I know the only friends she had were also his friends."

"Maybe an old friend who reached out?"

Kat shrugged. "Mom never mentioned anything to me. I wonder what the coroner's report says."

"If your stepfather killed her there could be collusion with the report."

"You mean he knew the coroner and the coroner covered for him?"

Airmid lifted one shoulder. "In that case the body will have to be exhumed."

"That's the thing—I can't force them to dig her up. I hope this mystery man has some clout."

Later in her bedroom Kat went over her trip to the precinct, replaying her conversation with the detective. He seemed competent and she had a feeling he would get to the bottom of it all. But what if she needed to go to court and testify against Jack? The thought of it was terrifying. For just a moment a strange idea flitted through her mind. What if the man who made the complaint was her real father? She shook her head and dismissed it as ridiculous. If he hadn't been in touch all these years why would he suddenly reappear once her mom was dead?

Some part of her longed to meet him and to know why he'd abandoned her when she was just a tiny baby. Her mom had said he was a good man, but if he was so good why hadn't he gotten in touch or made sure his child was provided for? A surge of anger moved through her at the thought of him leaving her mom like that. What kind of a man gets a woman pregnant and waits until the baby comes and then disappears off the face of the earth?

17

The dream started easily enough…soft breeze, the call of birds, a feeling of utter peace. She was floating again, her body light and free, her eyes closed, the water holding her like a mother's arms. 'This is more like it,' she thought dreamily. It was at that moment that she heard the horn—an ancient call to war? How would she know that? And yet she did. It was like that sound was emblazoned on her psyche somewhere. She was out of the pond before the echoes had dissipated, her heart rat-a-tatting against her ribs. When she raised her gaze in the direction of the sound her eyes fell upon Bran watching her. She took in his clean hair pulled back and tied with leather, the indigo tunic and the loose-fitting trousers hanging low on his hips, his bare feet. He was beyond good-looking, even more tantalizing than he was in real life. She wanted to feel his lips again—this time she wouldn't pull away. But just as that thought formed another burst from the horn made her jump.

"It's merely the hunting horn," he said. "Did it frighten you?"

Kat met his eyes. "Yes. I know I've heard that horn before, but when would I have?"

"Perhaps when you were a babe in arms? Noises of this nature have a way of sticking with you."

"A babe in arms? My mom never came to this place—as far as I know."

"Maybe your father brought you here."

"My father? I never met my father."

Bran chuckled, moving a step closer so that his arm brushed against hers. "I'm sure you met your father, Kat. Didn't you tell me you were a baby when he disappeared?"

"So as a tiny baby I'd retain this sound and my father's memory as well?"

"A newborn has access to his or her former life as well as to the world he or she is coming into. It takes a while to transition into the full reality of the new life."

"Reincarnation—you believe in that?"

"Yes, and many other strange and unfounded things as well, like mythology and spirits and destiny and fate. I know you don't want to acknowledge it, but now that we're in Otherworld I can tell you that I was sent here to protect you. But I didn't count on feeling about you the way I do." He reached for her hair, running his fingers through it, his mossy eyes focused on hers.

She fought the urge to throw herself at him. "I...I'm attracted to you too, but Airmid said that..."

Bran's eyes went dark. "Airmid said what?"

"That you had a family elsewhere—are you married?"

Bran let out his wonderful throaty laugh. "She's right—I have family here, in Otherworld. She's part of my family. And I am NOT married."

Kat suddenly realized that this dream was exactly like waking life, except for her surroundings and the clothes she and Bran were wearing. Looking down she noticed that her nipples showed through the wet shift, the rest of her body as visible as if she'd been naked. She crossed her arms over her chest.

Bran watched her, a smile curling up the corners of his beautiful mouth. "Would you like me to kiss you? The last time was hardly what I'd call complete."

Kat stared back at him. Yes, she would like him to kiss her and yes, the last one wasn't nearly enough, but...

"But you're afraid. Can you voice what it is that scares you about me?"

"I don't know you—you're different here than you are in...well... in my real life."

"I may dress differently so I don't stand out, but I'm the same person. Do you want to know my true name?"

Kat had read about 'true names' in fantasy stories and how you have control of those who gave them. "Bran, isn't it?"

"I was once a Welsh king, Bran ap Llyr. I had a son, Caradog. My father is Llyr and my mother is Penarddun. My true name is Bran Bendigeidfran, god of ravens and protection. My name means raven, holy raven or blessed crow."

"So you are married."

"No, Kat, I am not married and that life was very very long ago. Now I am known as Bran the Blessed after the raven which is the messenger between your world and mine."

Kat was tongue-tied, her thoughts jumbling into a tangle of threads that she couldn't unravel. What was this place? Was Bran an ancient Celtic god? She didn't remember him from her goddess book. But when he moved his hand to her chin and tilted it up to place his lips on hers she forgot all of it as she pressed against him, her arms going around his neck. The feel of his body against hers, the taste of his mouth, and the scent of cinnamon and fresh air, took away all thought.

It was a long time before they pulled apart, both of them breathless as their eyes met. Neither spoke, fearing to break the magic that held them captive.

"Are those ravens flying around—are they you?" she finally asked.

He smiled. "There is but one raven, Kat. And yes, we are one and the same." Minutes passed in which they stood very close, their hands clasped together. "You must go back," he finally told her. "It isn't time yet."

"What do you mean? For what? I don't want to leave."

"You have things you must complete in your world. You have opened up the beginnings of something that needs to be resolved. By the end of that inquiry you will know much more. But for now…"

"Will I see you there?"

"Maybe, maybe not. I am called upon to see you safe, but this other thing we've begun is not part of my assignment and will have to be reconciled before it can move forward."

"Who has the right to approve or disapprove?"

Bran cast his gaze around the darkening forest, the chill wind that had begun to move through the branches of the trees. Something was shifting. "It is time for you to go back." He kissed her lightly on the lips and clapped his hands.

When Kat woke her cheeks were wet with tears. But as to remembering the dream, any remaining wisps had drifted away. The only thing left was a hollow feeling in the middle of her stomach, as though something had been gained and then lost.

When she stepped out of bed a raven flew by her open window, it's raucous caw stirring something inside her. She ran to the window to catch sight of it, her earlier disgust and fear gone, as though the emotions had never been.

"Will you help me in the forest today?" Airmid asked when Kat walked into the kitchen.

Kat glanced at her, a hint of annoyance rising. Why would she feel annoyed with this woman who had done nothing but be her friend and help her get back on her feet? "Sure," she muttered, heading to the stove to heat water for the French press. The idea of one of Airmid's tea concoctions did not appeal.

"Another bad night?"

Kat shrugged, wondering why she could remember nothing of her night. Normally she could at least retain bits and pieces of dreams, and sometimes they were vivid in her memory the next day, but not this morning. "I don't really know if I slept or not."

Airmid looked troubled for a second before she pointed to the baskets lined up on the butcher block. "Once you've had some breakfast we'll take an Uber to the woods on the edge of the city. Can you use your cell phone to summon one?"

Kat nodded. "What exactly are we looking for?"

"Mushrooms, rosehips, chamomile flowers, and oxalis and dandelion—other things if we come across them. The weather is turning cold and I want to get some supplies in before they freeze back."

"What about the face creams?"

"I buy a lot of the supplies for those…I have to admit that the computer is coming in handy for ordering, now that I've figured out how to use the thing. But chamomile and rosehips grow wild. Wish it didn't take so much, though; it's almost worth it to order the oil rather than go through the lengthy process to extract it. I'm going to be really spoiled when I…" She stopped herself and put a finger to her lips.

"When you what?"

She glanced at Kat. "When I visit my family."

Kat knew she was lying by the expression on her face. "Where does your family live?"

Airmid stared blankly into the distance. "Out West."

"Like California?"

"Yes, California."

"What part?"

"Hmm…southern?"

"So Los Angeles?"

Airmid giggled nervously. "I always have a hard time remembering. My aunt and uncle live there," she said, turning away to break eggs into a pan. "I hope you don't mind eggs again. It's all we have until I go to the market."

"That's fine," Kat answered, sipping her coffee. Something seemed off today, as though the planet had tilted on its axis.

The Uber driver dropped them next to a wide dirt field that had been used to store heavy equipment. In the distance rain clouds were forming. It didn't bode well for foraging in the woods, but Kat grabbed the basket out of the car and followed Airmid. The driver shook his head, watching them, before he did a U-turn and drove off. "How will we find one to pick us up? I don't see an address anywhere and you told the guy how to get here."

Airmid turned from where she was hurrying toward the trees. "I hadn't really thought about that," she admitted.

Kat didn't like the feel of where they were, or the storm

approaching. She could see a homeless camp on the outskirts of where they were going; trash and used needles littered the sides of the path. "This is a bad place," she muttered.

"Not unless you let it be," Airmid whispered back.

Kat tried to push her fear down as she followed her off the trail and headed toward the trees in the distance.

Airmid was ahead when Kat saw her stop to talk to a man wearing a trash bag over filthy jeans and two different shoes. He was yelling and Kat couldn't hear what Airmid said, but a few seconds later he turned back to where he'd come from. Kat ran to catch up. "What did you say to him?"

"I told him we'd bring him some nuts and berries from the woods. He said thank you."

They entered the forest just as the clouds opened up, the wind sending branches flying. But as she hurried after Airmid it was as though they'd entered a completely different ecosystem. Birds were singing and the understory was filled with the smell of mushrooms and green things growing. They were a few minutes down the path when the sun came back, shafts of light filling in the spaces that a moment before had been enclosed in shadow.

"Check for chamomile," Airmid ordered. "I'm going to fetch some nuts and berries for our friends out there."

Kat watched her melt away and disappear, a shudder of fear making it's way up her spine.

"Don't worry, Kat," Airmid called from somewhere close. "I'll find you again."

She had the strangest sensation that Airmid had stepped into another universe, her voice muffled and unclear. A quick perusal of the area revealed rose bushes and the low growing chamomile, its yellow buds and flowers growing in profusion. Kat bent to her task, filling the basket in no time. She'd never seen a forest like this, she thought, gazing in surprise at the abundance of plants. It reminded her of the dream forest, with everything you were searching for right at your fingertips.

By the time Airmid returned, Kat's basket was as full as it could get. Airmid had two, one filled with nuts and berries and the other with mysterious green herbs and mushrooms of all kinds, including 'hen of the woods'.

"Good work!" Airmid cried when she spied Kat's full basket. A moment later Kat was following her down the path.

When they got close to the edge of the woods the sun disappeared again, the storm returning with a vengeance. Kat hugged her arms around her body as cold rain hit her full in the face. "It was lucky for us it stopped while we were in the woods," she said, hearing the howl as wind tore through the low hanging branches, scattering leaves and twigs.

"Yes, lucky," Airmid agreed, smiling. "I have to drop off the nuts and berries. And if you have your cell phone, could you call us an Uber?"

"What address?" Kat asked, wondering if she remembered their earlier conversation.

"Homeless camp by the woods on the north side of town," she answered, hurrying toward the tents in the distance.

Is it my imagination or is the rain falling all around her but not on her? Kat thought, watching her talking to the homeless people. *What the hell?*

The Uber arrived ten minutes later, and by that time Kat was thoroughly drenched and freezing cold. But Airmid was as dry as though she'd been standing under a roof. "How come you aren't wet?" Kat asked as she went ahead, wading through mud puddles to the waiting car.

"I'm drenched, Kat—what made you think I wasn't wet?"

When Kat turned to look at her, Airmid's hair hung in limp curls down her back, her dress soaked.

18

It was another two weeks before Kat heard back from the detective. Her cell phone rang early in the morning just before she stepped into the shower.

"The coroner's report said your mother died from a cerebral hemorrhage."

She turned the water off and wrapped a towel around her body. "What does that even mean?" she asked, sitting on the corner of the bed.

"Could be an aneurism, or a stroke."

"Can poisoning cause it?"

"Depends on the substance."

"Can we dig her up to find out?"

There was silence for a moment before the detective responded. "Cause of death is legitimate."

"But my stepfather said she'd been sick for a long time—I never heard a word about her having a problem like this."

"Can't help that. The law is the law when it comes to exhuming bodies."

"What about our mystery man? Have you heard from him?"

"Mystery...oh, you mean the man who brought the possibility of murder to our attention. Haven't seen him."

"And what about this coroner? Do you know him?"

"Not someone I'm familiar with, but I could ask around to find out his credentials. I wouldn't get my hopes up if I were you."

"If you hear from the person who made the complaint, will you let me know?"

"I'll be in touch. Sorry there isn't more we can do."

The called ended there.

A raven flew by the window taking her attention away from the sinking sensation in her stomach. "Can you help?" she whispered, watching dark wings soaring toward a telephone pole. The bird landed, turning its head to look at her, or so it seemed. *Am I really asking a bird to help me?* She mentally shook herself and went back into the bathroom.

Two days later Kat was at the bookstore looking up ways to poison someone when Bran came in. She stared at him, wondering why she wanted to run over and fling her arms around him. He looked as he always did with his ripped jeans and slightly stooped way of walking.

When he saw her his eyes lit up before a wary look appeared on his face.

"How are things?" he asked, watching her carefully.

She still felt the urge to kiss him but managed to suppress it. "Fine. What have you been up to?"

He shrugged. "Same old same old. Still working nights."

When she glanced at the bookshelf she could feel him

watching her. "What?" she asked, turning to face him.

"Nothing. Are you going to the studio tomorrow?"

"Oh. I forgot. I've been busy helping Airmid and dealing with the police."

"What about?"

"My mom's death. Didn't I tell you?"

"Not that I remember. Listen, Kat, I've got to get a move on. Take care."

"But...wait! Don't you want to know what's going on with the murder investigation?" she yelled out as he walked away. Several people turned to stare at her as she hurried after Bran. She followed him out the door and grabbed his arm. "I thought you were my friend."

"I am your friend. But you seemed irritated when I told you I felt protective. I've been trying to stay out of your business."

"But we've moved past that, haven't we? I mean, I thought after you borrowed my shower, and..." Kat was suddenly overcome with an emotion she couldn't identify. When her eyes welled she wiped at them angrily. "Are you mad at me?"

Bran shook his head. "How could I be mad at you? I..." He stopped himself and looked down. "I have to go now." He hurried off before she could stop him, his retreating figure disappearing into the shadows of a narrow alley.

When she ran after him all she saw was an enormous raven that rose up and disappeared into the sky. Must have been eating dead rat or some other disgusting thing, she thought to herself. But where had Bran gone so quickly? Did he live down there?

Kat walked home feeling utterly desolate and

bewildered at why she felt this way. Why was she so into him? They'd only kissed that one time. There was something, though…something she must have forgotten. Whatever it was niggled at the back of her mind but refused to reveal itself.

"A detective came by to see you," Airmid told her when she arrived home.

"Joe? He's a cop, not a detective."

"This man was dressed in jeans and a motorcycle jacket and was wearing those terrible sunglasses that have mirrors on the front. He said he had some information for you but that your phone wasn't working. He showed me his credentials but I didn't catch his name."

Kat pulled out her phone. "Forgot to charge it up," she muttered. "What should I do?"

"Call him. It must be important if he made a special trip to see you."

When Kat plugged her phone in and called Detective Johansson the duty cop told her he was gone for the day. She left a message. "I hope he has some good news," she said, turning to Airmid. "If we can't dig her up and do an autopsy I'll never prove anything."

Airmid didn't answer, her eyes glazed as she stared into the distance.

The next day Kat called the precinct again to make an appointment with Detective Johansson. The woman who answered put her on hold for a moment, and when she returned she told Kat a car would be sent to get her. Kat was surprised by the special treatment.

She waited by the curb, and when the car arrived she was happy to see it was Joe behind the wheel. There was something comforting about him. She slid into the front seat next to him. "Is there good news?"

Joe glanced at her. "I couldn't say. All I know is that I was told to come pick you up. I'm kinda low on the totem pole, I guess."

Kat laughed. "Sorry about that."

Joe glanced at her again, his eyebrows rising. "Could be worse. Do you have a boyfriend?"

Kat stared at him. "No. Why?"

He shrugged. "Thought you might like to have a cup of coffee sometime."

This time she took a better look at him. He was good looking in a way, with his fair hair and smooth cheeks. He had a boyish appearance that was kind of cute. And he was super nice. "Yeah, I think I would."

Joe smiled, revealing dimples in his cheeks. "I'm off tomorrow."

Kat realized suddenly that she'd missed the session at the studio. Oh well, proving her mother's murder was way more important than drawing. "Around nine would be good for me."

"I'll be there with bells on."

When they reached the station Joe reached across her to open the door. "See you tomorrow," he said, smiling.

She nodded and headed into the station, stopping by the desk to announce herself. Fifteen minutes later she was in a room sitting at a table across from Detective Johansson.

"Our mystery man came by yesterday to check in," he told her, looking down at his notes. "He said as far as he knew there was no history of stroke in the Davies family. He wants us to exhume the body. But in order to do that he has to get a court order. If he wasn't who he is this would never happen, but with his credentials there is a chance the judge will grant it."

"Who is he?"

"If he wants you to know he'll contact you. I've given him your information."

"But she was my mother—what's his relationship to her?"

"Are you saying no to his request?"

"I want to have her checked for poison or whatever, but I don't like this stranger going above my head. And what about Jack? Does he have a say in this?"

"We have yet to locate him. Once we do he will have the right to go against the request. It's now up to the courts to decide."

"Did you speak to the coroner?"

"Yes, I did. He was adamant that there was nothing untoward about his report. He told me that Siobhan Davies had been ill for some time."

"According to Jack. And how was she ill? Is there a doctor she was seeing, pills she was taking?"

"Once we locate and question Jack Turner we'll know more."

"That figures," Kat muttered. "But you're a cop—don't you have ways to locate a person?"

"Serial killers, maybe, but this case has not been at the head of the priority list for us, Miss Davies. The house he owned was sold nearly a year ago and there's no forwarding address."

"I hope this guy contacts me. Am I allowed to go to court to put in my two cents?"

"I'm sure you will. But that's probably months off. First we need to talk with your stepfather and determine the name of your mother's doctor. After we speak with him or her we can proceed. In the meantime I suggest you find a lawyer and do your own digging."

"But what if Jack refuses to talk to you? If he's guilty he won't want to be interrogated by the police."

"With this man's interest the investigation will be stepped up. And believe me, Jack Turner will be brought in for questioning."

"So the only reason you're doing anything at all is because this man, whoever he is, is either well known or rich?"

He gave a shrug and stood up, gathering his papers into a tidy pile. "I'll be in touch."

Kat just stared at him, her thoughts on the mystery man. Could he possibly be her father? If so she wanted to meet him.

Joe gave her a ride back, his worried gaze going to her several times as they circumvented traffic. "You seem upset."

"I am." She turned to stare out the window, unable to go on as tears welled. She didn't have the money to hire a lawyer unless he or she took it on a contingency. Could she sue Jack for taking her inheritance, or had her mother intended to give it all to him? And how much money was there? Proving Jack killed her wouldn't bring Kat any money, but at least Jack would go to jail. What lawyer would be stupid enough to take on a case like that?

"Do you still want to have coffee tomorrow?" Joe asked, pulling up in front of the apartment.

Kat nodded, trying to smile.

"I'll meet you here," he said. "And try not to worry. Johansson's the best detective we have."

Kat nodded and hopped out, anxious to get upstairs where she could let her frustration out.

"Slow down," Airmid said, placing a hand on her arm. "I don't understand what you're asking me."

"Can I hire a lawyer if I don't have the money to pay him or her?"

"There are court appointed attorneys for those who can't afford one. Why do you need a lawyer?"

"To dig into this case, that's why!" Kat burst into tears.

Airmid put an arm around her, leading her to a chair where she gently urged her down. "Not sure you need a lawyer for that. Perhaps with my help and maybe Bran's, we can 'dig in', as you call it. What is it you need to know?"

"Where my stepfather is and the identity of the man who brought the complaint! What if he's my father? But if he is, why doesn't he contact me?"

Airmid sat down next to her. "Maybe he's an old friend of your mother's, or perhaps he's a long lost relative."

"From what I've heard he has some pretty hefty credentials. The police are bending over backwards for him, and apparently he can get a judge to award him the rights to dig up my mom."

"If you don't want her dug up I'm sure he won't be allowed to do it."

"But I do want her dug up—I know Jack killed her, Airmid, and I want to prove it!"

"Well then, what's the fuss?"

"I want to know who this guy is!"

"Once you go to court you'll find out, won't you?"

"Or if he deigns to contact me. I don't get why he hasn't."

"Maybe he's worried that you'll fight him on it."

"That's not it. I'm sure the cops have told him what I suspect about Jack."

"Perhaps he's protecting you."

Kat grimaced. "Like Bran? Does everyone think of me as a person who can't take care of herself?"

Airmid rose to stir something on the stove. "I need to do some more foraging tomorrow—what are your plans?"

"I...I'm having coffee with Joe in the morning—nothing after that."

"Shall I wait for you then?"

"I guess, but I don't want to hold you up."

Airmid glanced out the window over the sink. "It will rain tomorrow afternoon. If you're not back by noon I'll go alone."

"Nine until noon?" Kat scoffed. "I don't even know the guy—I figure an hour at most."

19

Birds circled around the horse goddess's head, twittering in dulcet tones as she moved restlessly from one side of the balcony to the other. "Who is this man?"

Airmid shook her head. "How do I know? But apparently he has the police department cowed."

"Could he be her father?" Morrighan asked, sweeping onto the balcony from inside the castle

"I have the sense that Dagda has kept some pertinent details from us," Corra said, arriving in a rustle of gray feathers. "Is he so infatuated with you that he can't take the time to lay out our assignment correctly?"

"Infatuated?" Morrighan scoffed. "He loves me, Corra. As to this assignment, we know everything we need to know."

"Is that so?" Arianrhod asked. "Seems to me that it's becoming more and more complicated. First there was a girl to watch over, and now…a murder? And of course her infatuation with Bran."

"And Bran's infatuation with her," Airmid reminded

her. "He's been avoiding me since I confronted him about it."

"I spoke with him as well," Rhiannon added, glancing around. "I haven't seen him since, nor has the girl come back to the studio. What is she doing these days?"

"She's fretting about the police case and dating a man named Joe who is on the police force."

"Really? Well there goes Bran's chance." Corra chuckled.

"I wouldn't be so sure about that," Airmid whispered, moving toward the forest to listen. "Bran is at the apartment as we speak and it sounds as though they're having an argument."

"Bran never argues," Rhiannon said, moving next to her. "Oh my," she said, her eyes going wide. "That sounds very much like a lover's quarrel. I thought he was backing off."

"Lovers? I hardly think so. Bran would never take a step like that. He knows that Dagda would have his…well; we all know what Dagda would do. As to why he's at my apartment, I cannot say. I was happy when Kat told me about Joe."

"I suggest you head home before they kiss and make up," Rhiannon urged. "But don't appear from under the tree. That's where they are."

"Unless they've moved to the bedroom," Airmid muttered.

20

"**Y**ou don't even know this guy—who is he? Are you attracted to him?"

"Why do you care?" Kat yelled, glaring at Bran. The tree in the living room shivered with her words, birds scattering. "He's a good guy, Bran. He likes me and we've gone out a few times—what does Joe have to do with you?"

"I love you, Kat," Bran blurted, his face turning bright red.

"What? Since when?"

"Since...the first time I laid eyes on you. Gods, I can't help it," he mumbled, staring at the floor of moss and rock.

Kat trembled all over, her body cold and then hot. "You...I thought you wanted to protect me. Joe doesn't think I need protecting—he thinks I'm strong."

Bran let out a mirthless laugh. "You are strong. I feel protective because I love you, not because I think you're weak."

Kat met his gaze, a shiver of energy passing between them. The mist lifted from her eyes and she remembered how she felt about him. "I dreamed that…"

Bran took a step closer. "That wasn't a dream. I made you forget, because…because…"

"Because what? And how is it possible that I dreamed about you and you had the same dream?"

Bran took another step toward her, his hand going to her cheek. "I…"

Before he had a chance to finish his sentence Airmid flung the door to the living room open and stomped in. "What are you doing here?" she demanded.

"Airmid…!"

"Be quiet Kat. I'm talking to Bran who promised me…"

Bran turned to face her, his eyes welling. "I'm sorry, Airmid. I can't control it."

"Get out!" she yelled, grabbing his arm and dragging him toward the door. "Now!"

Bran gave Kat one last lingering look before he left the room. When the door closed behind him Kat ran and flung it open. "Bran!" she called out running to peer down the stairwell, but he was already gone.

Kat turned on Airmid, anger blazing inside her. "Who do you think you are? Bran just told me he loved me—why would you do this?"

"Because it's not allowed."

"Not allowed…why?"

"Because…because he's married."

Kat was dumbfounded, several conflicting emotions moving through her at the same time. "He can't be."

"Well, he is," Airmid said, turning toward the kitchen. "I suggest you concentrate on your new guy and let this one go—Bran's nothing but trouble."

The birds in the living room began a raucous chatter as though the argument had riled them all up. They flew in circles around the tree, their shrieks ringing off the walls. It was a second later that Kat realized what had upset them. An enormous raven was sitting on the windowsill. When she went to close the window the bird stayed put, its dark eye fastened on her. Tentatively she reached out to touch the smooth feathers, sure she would scare him away, but instead he pressed his downy head into her palm.

"Get that filthy bird out of here!" Airmid screamed.

The raven lifted on wide wings and disappeared into the gray of the sky, leaving Kat feeling utterly bereft. "How can you say you love nature and chase away a raven? What is *wrong* with you?" Kat ran for her bedroom and grabbed her suitcase out of the closet, stuffing her belongings in haphazardly. Living at the shelter was better than enduring this woman's baffling moods and this latest nastiness.

Airmid grabbed her arm on her way out, the woman's eyes filled with tears. "I'm sorry, Kat. I only want what's best for you."

Kat jerked away. "How do you know what's best for me?" She opened the door and hurried down the stairs without looking back.

Kat lugged her suitcase toward the women's shelter, hoping she could find the place again. It had been months since she'd been there. Her fingers went to the necklace around her neck hoping for some magical message, but she felt nothing but the usual tingle that she assumed came from the metal. When she felt a presence behind her she turned quickly, surprised to see Bran following her. "Go away. Airmid told me you're married."

Bran caught up to her and walked along beside her. "I am not married, Kat. I told you all about myself in your dream—don't you remember?"

Kat did remember, even recalling his true name, the one that gave her control over him, or so she'd read. "Bran ap Llyr, Bran the blessed, Bendigeidfran, god of ravens and prophecy," she intoned, wondering if he would now bow before her. "Was that you on the windowsill?" she blurted with a snort of derision.

He nodded, looking like he'd just lost his best friend.

"You expect me to believe that you can shape shift?"

"I don't expect anything, Kat. I just know I love you and I want you to trust me."

A car honked next to them, taking Kat's attention. "Hey! Don't we have a date for dinner?" Joe called, slowing.

Bran tugged the suitcase out of her grip. "Go. I'll take this to my apartment—I have an extra room. It's got to be better than the shelter." He pulled a piece of paper and a pencil out of his pocket and jotted down his address. "Have him drop you here."

She gazed at Bran, trying to decide what to do. The shelter was not where she wanted to be, but...

"Please just trust me, Kat. I'd never hurt you or lie to you. I promise." He crossed his fingers over his heart.

She took the address and stuffed it in her pocket and headed toward Joe waiting in his cruiser. He had the light on but the siren was quiet, cars going carefully around him without honking.

"What was that all about?" Joe asked when she climbed in beside him.

"I got kicked out of my apartment and Bran knows a place where I can stay."

Joe smiled. "Nice to have a friend like that—someone who has your back."

The entire scenario from her dream hit her with such force she let out a gasp. After Bran revealed his name he'd kissed her like she'd never been kissed before. But was Airmid telling the truth—was he married? And what about this nonsense about shape shifting?

"You okay?"

"I think so. Still reeling from my sudden homelessness."

"Good thing your friend happened along."

"Yeah, good thing."

Dinner at the taco place Joe chose was fine, but Kat was distracted, trying to work out her plan for the near future. She couldn't move in with Bran, especially if he was married. In fact she shouldn't even stay with him for one night. But she had a memory of him telling her that the marriage happened a long long time ago—how long? He was barely twenty-five years old. His words came back as though he was standing next her. *"No Kat. I am not married."* But Airmid said he was. Who should she believe?

By the time they left the restaurant Joe was somewhat disgruntled, a frown on his face. In the car she handed him the paper with Bran's address. "I'm sorry for being so distracted," she said, trying to smile. "I don't know what to do now. I don't have a job, so no money for a place to stay, this case is going nowhere, and that man has not bothered to reveal his identity. I'm lost, Joe."

A few minutes later Joe pulled up in front of a nondescript building. "I know you are and I wish I could help." When he reached for her and pressed his lips to hers she pulled away.

"Too much too soon," she told him when she saw the forlorn expression on his face.

He nodded. "I get that. Hope we can do this again, Kat. I like you a lot."

Kat smiled and nodded, unable to give him any encouragement. Right now she felt like her life had been turned upside down. Again.

Once he drove away Kat took a look at the building in front of her. It was glass and metal, much newer than the one where she'd been living for the past few months. When she glanced up at the sky she saw charcoal clouds rolling and bumping. A storm was coming. The wide door stood open and she entered a pure white vestibule, looking down at the paper in her hands. Apartment number seven. *The number for good luck,* she thought hopefully as she hunted for the door.

hat have I done? Airmid moved aside tree branches in the apartment living room. A moment later she was in the castle, the sound of birds and the snuffling of skunks and other animals rustling around her. There were no other goddesses there, her abrupt visit made in haste. She hurried outside, rushing into the garden to call out their names, one by one.

"What is wrong?" Corra asked, appearing by her side.

"I have alienated our charge. I told her that Bran is married. She's left my apartment and I have no idea where she's gone. I know she will not forgive me for what I have done." Airmid dissolved into tears, wiping ineffectually at her eyes with her long sleeve.

"Why would you do this, Airmid?"

The tone was less than kindly. "Try to understand, Corra. Bran was about to make the biggest mistake of his life, and Kat...she..."

"What mistake?" Corra interrupted. "I have seen his future and this young woman is a part of his destiny."

"How can that be? Gods are forbidden from consorting with mortals."

"And yet Rhiannon has a child with a mortal."

"Pwyll is a prince who lives in Otherworld. This situation is not at all like that."

"And yet it seems Bran may love her. How can you keep them apart? It is not possible unless the Dagda forces his will upon Bran."

"Maybe the Dagda is who I must speak with. Bran doesn't understand the gravity of his actions."

"Did you not hear me? Why are you so dead set on keeping them apart? Are you in love with him?"

Airmid colored. "I…I don't think so. Honestly, I'm not sure."

Corra shook her head and pressed her lips together. "This is pure jealousy, an emotion unbecoming of a goddess. How *could* you?"

Airmid found a stone bench and sat heavily, her head in her hands. "I…I can't believe this is happening to me. I've always been a free spirit."

"You must make amends for what you have set in motion, Airmid. That young woman was meant to stay with you until this matter was resolved. Now she wanders alone with no one to help her."

"Maybe we can coax her into Otherworld through her dreams?"

"And what will that accomplish? If she is meant to be with Bran, and you have soured her feelings for him, she is without support of any kind."

"She has another boyfriend, a cop named Joe."

"And yet the last time we gathered together she was in

your apartment arguing with Bran. Is that when all this happened?"

Airmid nodded. "I made him leave and I called his raven shape a filthy bird and screamed at Kat to get rid of it."

Corra's mouth dropped open. "My gods! I am not the one with authority to say this, but it is my opinion that you should stay away for now. Allow Rhiannon and others to deal with this poor woman."

"Perhaps you're right. I want to apologize to her, but I know in my heart there is nothing I can say to make up for this. I have betrayed myself."

"That is true. I suggest a trip to your healing spring. You must heal yourself, Airmid—rid yourself of envy before you return."

Airmid nodded and hurried toward the castle. A few moments later she disappeared into the forest, her focus on the healing spring and submerging herself in the waters. Tears flowed down her face without cease, shame and self-loathing propelling her forward.

Once Airmid was gone Corra shifted into her crane shape and flew off to find the other goddesses. Her inner sight had shown her many things. It was time for an emergency meeting.

22

Kat knocked on number seven, her hands shaking. The door opened a second later, Bran standing there wearing a pair of sweatpants and a ripped T-shirt.

He smiled and opened the door wide to let her in. "Didn't know if you'd come, but I figured since I was holding your belongings hostage you'd at least come by to pick them up."

Kat walked by him into a modern apartment filled with light. Two walls were devoted entirely to windows, a hallway leading off the living room into another section. It seemed larger than it should, with more windows than possible, considering where it was situated on the first floor. The furniture looked Scandinavian, maybe Ikea? The kitchen was filled with stainless steel appliances and counters of black granite—masculine but not cold. "This is…amazing. How can you afford it?"

"I know, right? I totally lucked out. It belongs to a friend of mine who moved to Europe. He lets me stay here as a caretaker."

"So you pay nothing? Where are your roommates?"

"Moved out. I guess I'm too anal for them," he chuckled. "Can't help it if I like things neat. And it was one of my agreements with Trent."

"A man who dresses like a bum and hardly ever showers but likes things neat—that's an oxymoron."

"What kind of a moron?"

Kat laughed, her nervousness disappearing when his teeth flashed in a grin. "Okay, Bran. Time to be grilled."

"Grilled as in cooked alive?"

"Maybe. It depends on your answers."

"Let me show you your bedroom first." Bran headed away and Kat followed him down a long hallway that opened into another large room with a bed against one wall. There was no door. More Ikea, from what she could tell, another wall of windows looking out on a forest of green. "What…how is there a forest there?"

Bran shrugged. "Don't know, but there it is."

Her suitcase waited on an old-fashioned luggage holder. "Wow."

"You like it?"

"The layout of this place is like an artist's studio or something out of a futuristic novel—all open and clean."

"An artist's place wouldn't be so clean, I bet."

"Yeah, maybe not. Has Rhiannon been here?"

Bran frowned. "Are you still thinking I have something going with her?"

"No," she lied, "But I know you're good friends."

"With no extra benefits." His moss green eyes met hers.

Some sense of support and hopefulness she hadn't felt in a while stole through her. She wanted to move closer, to be in his aura, but she stopped herself, turning away to check out the bathroom hidden behind a curved wall. It was all black and white tiles and glass, an enormous tub that could fit two people taking up a lot of the space. She couldn't wait to get in it. "No doors at all?"

"No doors at all, but I never come in here. You'll have all the privacy you need."

What if I don't want privacy? she wanted to ask, but instead she went to the bedroom to gaze out a set of casement window that stood open to the elements.

Instead of the cold gray sky, she was met with a warm breeze and a dazzling sunset. "Is this magic? It was gray and cold when I got here."

Bran smiled. "I did it for you," he joked.

When she turned he was gazing at her, an expression in his eyes she hadn't seen before. The tingle started in her toes and moved up quickly, taking her breath away. She had to turn away to compose herself. "What about what Airmid said?" she asked with her back turned.

"About what?"

Kat faced him. "About your marriage."

"I already told you I'm not married. Not sure why she keeps saying that."

"Maybe she's in love with you."

Bran's eyes widened. "Airmid?" he shook his head dismissively.

"She chased the raven away."

"I know."

Kat felt light-headed, dizziness making her sway. Bran moved close to steady her. "You okay?"

"Not really."

"What can I do to help?"

She shook her head. "Tell me that you're not a raven?"

"How can I be a raven when I'm standing here in human form?"

Kat didn't want to ask any more questions for fear of what she might learn. "Can I have a cup of tea?"

"Sure thing," he said, leading the way back to the kitchen.

They chatted about this and that as Bran made tea and produced a plate of oatmeal cookies. "How was the date?" he finally asked.

"It was …fine. Joe's nice."

"And how do *you* feel?"

"I…like him…" she let the sentence hang, unsure how much she wanted to reveal. They were all alone here—anything could happen.

"I won't do anything you don't want me to," he said in a serious tone. "I meant it when I told you you could stay here without fear of me coming on to you."

"You said that?"

"Not in so many words, but I tried to get the point across. You need to unwind, Kat. You've had some major trauma, especially with what just happened at Airmid's. Me making a pass would not be good for you right now."

"How do you know?"

Bran frowned, staring at her. "Whoa—what are you saying?"

"I'm saying I remember our kiss and I want more."

"Are you sure?"

"Yes, Bran, I'm sure. I don't want to have sex—at least

not yet—but I would like to kiss you again."

Bran let out his throaty laugh, shaking his head. "What are we waiting for?" He grabbed her hand and dragged her into the living room and pushed her gently onto the leather couch. He sat down next to her and stared at her. "You are really beautiful," he murmured before his mouth moved to hers.

Kat melted into his arms, letting go as they explored with their tongues. Her body felt really alive for the first time since her mother's death. And oh, how she wanted to take this further. But her inner voice warned her no. Bran had pushed her sweater and her bra strap off her shoulder, and his warm mouth was traveling downward, when she realized that if another minute went by she wouldn't be able to say no. Her heart was already pounding, her body molten as though she'd jumped into a vat of hot lava. When she pulled back he sat up, his eyebrows pulling together. "Did I go too far?"

She smiled and shook her head. "But if you kept that up, I..."

"Yup—me too." He took her Celtic knot necklace in his fingers, gazing at it with a frown. "Where did you get this?"

"My mother gave it to me—why?"

He pulled a pendant out from under his shirt. "It's similar to mine."

Kat examined his, comparing them. "Weird—where did you get yours?"

"I...it's my heritage, Kat. It's a family heirloom. Do you know where your mom got yours?"

"She told me my father gave it to her."

Bran let the silver knot fall into the hollow between her

breasts and stared at the dark windows that now reflected the room, his brow furrowed in thought. With the dusk, the lights inside the apartment had come on automatically. A moment later he turned to her. "It's getting late. Shall we call it a night?"

"Yes, but I'm not sure I'll be able to sleep."

"Me neither, but I think you're right about taking things slow."

"We hardly know each other," she said, staring into his eyes that seemed to be swirling in some kind of magical way. She could see her necklace reflected in them. And he had one just like it. Her fingers went to the knot around his neck, a tingle running up her arm.

His gaze met hers, his hand enclosing her fingers that were wrapped around his pendant. "We may know each other better than you think we do," he said, letting go.

When she released his pendant he stood and pulled her up, his fingers twining through hers before he led her down the hallway. When they reached the opening to her room he leaned down to kiss her lightly on the lips. "Goodnight," he murmured.

When Kat gazed into his eyes she nearly changed her mind about things, the need for him tugging at her. *No,* she told herself sternly. *What if he's been lying this entire time? You need to get a grip.* For one moment she worried about not having a door to lock, but when she noticed the softness in his eyes her worry went away. He turned and left her there, disappearing down the curve of the hall.

23

After waking in the middle of the night and going over the events of the day before Kat decided that she needed to go back to Airmid's apartment and hash things out. The woman had been a big part of her life for several months and she hated to just drop the friendship. Maybe Airmid had a logical explanation for why she acted the way she did.

When she woke again the sky was pale gray, her thoughts immediately going to Bran and making out with him the night before. She smiled and stretched before climbing out of the comfortable bed.

When she came into the kitchen there was a pot of coffee, a pitcher of cream, a mug, and a plate of sticky buns sitting on the counter, a note next to them.

Had a few errands to run. Make yourself comfortable. Extra key is on the hall table. See you later.

She poured a cup of coffee and went into the living

room to admire the view, but what she'd seen the day before was not there. Now it was what she'd expected— tall buildings, a sky filled with dark cloud, and the sound of traffic. She didn't even try to puzzle it out, heading to the couch to finish her coffee and figure out her day.

Once her cup was empty she refilled it and grabbed a sticky bun before heading to the bedroom to get dressed. It was a cold day and she needed her one pair of heavy socks, a warm sweater and jeans. After dressing she picked up the sticky bun crumbs she'd strewn across the floor, depositing them into the trashcan in the bathroom.

On the chair next to the table that held the spare key she found a warm jacket, obviously left for her to wear. It was waterproof and had a fur-lined hood and it fit her perfectly. Next to the key she found some cash with another note: *If you need an Uber*...

How had he known that she had no money? She'd been in such a hurry she'd left her cash in the dresser drawer at Airmid's. And she had little memory of the trip here with Joe—she'd been too preoccupied. She'd never find her way back to Airmid's apartment. She smiled to herself thinking about his thoughtfulness.

The Uber driver dropped her off in front of the apartment building and took off, his tires spinning in the puddles. She hurried to the entrance door and pulled out the key she still had, fitting it into the lock. When she reached 333 the door was ajar, voices wafting from inside. "Airmid?" she called out, pushing the door open. A middle-aged man stood in the doorway into the living room, his pale eyes regarding her curiously. Behind him a man and woman in their twenties were looking over the apartment. "Are you here about the rental?" he asked.

Kat moved inside, peering into the living room. The apartment was empty, no sign of the tree or anything else that had been here just yesterday. "Where's Airmid?"

"Who? This apartment has been empty for several months now. These kind people are considering renting it. Shall I add you to the list? We've had quite a rush of interest since I lowered the price."

Kat stared at the floor where the tree had been. There wasn't a pebble, a piece of moss, or a twig left behind. "I...no. I thought a friend of mine lived here but I must have been mistaken." She backed away and fled through the door, her heart beating erratically as she raced down the stairs.

When she reached the ground floor it was pouring rain outside, a cold wind blowing. She huddled under the roof to wait it out, her mind completely blown. There was no way Airmid could have stripped that place and cleaned up in one night—no way at all. So what had this been—some kind of dream sequence like the ones she'd had with Bran? But the apartment was real, the layout one she recognized, the number the same. When her phone rang she expected it to be Airmid with some fantastical tale explaining what she'd just experienced, but instead it was Detective Johansson.

"Think you'd better come on down."

"What's happening?"

"I'll tell you when you get here. How soon will that be?"

Kat searched in her pockets for the remainder of cash.

She was pretty sure she had enough for another Uber. "Half hour?"

"Good." The phone went dead.

The rain had stopped by the time she reached the station, thin sunshine attempting to peek through the thick cloud cover. She suddenly realized that today was the anniversary of her mother's death. An entire year had gone by.

Inside she was ushered to a room to wait for the detective, nerves making her hands shake. Having a sticky bun and coffee for breakfast had not been the wisest of meals. When he arrived his expression gave nothing away, his blue eyes fastening on her for a moment before he sat in the chair across from her.

"We found your stepfather," he told her without preamble. "He is livid and denies any wrong doing. He's already hired a team of lawyers to fight this."

"Did you speak to him in person?"

He nodded. "We brought him in for questioning, but got little out of him. He called his lawyer right away."

"What does your intuition tell you?" Kat asked, watching him.

He smiled, which changed his demeanor from cop-like to almost human. "Judging by his reactions to the questioning, and feeling it necessary to call a lawyer? I'd say he has something to hide."

"Does he know I'm involved?"

"I didn't mention you, but he brought you up, complaining about your threats."

"My threats? That's rich. And he knows about the mystery man?"

"He does now."

"Did you reveal the man's name?"

"Had to since the man is basically accusing him of killing Siobhan Davies and wants to exhume the body."

Kat stared at him. "Are you planning to tell me who he is?"

"Not until he agrees. He doesn't want to get you involved."

"Someone else protecting me," Kat muttered, looking down at her boots.

"What's that?"

"Nothing. Did you get the doctor's information?"

"Jack Turner refused to give us anything, including the name of her doctor."

"That's because she didn't have one. What's next?"

"We go to court."

Kat used the rest of her money to Uber back to Bran's apartment, her thoughts on what going to court really meant. It was time to get a lawyer, but how could she without any money? And why in hell didn't the mystery man reveal himself to her? She could be a valuable asset to him. *Damn it all to hell*, she muttered to herself.

Once the Uber dropped her off in front of Bran's apartment she hurried inside to number 7, and inserted the key into the lock. She closed the door behind her and called out for Bran—she needed to talk over recent events with a friend, but the apartment was as silent as a tomb. Another note lay on the kitchen counter:

Had to make an unexpected trip home. Not sure when I'll be back.

Please stay and enjoy the apartment. There's food in the fridge and lots of coffee.

Kat was utterly baffled by Bran's note. Her first thought was to move to the shelter, but when she visualized the place, and remembered what it felt like to be there, she thought better of it. Today was art studio day but she'd left all her supplies at Airmid's non-existent apartment. Was her entire life a fantasy she'd made up? After standing in the middle of the kitchen for probably ten minutes she pulled out her phone and called Uber, deciding to use her last few dollars to have the driver take her to the studio. Maybe Rhiannon could explain what was going on.

When she reached the warehouse the studio was locked up tighter than a drum. A notice on the door said the space was for rent. When she peered through the smudged and filthy windows there were no easels and the floor was pristine. Last time she'd been there the floor had been covered with remnants of paint and chalk. She was still standing there when Joe happened by, his cruiser slowing when he noticed her. "Hey, lady!" he called out. "You trespassing?"

Kat turned to see him grinning at her and headed toward him, her thoughts tumbling in confusion.

"Get in," he ordered when he saw the expression on her face. "You're as white as a sheet."

She felt like a robot as she opened the door and slid inside. A moment later she dissolved in tears.

24

Despite the fact that he was on duty, Joe took her to a coffee shop and made her tell him what had happened. Only one day had passed and it felt like the planet had tilted and gone so far off kilter that she worried she might slide off.

Instead of holding certain details back Kat let it all out, from Airmid's disappearing apartment, (she left out the part about the tree), to Bran's sudden need to leave, to the absence of the studio. "And on top of that I need a lawyer," she managed to blurt out, wiping at her eyes.

Joe nodded, taking hold of her hand. "Johansson told me. That stepfather of yours seems like a real piece of work."

Kat glanced at his concerned face. "What should I do?"

"You have a place to live but no job. I know someone who's looking for a file clerk. Would you be willing to do that kind of work?"

"Anything at this point. But that won't be enough to pay for a lawyer—how much does it pay?"

"Fifteen an hour probably. You can get a public defender, Kat."

"But how good will he or she be?"

Joe shrugged, twining his fingers through hers. "Some are really good, others aren't. You have to take your chances—what other choice do you have?"

She nodded, pulling her hand out of his and placing it in her lap. "How do I go about it?"

Joe narrowed his eyes in thought. "Best idea is to take you to the precinct to talk with Johansson. I'm sure he can figure it out."

A half hour later Kat was in the front room of the police station waiting for Johansson. When he finally appeared he seemed harassed, as though her being there was interrupting his day. "Sorry," she said when he gestured for her to follow him. "Joe said that..."

"Joe's thinking with his dick right now," he interrupted as he led her into the back. "Sorry for the crudeness, but he shouldn't have stepped in—he's a traffic cop, and the way he feels about you isn't helping."

"Anything new with the case?" she asked, trying to deflect his terrible mood. She followed him into a room and sat in a metal chair across from him.

"If you feel you need a lawyer I'm sure...*he*... can get you one."

"I'm really sick of this. I haven't a cent to my name and this man seems to be able to do pretty much anything. Can you please tell him that I'm destitute?"

Johansson's eyes bored into hers. "Can't you get a job?"

Kat sighed. "Joe mentioned a friend who has an opening, but minimum wage won't do much good. I had a good paying job before..." her voice trailed off, a lump forming in her throat.

"Let me talk to Mr. Anonymous and see what he has to say. Knowing him he'll probably spring for a lawyer for you. He wants to get on with this, and right now it's lagging until we can get a judge to hear the case. Your stepfather has put the brakes on it."

"How can he?"

"He was there when she died, he has the coroner's report and he was married to her."

"Crap," Kat muttered.

"Exactly. Now can you please get out of here so I can get some work done? This is not my only case. I'll be in touch as soon as I can get word from our friend. And *please* don't encourage Joe. He's vulnerable to damsels in distress."

"I'm trying not to, but he…"

"Yeah—he can be persistent. I'll assign another driver if we need to pick you up again. Leave your new address with the desk on your way out."

Kat left the station, avoiding Joe when she saw him hanging around by the curb. But then she thought better of it—how was she to get from here back to Bran's apartment? She hurried over to the cruiser and climbed inside.

"Back to the apartment?" he asked, his eyes bright.

She nodded.

"Want to have dinner after I get off work?"

"No, Joe. I'm sorry but I have something going with Bran. And besides that I have to sort out my life, which is a royal mess right now."

Joe looked over at her, sadness in his eyes. "I thought we were good together."

"I like you, but not in that way—I'm sorry."

"You still interested in that job?"

"Yes."

"I'll text you the info."

For the rest of the trip he stared straight ahead without looking at her once. When he reached the apartment she got out of the car and turned to say goodbye and thank you, but he was already racing away, his tires squealing. *So much for being friends with Joe*, she thought morosely.

Bran still wasn't back; the apartment felt cold and lifeless without him. She wandered from room to room, finally arriving at his bedroom. She lay down on his bed and pressed her face into the pillow where his special scent still lingered—cinnamon and cedar. Tears welled and dripped down, soaking his pillow.

A black raven stared at her from the window, but when she got up to check, it wasn't there. Am I dreaming? She remembered lying down on Bran's bed, but she was no longer in the apartment. A trail led through a dark wood and she followed it, hoping to run into Bran, but by the time she reached her pond she figured she was on her own. Birdsong was loud in her ears, the soft breeze caressing her cheek like a lover. She stripped off her light shift and waded into the water.

Being here no longer soothed her as it had in the past. Now she was beset with worry about her life, Bran's absence, and the case against Jack Turner. And what about Airmid's sudden disappearance? Had anyone ever seen the woman aside from Bran? Was she even real? Kat sighed and floated, kicking her feet to propel herself from one side to the other. Cattails waved in the breeze, fluff coming loose and floating around her before landing on the surface of the water. How could a dream feel so real?

A low hanging sun moved across the sky—she could see its progress—okay, that was definitely dreamlike. When it set the sky went from blue to all colors of the rainbow before stars began to show up, massing to become constellations. She watched them, tracing the big dipper, Orion, the hunter, Taurus, the bull. They looked almost close enough to touch. When the moon rose the stars were obscured, the orb so bright it hurt her eyes to look at it. A bird flew by, dark shadow against the brightness. A raven. She laughed when she saw it, her voice echoing in the night stillness.

A moment later Bran had shed his clothes and was wading toward her, his dark eyes on hers. A few seconds after that she was cradled in his arms and he was carrying her to shore.

They lay together in the tall grass, their eager lips meeting in a kiss. And when their bodies came together she let out a cry that rippled, sending bright colors streaming through the air like fluttering ribbons. She felt his heart and hers beating in rhythm as though they were one heart. They lifted together, floating on a sea of brightness, their breath, the same breath, their two bodies melding into one. Together they reached the pinnacle, bright stars shimmering before splintering into a million fragments that lit up the night sky.

Kat woke in Bran's bed. At some point she'd crawled under the covers. The window stood open, a cold wind blowing across the room. Rain lashed and dripped from the roof and puddled on the wood floor. When she swung her feet out of bed she was hit with the remnants of the dream, her mind reeling with what had happened between them. *It's only a dream,* she thought to herself—*my mind's way of escaping reality, and having a magical moment with Bran.*

From what she remembered of the sex it had been

mystical and otherworldly—unbelievable in the full sense of the word. There was no way it could have happened. And yet…and yet her body registered something she couldn't ignore, her leg muscles weak and aches in places that couldn't be denied. When she went to take a shower and took a look in the mirror her eyes were bright, the area around her mouth red and chapped as though from rubbing against his stubble. She chose to ignore it as she stripped off her clothes and climbed into the shower. But when she came out and reached for a towel she realized that what she'd been wearing was not the jeans of the day before, it was the gossamer tunic she'd had on in the dream. And when she pressed the pale garment to her nose she could smell him. The two worlds collided in an explosion, her senses overloading as she took in the significance of this. What was happening to her?

25

The meeting was held in a neutral spot in the middle of a large meadow, the gods and goddesses gathering to discuss the matter. Airmid was on trial for her behavior, as was Bran. Angry whispering accompanied frowning stares as they awaited the Dagda.

"Well, this isn't going to be pretty," Bran said, watching them. He and Airmid sat on grass in the middle of the circle awaiting the great god, the one who would take the testimony and give his verdict.

Airmid glanced at Bran, her lips tight as she tried to hold herself together. "I never meant for this to happen. If it hadn't been for your behavior I never would have acted like that."

"My behavior? All I did was care for Kat. What have I done that is so against the rules?"

"You…kissed her and would have taken it further if I hadn't stopped you. Don't deny it."

"And why was it your job to stop me?"

"I…I couldn't let Kat get caught up with you that way—it is forbidden!"

His eyes narrowed. "Are you sure that was your only motive?"

"Are you accusing me of...?" the rest of her sentence was cut off as the father god appeared, his anger palpable. He was enormous with wild dark hair, his eyes the deep winter blue of a stormy sea. He wore a tunic of leather over a homespun long sleeved shirt, and trousers of loose wool, his feet clad in heavy boots. A cape of heavy wool lay across his wide shoulders, a clasp in the shape of a Celtic knot holding it closed.

"What is the meaning of this?" he shouted. "I have better things to do with my time than listen to mean-spirited gossip."

"There are laws," Corra said, standing. "When we become aware of wrong doing we must bring it to the attention of all."

Morrighan let out a hiss of annoyance, moving from her place in the circle to stand by Dagda. "I am not part of this," she told him, trying to soothe his anger.

He glanced down at her, his eyes softening for a second before he turned to the rest of those assembled. "We have two accused, it seems," he said, staring at Airmid and Bran. "Will someone speak for them or will they speak for themselves?"

Rhiannon stood. "I will speak for Bran. In my estimation he has performed the duties placed upon him to the best of his abilities. My vote is in his favor."

When Rhiannon was finished Airmid rose and spoke. "I only lost my composure for a moment—I do not think it is reason to punish me. I was trying to keep the rules regarding humans and gods in place. I acted on impulse because of Bran's indiscretion regarding our charge."

"But from how you explained it to me," Corra said, glancing at Dagda, "in the process of doing what you deemed to be correct, you alienated our charge and ruined our mission. The young woman is now completely alone and without our support."

Dagda's eyes narrowed in anger. "I had a very specific reason for what I asked of you. There are certain details that are yet to be revealed, and now we are at an impasse. What I will say is that this woman's future is pivotal to our continuation. She is a link between the human world and Otherworld. It is why I asked of you what I did. What have you to say for yourself, Bran ap Llyr?"

Bran started, standing hastily. "I am in love with this woman and have tried very hard not to pursue her in that way. But I have to admit I have been unsuccessful."

"And have you told her who you are?"

Bran nodded. "I have, but I am not sure she believes it. There is a bond between us that I cannot explain."

Dagda stared into the distance for a moment before he spoke again. "This is an understandable transgression. We are all subject to our emotions, despite being gods. But from this moment forward I expect you to cease all contact with her." He turned to Airmid. "Your rash behavior is the cause of this gathering. If you had handled this with more discretion we would not be assembled here."

"I...I guess my emotions got the best of me," she said, staring down at her feet.

"Because you have feelings for Bran," Corra added. "Admit it, Airmid."

Airmid's eyes flashed, her anger rising. "What I feel or don't feel is none of your business, Corra. We all have a right to our private thoughts." She glanced at Bran next to her. "I was worried that Bran would take this thing too far and regret it. The rules are clear and there to be followed. No fraternization between the gods and humans. I saw the look in his eyes when he was around Kat. And because of who he is, she had no way to resist him."

Dagda turned his dark gaze on her. "So your excuse is that you were attempting to stop a god from using his powers to lure an innocent?"

"That is correct."

Dagda let out a heavy sigh. "The entire purpose of the task I put before you has been ruined. I see no way to salvage it other than to watch from afar and attempt to deflect any evil that befalls her. I am doing what I can, and I expect everyone here to do the same, *without* appearing to her in the flesh. Is that understood?"

There was mumbling and a collective nod.

"As to punishment," he said turning to Airmid. "That young woman is now aware of the magic with which you created your environment and has witnessed you going from one world to the other. You will remove those memories from her mind. And once that is completed you will have nothing more to do with her. And Bran, as I said, the same goes for you."

"But…"

"I am well aware that she is now living in an apartment you set up for yourself. Not the best of choices considering your feelings for her. You will have one more meeting with her to clear her mind and at the same time return the apartment to its original state. Make sure she's on the lease and has paid up for six months."

"But she has no money and no job."

Dagda narrowed his eyes. "Be creative, Bran. I'm sure you can plant some ideas in her head to explain it all. Find her a job."

Bran glanced away, his eyes dark with pain.

Dagda swept his gaze across the group before turning on his heel. The meeting was over.

26

K at was sitting at the kitchen table drinking coffee when she heard Bran's key in the lock. It had been three days since she'd last seen him. She hurried to the front door as it opened and flung herself into his arms. "Was that a dream? Did we...I mean...oh my god, Bran!"

Bran gently removed her arms from around his neck, his face registering pain and another emotion that she couldn't decipher. "We need to talk," he said, leading the way into the kitchen. He sat down and put his head in his hands.

"What's wrong?"

"You know I'm a god, right?"

Kat shook her head. "I know there's magic around you—I was right there with it a couple of nights ago when we...but a god? I can't really buy that."

"I'm not allowed to do this, Kat. Gods are strictly forbidden from...being with humans in this way. I love you, but...I have to do something that pains me greatly."

"Before you do whatever this is, can we...? I mean...I'd like to have sex, here in your bed in this reality."

Bran stared at her, several emotions moving across his features. "I...want that too, but I've been ordered to..."

Kat took hold of his hand, pressing it to her breast. "I don't know who has the right to order you to do anything, but right now I want you to make love to me. What can it hurt?"

Bran stared at her for several moments as emotions worked across his features. He finally let out a sigh and tugged her to her feet and led the way down the hall. Once they reached his room he turned to her. "Are you sure about this? You said you wanted to take things slow—I don't want to push you into..."

"Shut up," she said, pulling off her sweater. "And get undressed before I rip your clothes off."

Bran frowned for a moment before he unzipped his jeans.

"Don't you want to?" she asked him, pausing in the hasty removal of her clothing. "If you don't want me, I..."

"I want you, Kat, more than you'll ever know." His eyes welled with tears.

Kat stared at him. "You're...you're crying. Why?"

"Because I love you, and I..." He pulled her close and buried his face in her neck.

"I love you too." She held him, her fingers working through his hair. "It's why I want to make love with you."

"Don't you want to know where I've been and what I've been ordered to do?"

"I don't care about that right now."

Bran moved to sit on the bed, his eyes sad. "Come here," he ordered.

When she came close he pulled her down next to him.

"I'm supposed to wipe your mind of all memory of me. How can I make love to you and then do that?"

"I would never forget you no matter what you did. Who told you to do that?"

"The great god, Dagda," he muttered.

"Dagda…" she repeated, staring into space. "Dag. My father's name was Dag."

"What??"

"His name is Dag—Mom told me. He never told her his last name."

Bran's eyes widened. "That would certainly explain a few things," he muttered.

"You aren't really a god, Bran—seriously. And this Dagda dude—who is he supposed to be? Is this a game of Dungeons and Dragons?"

"Dungeons and…" Bran looked confused. "Dagda is the father god, a chieftain who wields immense power and control in Otherworld."

"What color is his hair—and his eyes?"

"Dark curly hair and blue eyes—the man is immense and rock solid."

Kat's mouth fell open, her earlier skepticism diminishing. "Could he…no, it's not possible—gods? You're telling me that this Dagda is a god, and that maybe he and my mother…?"

"Had a child together?" Bran nodded. "It is quite possible and would make sense under the circumstances."

"But gods don't really exist. This is crazy."

Bran watched her for a moment. "Don't be afraid of what I'm about to show you," he said, standing.

"What are you talking about?" Her question was

answered when he began to glow, getting brighter and brighter until she could barely stand to look at him. His face became even more beautiful, his lank hair turning golden and shining. His moss eyes swam with magic. He looked like himself except more—so much more. She closed her eyes and when she opened them again his arms had turned into raven wings, the rest of him transforming in front of her eyes. "Stop!" she shrieked, moving backward on the bed.

A second later he was himself again, his eyes filled with worry. "I'm sorry, Kat. But you need to believe me."

She stared at him, her mind everywhere at once. It wasn't possible, and yet she'd just seen him turn into a raven. "I…I'm freaking out, Bran."

He moved next to her and wrapped his arms around her. "I know you are," he murmured into her hair. "I'm sorry."

"What about Airmid and that tree?" she asked, pulling away.

"Earth goddess."

"Oh my god. And Rhiannon? When I went by the studio she wasn't there—the place was shut up like it had never been…"

"Horse goddess."

She gazed at him next to her. He looked like a normal human being—maybe more street person than most, but definitely not a god. She tried to tell herself that what he just showed her was the truth, but her mind refused to take it in. Even her dream couldn't explain this. No wonder she'd felt jealous of Rhiannon—the woman was a freakin' goddess! *No!* her mind screamed. *This is just illusion—there are no gods or goddesses. Did he give me some drug like LSD or maybe ecstasy?* But she'd had nothing but the coffee. *Caffeine poisoning?*

But a moment later when his lips met hers she forgot everything, her mind going blank. Somehow they both ended up naked and in bed, his kisses taking her places she didn't know existed. He devoured her whole, his hands and mouth awakening her to another existence that had nothing to do with this one. Her need matched his in its intensity, both of them lifting on the wings of the raven and entering some ethereal world that she now knew belonged to the gods.

"If you *are* half goddess," he murmured as his mouth travelled across her overheated skin, "there is no rule to prevent us from…" But Kat didn't hear him, her mind shattered completely as she entered a universe filled with sensation so intense it utterly consumed her.

27

K at woke in her studio apartment feeling like she'd either run a marathon or had wild sex all night. She laughed to herself as she rose and pushed the Murphy bed up against the wall. She hadn't had a serious boyfriend since she was nineteen, and that jerk's behavior had put her off men ever since.

Her cat meowed, demanding breakfast. "Okay, I'm up," she told him, heading into the tiny Pullman kitchen.

A vague memory flitted through her mind of a spacious modern apartment filled with light from the large windows that looked out on a view of trees. She chalked it up to some dream fantasy as she grabbed a can of cat food and opened it, dumping it into the small dish on the floor. Bran went at it as though he hadn't eaten in a month, his dark fur gleaming like raven feathers. Because of his black fur she'd named him after a god who could shape shift into a raven; Bran the blessed was listed in the book her mother had given her. The name gave her a warm feeling, maybe because of her mom who had been particularly enamored with the Celtic pantheon of gods and goddesses.

As she made coffee she thought about what she needed to do today. Her rent was paid up for six months, but the rest of the money she'd saved from her last job was nearly gone and wouldn't cover her living expenses, including her cell phone. She glanced at the newspaper lying on the counter and the ads she'd circled the day before. One boutique was looking for a sales clerk to sell their line of natural cosmetics. She liked the idea of that and was interested in the process of making them—the small store wasn't far from where she lived.

She dressed in a wool skirt, tights and boots and a stylish wool sweater that came down over her hips. From the little she could see out her filthy window, the sky was dark, with a threat of either rain or snow. Over a year had passed since her mother's death—it was time to move forward, despite the weather and her aching muscles.

An hour later she was standing inside a small boutique called Cerridwen's Cosmetic Cauldron, and facing a woman she'd met at the shelter a year ago. The change in her was unbelievable. Her white hair had been cut and hung in a neat bob to her shoulders, her outfit of bright turquoise and orange bringing out the vivid blue of her eyes.

"Kat!" she cried out, taking Kat's hands in her own. "How are you?"

"I'm okay. I wondered what happened to you and why you disappeared."

"My daughter was running this place and decided it was too much for her with two children to take care of."

"Does she own it?"

"Yes, indeed she does. I am now manager and chief

165

cook and bottle washer." She laughed. "Are you here about the job?"

"I am. I saw the ad and I have an interest in herbal formulas. I like the idea of clean cosmetics that use natural ingredients."

Gwen showed her around, pointing out the different jars of rose hip cream and argan, coconut oil and shea butter concoctions. The packaging was simple, with brown recycled paper and green twine. "The job pays $25 an hour with increases depending on how well you do. We like to reward our workers here."

"Do you make the cosmetics?"

"My daughter makes most of them and we buy from other green companies. When can you start?"

Kat laughed. "Yesterday?"

Gwen clapped her hands. "Perfect! Now tell me, have you solved your mother's death?"

"Did I tell you about that?"

"Yes, you did, dear. I was very worried about you, but you seem so much better."

"Some mysterious benefactor has been in contact with the police about my mom. He's attempting to have her body exhumed and tested. So far he hasn't revealed himself to me, but he seems to have some cred considering the fact that the police are bending over backward to do his bidding."

"And your stepfather?"

"That's another story. He's of course trying to block it."

"Well, I hope this person is able to unblock it—he must be quite powerful or a long lost relative to get this far."

"I thought mom was an only child, but maybe he's a

brother she never mentioned?"

"What about your real father, Kat?"

Kat shrugged. "Mom never told me his name."

They stopped talking when a customer arrived. Gwen sold her some products and then turned back to Kat. "Can you start tomorrow? I'll be here this week to show you the ropes but I would really like some time off. I'm getting too old to be on my feet this long."

"What time?"

"Hours are from ten until four-thirty and we're closed Mondays. You need to be here at nine-forty-five at the latest."

Kat walked back to her apartment feeling elated. Twenty-five dollars an hour was good pay for a store clerk, and maybe with time her pay would go up. She stopped into the bookstore on the corner on her way home, but once she got inside she had the strangest sense of expectation. She glanced around, wondering why, but nothing jumped out at her. A man with his back turned caught her attention, his dark blonde shoulder length hair and torn jeans reminding her of someone, but when he turned she didn't know him, her racing heart slowing as he left the store. For the life of her she couldn't recollect who he reminded her of or why her heart had begun to pound.

Her cell phone rang just as she reached the apartment; her hands were so full of grocery bags she nearly dropped the phone.

"Miss Davies? This is Detective McCormick. I have some news regarding your mother's exhumation."

"Yes? What is it?"

"The judge has given the go-ahead to…" he stopped in mid-sentence. "Sorry, I almost revealed something that I've been specifically warned not to," he muttered. "In any case, the exhumation will happen as soon as the ground is soft enough to dig."

"This is January—that won't be for months!"

"We often have a thaw in early February. With the heavy equipment it may happen sooner than you think."

"I guess the man who is ordering this is still keeping his identity secret? Since I'm a relative isn't he required to meet with me and get my permission?"

"That's why I'm calling. You need to come in and sign some papers."

"Papers to give him the green light?"

"Yes ma'am."

"I don't think I'll do that," Kat stated.

"You…don't want her exhumed?"

"Of course I want to find out what killed her, but I'm not going to sign a document giving a complete stranger the right to dig her up!" she yelled.

A few seconds of silence went by before he said, "Perhaps you should come in and talk with Detective Johansson. He's lead on this case."

Kat let out a sigh. "I'll come in, but I'm not going to sign anything until that man introduces himself."

"I'll patch you in to the desk so you can make an appointment," he said just before he put her on hold. Fifteen seconds later the duty officer answered. She made an appointment with Johansson for early the next morning before she had to be at work. Hopefully she wouldn't have to wait. It wouldn't do to be late on her first day.

The rest of the day was spent figuring out what bills she absolutely had to pay and which she could put off until her first paycheck. By the time night arrived her eyes hurt and she was bleary with fatigue. She cooked up some beans and made a salad before heading to bed.

Kat was in a dark place that seemed wrong somehow. She knew she'd been here before—she recognized it, but this time it seemed almost ominous. The forest ended in a vast valley devoid of life. Where were the wildflower meadow and the pond, the call of birds and the chirp of frogs? A gray fog obscured the view for a moment, chilling her. It was day but the sky was filled with dark clouds as though some malevolent force was looking down on her. Something niggled at her as if she'd forgotten something important. And that's when she saw him, a man walking toward her with a solemn look on his face. She backed away and began to run.

"Kat!" he called out, hurrying after her. "You know me—I'm Bran—I've met you here before, don't you remember?"

A vague deja-vu went through her when she heard his voice. Who was he? Her brain felt like it was smothered with cotton wool, her thoughts jumbled. This was a dream she'd had before. Had he been in it? As he caught up to her she figured she was about to find out.

He was breathless, his hair pulling out of the strip of leather he'd tied around it. "We can't meet in your world, but no one knows I'm here."

She stared at him. "My cat is named Bran. Who are you?"

The man smiled. "I couldn't resist leaving you with some part of me, that's why I left you a cat that had my name. I am Bran ap Llyr—the god of protection and prophecy. We love each other."

Kat frowned. "How can I love you when I don't remember ever meeting you?"

"I had to take away all your memories of me. I was forced to do it."

"Can you put them back?"

Bran stared at her for a few seconds before he waved his hand in front of her face, bombarding her mind with imagery—Bran, slope-shouldered, walking next her, Bran taking her to the art studio, Bran inviting her into his spacious and amazing apartment, Bran giving her a cell phone, Bran here in her dreams, dressed as he was now—Bran making mad passionate love to her. She let out a cry and put her hands up to her head.

"Sweet Kat," he said taking hold of her hands. "We can meet here even if we can't meet in your world. I've put a spell on this place so that we will not be discovered. But you will not remember me in your waking life."

When she gazed at him she knew him, her eyes filling. "Why?" The question hung in the air, a mist wafting around them. The forest and valley disappeared as they were cocooned in a soft white world. She waited for his answer as he moved closer, his hand going to her cheek.

But instead of answering he pulled her into his arms and kissed her.

The cell phone alarm went off, waking Kat out of a deep sleep. She started, looking at the time. She had to get to the police station by eight and then to work by quarter of ten. When she jumped out of bed her body ached just as it had the day before. Was she coming down with the flu? She hurried into the shower, trying not to notice her swollen eyes or the dark circles under them. *Definitely getting sick,* she thought to herself.

Bran meowed at her in the kitchen and she distractedly opened up a can and dumped it into his dish. Something went through her mind about his name, but the thought was gone before she could grab hold of it.

Thanks to Uber she made it to the station in time, her nervous energy tapping out a rhythm on the floor with her foot as she waited for Johansson. She didn't know what she was going to say or really how she should respond to this latest disregard. *How dare he,* was a thought that she'd had nonstop ever since the other cop had mentioned the document.

Johansson appeared and made a 'follow me' gesture with his hand before leading the way into the back. Once they were seated he put down his file folder and opened it up. "Some papers to sign to get this thing going," he muttered, handing her a stapled document and a pen.

She folded her arms over her chest. "No. Not until I meet him."

Johansson let out a huff of annoyance. "That isn't happening. If you want to prove your mother was murdered you need to go along with the program."

"He needs my signature and I need to meet him."

Johansson glared at her, his eyes hooded and annoyed. "He's ready to go with this—why are you holding it up? I thought you wanted to prove that Jack Turner killed her."

"Speaking of that, how did he slide by my stepfather's stop and desist order?"

"Judge overrode it."

"How does a person who is not even related do that?"

"He *is* related," Johansson admitted before realizing his folly. "Shit."

"Brother? Nephew? Who is he?"

Johansson stared at her without speaking.

Kat looked over the document, trying to find out who had signed, but there was no other signature. "It doesn't have his name here."

"That's right."

"I'm not signing until I meet him." Kat stood.

"I'll run it by him but I doubt very seriously he'll bow to your threats. He may even go around you. It seems the judge is in his pocket."

Kat's mouth opened. "He has that much power? That has to be against the law! She was my mom, for god's sake! Who *is* this guy?"

"I'll call you after I hear from him, but I hope you change your mind. I know he wants to do the right thing."

"The right thing is not staying completely anonymous!" Kat stalked out of the room and headed for the door. This dude had everybody eating out of his hand. Just as the Uber driver arrived an enormous raven flew by so low that she had to duck. It made a horrible raucous noise before flying up and disappearing into the mass of dark clouds.

"I hate those birds," the driver said as she climbed in.

Kat stared out the window wondering why she felt like crying. Was it because of this man who refused to meet her, the feeling of having no control over her life, or the idea that had flitted through her mind that the raven was in distress?

28

"**B**ran is going against the Dagda's orders," Airmid whispered, looking around furtively. Rhiannon stood next to her, the healing pool behind them. The air was alive with the sound of insects, birdsong and the chirp of frogs. The thicket behind the pond shimmered with magic, blue lights flickering within the flowers and plants that grew there.

"How do you know that?"

Airmid colored. "I've been watching him. He's done something to the intersection of Otherworld and Kat's world. It's unreachable by normal means—he's blocked it off."

"Were you planning to meet her there? If so I think it's a bad idea."

"No. I'm obeying the rules. And with the magic Bran has erected it would be impossible for me to reach it anyway. What he's doing worries me."

"Why, Airmid? Are you jealous or are you concerned?"

Airmid huffed in annoyance. "Just because Corra started a rumor doesn't mean it's true. Bran is a good friend and I worry that if he's playing fast and loose with the rules that Dagda will come down hard on him. I know the Dagda and he is not one to forgive."

"I miss her as much as you do," Rhiannon said, picking up on Airmid's distress. "But she's doing fine. Cerridwen is down there."

"How is she still there when the rest of us were called back?"

"She was not part of the debacle that ensued. As far as Bran is concerned, you have to let him do his own thing. He's a full grown god and he knows the punishment for going against the Dagda."

"I've never seen him act like this," Airmid said, gazing into the distance. "He's always been so level-headed."

"Do you think he's cleared her memories? And if not, what does that mean?"

"He cleared her memories—of that I am sure. But he's set it up so that he can meet her in her dreams."

Rhiannon shook her tangled mane of red hair and pressed her lips together. "I suggest you concentrate on healing yourself and getting on with your work. Worrying about Bran's behavior will get you nowhere."

Behind them the pool lay in shadow, fireflies flitting across the still water. The sun was low on the horizon, the color of the sky deepening as dusk approached. Airmid pulled off her light shift and stepped into the pool. "Join me if you wish, Rhiannon. The water does wonders for all ailments, both mental and physical."

Rhiannon let out a short laugh. "And so does riding my mare," she said, pointing at the beautiful white horse waiting for her. "Please take care, Airmid. If Dagda finds out that you've discovered a transgression and have not reported it, you will be punished along with Bran. I will keep all this to myself for now, but..."

Airmid raised her hand as she slid down into the warm water. "Don't say it. I know. You'll call a meeting and I will be on trial again."

"It would be for your own good," the horse goddess said before climbing onto the bare back of her mare. The birds circled her head as she galloped away, red hair flying like a flag behind her.

Airmid let herself sink, the water closing over her head. She opened her eyes and watched the waterweeds pulsing with the rippling movement, the last rays of the sun shimmering as they shifted and changed color. Was she in love with Bran—was that the reason for her concern? She no longer knew. What she did know was that he had broken through a barrier that was never supposed to be crossed. His need for this woman must be monumental to explain taking such a risk.

She said the healing prayer, letting her thoughts drift as she concentrated on restoring her psyche. Her time on earth had brought something that she never would have guessed, and now that she was back in Otherworld she missed it greatly. She'd formed a bond with Kat and with other humans she'd come into contact with. Yes, earth was polluted, and yes, there was violence and despair, but there was also the unpredictable and the unexpected kindness and love that sometimes appeared out of nowhere.

She wasn't in love with Bran, she was jealous of his willingness to jeopardize his status as a god for this woman on earth. With a rush of water Airmid rose to the surface, sparkling drops spraying in all directions. A plan formed, vague and dangerous.

29

By the time Kat reached Cerridwen's Cosmetic Cauldron she'd worked herself into a rage. How could this man be so arrogant? Up to now she'd tolerated his control issues because she wanted the same thing he did, but she'd always expected to meet him. Why was he so insistent on not meeting her, and what could she do about it? Could he actually get a judge to say yes without having her signature?

She was bound and determined to take her power back—this was her mother they were about to dig up. She had more right than anyone to give it a green or red light. She had to talk to the judge, which meant she had to have a lawyer or some kind of representation. How could she do that with her bank account in the state it was in? And on top of all that her body stilled ached in weird places and she felt very close to tears. This had to be some kind of flu.

"It sounds like a virus, Kat, and if you aren't sleeping well due to all this nonsense with your mother, it won't get better," Gwen told her. "I have some remedies that will help with this."

At that moment a customer came in and Gwen nodded for Kat to help her as she disappeared into the back. After selling her on a jar of rosehip and shea butter based wrinkle cream, Kat rang her up and placed the items in a small brown bag and tied it closed with green twine. "Thanks for your purchase," she said before the woman smiled and left the shop.

When Gwen returned a few minutes later she handed over a small packet of ground up herbs. "Take a teaspoon in warm water before you go to bed. I guarantee you'll feel better by tomorrow."

Kat placed it in her bag. "Thanks. I didn't realize you were so knowledgeable about herbs."

"Oh yes. My daughter was my student for years before she opened the store." She smiled when another customer came in, letting Kat help her as she busied herself with something behind the counter.

By the end of the day Kat was exhausted and ready to head home.

"You did well today, Kat. You're a quick study and good with the public. Next week I'll leave you here on your own and see how things go. You can always call me if you get into trouble." Gwen gave her a hug as they left the shop together and then said," Don't forget to take your herbs tonight."

As soon as Kat entered the apartment Bran demanded to be fed, irritated that she'd been gone all day. "Sorry, Bran, you'll have to get used to it," she told him, scooping a can of shrimp and tuna feast into his dish. As she brewed tea her earlier anger returned, her mind taken up with how to stop the mystery man from bullying her. And then she thought of Detective Johansson and how he was going along with it all. It had to be against the law. Before she could stop herself she'd pulled her cell phone out and punched in the police station numbers. When the duty officer answered she told her she wanted to lodge a complaint. "Against Detective Johansson," she told her.

She went to bed early, remembering to take her herbs before pulling the Murphy down. They didn't taste too bad. As soon as her head hit the pillow she entered a space of nothingness, white on white, as if her brain had filled with cotton wool. The white on white turned into gray blankness as she fell into a deep and dreamless sleep.

'Where are you, Kat?' Bran paced as he waited, worry lines crisscrossing his forehead. 'Have you found someone else so soon?' The question made him squirm with unease. If she wasn't with someone she would be soon—she was a beautiful woman and she had no memory of him or how they felt about each other. He let out a howl of pain, scattering the birds that clung to the dark branches surrounding where he stood. Fog swirled around him, holding him fast within its safety and muffling all sound. There were only two possibilities of why she wasn't here. She was either with someone else or not sleeping.

Bran waited until dawn before he left the sanctuary he'd created. His shoulders were hunched as he took himself back to Otherworld, pain evident in the way he walked and in his red-rimmed eyes.

Kat woke in the morning feeling drugged. She looked at her phone, noting that it was time to get a move on. The window revealed another nasty day. She let out a heavy sigh and swung her legs out of bed.

In the shower she remembered her call to the station. But what good would that do without a lawyer to back her up? Johansson needed to explain his willingness to allow a complete stranger to run the show. Money could not be allowed to override the law.

The mirror over the sink revealed a drawn face with dark circles under the bloodshot eyes. She didn't have the aches she'd had the day before but something bothered her, some emotion aside from anger that she couldn't identify. She felt like she'd lost her best friend.

She dressed warmly, fed the cat, grabbed her umbrella and headed out to walk the two miles to work.

"I have to stop him," Kat told Gwen once she reached the shop, "but I have no money for a lawyer and I don't think some court appointed public defender can go up against this bully."

"I can loan you the money, Kat. And I have the name of a very good attorney who I've used in the past." She reached into the drawer behind the counter and pulled out a business card and handed it over.

Kat took it, looking down at the name written in gilt letters in a fancy font: **FORSETI—ATTORNEY AT LAW**

A phone number was listed below the name. "Italian?"

"No," Gwen replied. "The name is old Norse…he's of Scandinavian descent."

"Will he…I mean, should I mention you?"

Gwen smiled. "Yes, I think you should. It will speed things up a bit if you do."

At noon Gwen told Kat to call the lawyer. There were no customers in the shop and the weather had gone from threatening rain to a downpour. "He takes an hour for lunch. He will be at his desk or at a café right now."

The voice that answered the call was deep and resonant, already engendering confidence. "This is Katel Davies and I have been referred to you by Gwen, Cerridwen..." she stopped, realizing she didn't know her last name.

There was a rumble of pleased laughter. "Gwen referred you? How is she?"

"She's...she's fine. I work for her at her shop."

"She has a shop now, in the city? Hmm..." There was a pause before he asked, "What can I do for you, young lady?"

After she explained what was going on he asked to speak with Gwen. She handed the phone over, surprised when the older woman disappeared into the back room. Kat could hear her girlish giggle and the lyrical tones her voice took on as she spoke with him. It was ten or fifteen minutes before she came back to the front. "He wants to set up a time and a place to meet," she said, holding the phone out.

When Kat got back on the phone it was on speaker, Forseti all business, his clipped tones organized and focused. "Gwen tells me you live not far from where she works. Would you like to meet me in the coffee shop she mentioned that is two doors down, or..."

"Yes, that sounds fine. But when?"

"Since time seems to be of the essence, I'd say today

after you get off work. Can you be there by four forty-five?"

Kat glanced at Gwen who nodded. "Yes, that sounds fine."

"And please bring Cerridwen along. We are old friends and I may require her assistance in this matter."

The rain had stopped by the time Kat and Gwen locked up and left the shop. They'd had few customers due to the weather, although a couple of middle-aged women had come by because they'd run out and were desperate.

As soon as they entered the coffee shop Kat picked out Forseti, knowing him by his wide shoulders and the long flaxen hair that spoke of his heritage. His features were Nordic, his mouth wide and facile, turquoise eyes intelligent and knowing. He wore a dark suit with no tie, a blue shirt that matched his eyes open at the neck. She could imagine him with a crown on his head and a sword hanging on a belt around his hips.

When he saw Gwen he smiled, revealing deep laugh lines and dimples in his pale cheeks. Kat placed him somewhere in his late fifties or early sixties, although it was hard to tell aside from the few strands of gray threaded through his wavy hair. He strode quickly to Gwen and pulled her into his arms, muttering some foreign words as he drew her close. She bent her head and giggled before pulling away to introduce Kat.

The next few minutes were taken up with ordering tea and coffee and settling around the table next to the window that looked out on the rain soaked street. Once the drinks were served Forseti got down to business.

"I have already contacted the station regarding the case, Kat. Is it all right if I call you Kat?"

"Of course."

"The detective in charge, a man called Johansson, is planning to meet with us at eight thirty in the morning. That is if your employer will let you off for an hour or two?" He glanced at Gwen, who nodded. "Should have her back by ten," he told her.

"Did he reveal the man's name?"

Forseti shook his head. "I need a court order. But don't worry, I can get one easily enough." His eyes narrowed dangerously. "I also have friends in high places."

Kat felt a shiver watching him. He was formidable. "What happens then? It's not like I don't want to dig her up—far from it. But…"

"You want to be the one in control," he interrupted. "You're the daughter and have a right to call the shots. First I'll file a writ to stop him and then we can discuss how to proceed from there."

"And will I get to meet him?"

Forseti stared at his cappuccino, a frown marring his smooth forehead. "I'm afraid he has the right to remain anonymous, but according to law he does not have the right to go over your head in this matter. He may be using some magic to get what he wants."

"Magic? What are you talking about?"

Forseti smiled, rubbing his fingers together in the sign of money being exchanged. "He's getting his way by greasing a few palms, and if I can prove it we can stop him."

"And what about my stepfather? Did Johansson mention him?"

Forseti nodded. "I think I can have him subpoenaed and brought in for questioning a second time. Not sure what your mystery man had in mind, but as soon as we discover poison or any other lethal substance in her body, Jack Turner will be arrested."

"I hope I'm right about this," Kat muttered, feeling suddenly afraid of what she'd set in motion.

"You are right," Forseti assured her.

She glanced at him. "How do you know?"

"According to Johansson this Turner guy has a record leading back to the early sixties. There's been at least one other suspicious death of a wife."

"He killed another woman he was married to?"

"Never proven, but yes."

Kat was stunned. Johansson had never mentioned it.

When the meeting ended Forseti and Gwen headed off together arm and arm. If there hadn't been such an age difference she would have thought there was something going on between them. She walked home in the drizzle, not even feeling it. She was pleased with Forseti. He exuded confidence and already had a plan of attack. She looked forward to his next move.

That night she took another teaspoon of powder, determined to stave off any further flu. Better to keep it up until she was sure the bug was completely gone.

irmid was sitting cross-legged on the grass by the healing spring when she spied Bran approaching, his gaze on the ground. When she yelled hello he looked up, frowning for a second before he joined her.

"Where are you coming from?" she asked him innocently, knowing full well where he'd been. It was just after dawn and this was the time he'd be returning from his tryst with Kat.

He shook his head, his eyes red rimmed with misery. "You probably know what I've done. Just please don't mention it to anyone who might alert Dagda. Trouble is Kat hasn't been dreaming. I think she may be with another man and staying up all night." He put his hands on either side of his head. "I'm going crazy."

Airmid's recently concocted plan began to take root as she listened to him. "I doubt she's with someone else," she said honestly. "Kat isn't that sort. Even if you wiped her memories there's a part of her that remembers."

"You think so? I left her that cat, the one named Bran, hoping I could keep myself in some back part of her mind."

Airmid gazed at him, trying to find words to tell him what she'd been thinking. Finally she said, "I miss life down there. It's boring here and I'm sick of the same old haunts and the same gods and goddesses and their same silly complaints. I miss the unpredictability of life there, the surprise that I feel every time I talk to one of them. I've been thinking…"

"Uh oh," Bran said, grinning for the first time. "I know that look."

"You can be part of it if you want. I'm going back."

Bran frowned. "And what about Dagda? You think you can do this without him knowing?"

"You set up that place to meet Kat. Does he know about it?"

"Not yet, but it's early days. And being on the surface is different. He has spies. If I were you I wouldn't trust any of your friends."

"Rhiannon has already threatened me."

"That's what I'm telling you."

"Would you be willing to work together on this? If you go down, Kat may not remember you, but she'll still be attracted to you. You can start over."

"Or I can make her remember me like I did in her dreams."

"But then she'll remember all of it, Bran. I don't want that."

Bran looked thoughtful. "I can't do it piecemeal. But I'm not sure what you're worried about."

"I don't want her to hate me if we run into each other!"

Bran stared at her. "What exactly did you have in mind? Are you going down for her or for yourself?"

"For myself."

"Well then, stay out of her life."

"I will if you promise not to restore her memories."

Bran let out a heavy sigh. "I guess starting over wouldn't be so bad—that is if she hasn't found another boyfriend."

"She hasn't."

"How do you know?"

"I've been watching her."

"We were explicitly told not to!"

"And what have you been doing? Give me a break."

Bran chuckled, rubbing at the beard growing on his chin. "Okay—tell me what you have in mind."

31

Kat stood with Forseti in front of the judge, her knees knocking. She glanced at the lawyer, scared for a second when she saw the glint in his aqua eyes.

"This young woman has a right to be in charge of this undertaking," he told the judge. "This man masquerading as a relative is no such thing."

"And how do you know this?" the judge demanded. "From where I sit he is indeed a relative, and a close one."

"Then why won't he agree to meet me?" Kat cried out.

The judge turned his dark eyes on her. "He has his reasons. I am not privy to what they are."

Forseti put his hand on Kat's arm, giving her a look before he faced the judge again. "Katel Davies is the daughter of the woman named in this case. It will be her decision whether or not the body is exhumed. So far she has been in agreement about this issue, but with this man's reluctance to reveal himself she's reconsidering." When he finished talking he waved his hand in front of his face as though chasing away a fly.

"I will see what I can do to reconcile this matter. Two people who want the same thing should be able to come to some agreement. I will tell you that he's very used to getting his own way. If you will accompany me to chambers we can discuss this further," the judge told Forseti, glancing at Kat.

"Wait for me out in the lobby," Forseti whispered before he followed the judge.

Kat found a bench and sat down, wondering what the judge had to say that she wasn't allowed to hear—probably the man's name. As she waited for Forseti Kat's head lolled back against the wall, dreams taking her away.

She was in her familiar forest but it was empty—when she walked toward the pond the entire place seemed like a movie set that had been deconstructed, with bits and pieces lying here and there. It disturbed her terribly to see what she'd thought of as live trees lying on their sides or barely propped up, the pool where she'd floated empty of water and not one plant anywhere around. The entire area looked like an abandoned stage, no sky, just blankness above, no birds, no frogs and no insects. No life of any kind.

"Kat?"

The voice roused her, her eyes opening to Forseti staring down at her. "You were out cold," he said, holding out his hand to pull her up. "You must be really tired to fall asleep in this place," he chuckled, looking around at the people hurrying by, the buzz of conversations as they went in and out of courtroom doors.

She shook her head to clear the cobwebs from her mind, unable to remember one thing about what she'd dreamed. All that was left was a hollow feeling. "How long were you gone?"

"Half hour?"

"And…what did he say?"

Forseti smiled an evil smile. "This man who's bullying you is a former colleague of mine. Not a man to mess with. But I think we've got him by the balls now."

"How so?" she asked as they walked side by side toward the exit.

"I'm the god of justice and I have more magic than he does."

When Kat turned to stare at him his mobile mouth was curled up in a smile, his eyes bright. His words seemed to indicate that he was enjoying this immensely. "And who is he?"

When they reached the door Forseti swung it open, letting her walk by him before following her out. "You don't want to know."

"Yes, I do!" she yelled.

"Calm down, Kat. All will be revealed in due time."

"So Forseti told you that he's more powerful than this man who's pulling every string there is?"

Kat laughed. "Yup. He said he's the god of justice and he has more magic."

Gwen let out a snort. "Maybe, maybe not. Time will tell."

"So you know who this other man is?"

"No, I have no idea."

Kat glanced at her, wondering if she was lying. She could usually tell. "Forseti knows him, so you probably do too, right?"

Gwen shrugged, her expression brightening when a customer came in.

With how happily Gwen turned her attention, Kat was sure the older woman knew the identity of the mystery man.

Once the store was empty again Kat grilled her, but could get nothing out of her.

It was late afternoon and Kat was in the back doing inventory when she heard Gwen say, "What are *you* doing here?"

"I had to come back," a woman's voice said.

"You know how Dagda will react to this, do you not?"

"I don't care. I am sick of taking orders from that tyrant."

"He's doing the best he can…considering the circumstances," she said, lowering her voice to a whisper.

"And what have you done to help this girl sort out her life? Seems to me you're making it more complicated with your meddling."

Gwen laughed. "You know about Forseti?"

"It's easy enough to determine these things, Cerridwen. Do you think me stupid?"

By now they were both whispering and Kat wondered whether she should come out or stay where she was. She was surprised her hearing was so acute.

"And what will happen when those two decide to battle it out?"

"It will be as it always is—one will win and the other will lose."

"Why is Dagda involved in this?"

"He has a dog in the fight, I guess. But what that dog is, no one knows. It seems to amuse him to take control down here, and have everyone bowing and scraping."

There was a humorless laugh before the stranger said, "I hope you know what you're doing."

Kat couldn't stand it another minute, emerging just as a dark haired figure exited the store. By the time she reached the door there was no sign of her. "Who was that?"

"Just an old friend who dropped by to say hello," Gwen said, turning away to fiddle with something behind the counter.

"Who is Dagda?"

Cerridwen turned to stare at her. "You heard that?" she asked, incredulous.

"I did."

"Dagda is another lawyer who may go up against Forseti," she answered.

"Who is this Dagda representing?"

"The...the person who is keeping his identity a secret."

Kat was positive that this was not the whole truth, but the look on Gwen's face stopped her from asking more questions.

Kat's twenty-first birthday came and went, an event that barely registered until it was over. She thought of how her mother had always made a fuss over her birthdays, making a special cake and giving her gifts she didn't need. "Wish your father was here to see what a lovely young woman you've become," she'd said on Kat's eighteenth. She was twenty when her mom died, her hopes of a happy future disappearing in the wake of that terrible day.

As the days went by Kat noticed several instances when her hearing seemed unusually acute. One time she was in a grocery store and heard a conversation going on that seemed like the people were right behind her, but when she checked she found out that they were two aisles over. The second time was in the bookstore when she heard two male voices discussing some kind of nefarious deal gone bad. When she checked there was no one in the store, but outside the closed front door two men stood together talking. *Should I get my ears checked?* she wondered. But then she thought it would be odd to go to a doctor because you could hear really well.

Her sight had sharpened too, her distance vision like she was looking through binoculars. Everything looked clearer than it ever had, and sometimes she saw things in the ether that couldn't be there, like wispy spirits and strange fairy-like creatures with wings like dragonflies. It worried her, but she had no one to discuss it with now that Gwen had seemingly turned against her—or at the very least wasn't being honest. It was coming up to the time for her to take over the store without Gwen's help— she was looking forward to being alone in the shop.

Kat was in the used bookstore when a man came up to her to ask directions. His mossy eyes pulled her in, the easy smile on his lips reminding her of someone she'd known in the past. He was lanky, wearing jeans that had seen better days, and a leather jacket over a T-shirt that had a picture of some band on the front. His hair hung in untidy tangles to his shoulders.

"I'm Bran," he finally said after she'd stared at him for probably a full minute.

"Bran?" She laughed."My cat's name is Bran."

"Really? We must be destined to meet then," he said, waggling his eyebrows. "Did you know that Bran is the name of a Celtic god?"

"Yes—actually I do. I have a book on the subject."

"Hmm…why do you have a book on Celtic gods?"

"My mom gave it to me. She had a thing for them."

"Sounds like a person I'd like."

"She's dead," Kat said abruptly.

Bran frowned, a look of pain crossing his features. "Sorry, Kat—didn't mean to open old wounds."

Kat blinked. "Did I tell you my name?"

Bran looked taken aback. "Yes, I think you must have— how else would I have known it?"

Kat didn't remember mentioning her name, but he must be right—she was distracted today and wasn't tracking properly. In response to his worry about opening old wounds she waved her hand in a dismissive gesture. "It's been over a year now, but…" She stopped herself before she blurted out everything about the exhumation and her frustration with the mystery man and the fact that she knew beyond a shadow of a doubt that her stepfather had killed her mom. What was it about this guy that made her feel so close to him? Maybe it was because she had no one to confide in. "Anyway, thanks for caring."

Instead of pursuing the conversation Bran turned to leave. "Got to go. Maybe see you around?"

Kat opened her mouth and closed it. She didn't want him to leave. "I hope so," she said, hoping she didn't sound too wistful. She watched him walk out the door without looking back, wishing...she didn't know what she wishing, or why.

32

"**A**re we about to be hanged?" Airmid whispered when she ran into Bran on the street outside the bookstore.

"Not quite yet, but it's only a matter of time," he responded, grimacing.

"Lucky for us Dagda is caught up in this court case about Kat's mother."

"Exhumation or no exhumation."

"Forseti represents Kat—remember him, the Norse god of justice? The main issue is that Kat wants to know who the man is that's running the show, but Dagda refuses to reveal himself to her."

Bran frowned, gazing at her."And you don't know why this is happening."

"No, I don't. Do you?"

Bran let out a lengthy sigh. "Before I wiped Kat's memory she told me her father's name was Dag. She's never met him. If Dag is short for Dagda she's half goddess and this bastard is keeping this information from all of us, including her. And if it's true I have a perfect right to be with her."

Airmid's mouth dropped open. "That would certainly explain his erratic behavior and why he's so interested in this case. The deceased woman was the mother of his child."

"And it explains why he wants all of us safely in Otherworld—so we won't find out."

"What about Cerridwen—does she know?"

"I'm not sure since I haven't spoken with her. Didn't she and Forseti have a fling a century or two ago?"

Airmid laughed. "That would explain her attitude. If what you think is true, do you think Dagda wants to bring Kat's mother back from the dead? It seems weird that he's so involved in the exhumation."

Bran blanched. "I hope not."

"But he does have the power to do that. Why else would he be involved in this?"

"Good point, but it seems extreme, even for him."

Airmid moved off the sidewalk as two people hurried by. "Have you seen Kat?"

Kat's in there," he said, indicating the bookstore with a flip of his fingers.

"And?"

He shrugged. "And nothing. I don't want to rush her and make her think I'm some weird stalker."

Airmid smiled. "Good self-control, Bran. I wouldn't have expected it."

"She remembers me. I could tell by how she stared. It won't be difficult to restart things."

"Don't be too cocky. Being sure about something never ends well."

Bran nodded, tugging her toward an alley when he saw

Kat come out of the store. "Where are you staying?" he asked once they were in the shadows.

"In the woods north of town. There's a homeless camp there."

Bran snorted. "And are you providing them with your version of food?"

"Of course," she grinned. "Acorns and nuts and berries and wild herbs—an occasional rabbit when I can force myself to murder one. And where are *you* staying?"

Bran flushed. "Got myself an apartment in Kat's building."

"I guess that makes sense since it was you who put her there."

"That's what I thought. I can't wait to get things going again," he said wistfully. "I want her to remember our last night together before I took away all her memories. It was pretty fucking magical." He stared at the ground. "That's the night she realized the connection between her dad's name and Dagda and finally believed me about the goddess and god thing. I'd decided not to wipe her memories, but then I figured if I didn't, the great Dagda would find out and cut my balls off or something. And I really don't want to be a eunuch."

Airmid chuckled. "Do you think Dagda will eventually reveal himself to Kat?"

"I have no idea what's on that bastard's mind. I think he may have lost it. And when Morrighan finds out what he's been up to there will be hell to pay."

"It doesn't seem fair to keep Kat out of the loop. Don't you feel weird around her now?"

"I'm only with her in her dreams. In her waking life she has no idea who I am."

"And this seems like a good basis for a relationship? Trust is the most important component."

Bran stared at her. "You're saying I should restore her memories despite what Dagda will do to me?"

"I don't know—it just seems mean, that's all. And you love each other, don't you?"

"I definitely love her, and the last time we were together in this reality she loved me too. I was in love with her way before I knew she was a goddess."

"You don't know that for certain, Bran. It could be a coincidence."

"That her father's name is Dag and that Dagda is hell bent on digging her mother up?"

"You're right. It's pretty conclusive. Does everyone know or just us?"

"I'd say Cerridwen probably knows because of Forseti. As to the rest of them, probably not."

"Maybe if we all ban together and confront him, Dagda will back down."

"Has he ever backed down?"

"Well, no. But…"

Bran let out a sigh, rubbing a hand over his stubble covered chin. "If things go south with Kat I might be more inclined to put my life in jeopardy."

"He's breaking the rules, Bran, and lying about it. We may have to hire Forseti for ourselves."

Bran brightened, his eyebrows lifting. "Now that's not such a bad idea."

"For now let's steer clear of Dagda, at least until we've determined how he plans to proceed."

"Don't worry—I'm not a complete idiot."

Airmid laughed. "Just a plain idiot then?"

Bran made a face and then glanced up and down the alley before he became his raven self, rising up on wide wings to disappear into the bleak and dismal sky.

Airmid watched the dark bird for a moment before checking the alley and vanishing into thin air, landing not far from the homeless camp. Joy bubbled up when a woman called out her name. Airmid waved and hurried toward her newfound friend.

33

Kat was checking out her tenth customer of the day when Gwen arrived, her normally pale skin flushed from the cold air. "Forseti mentioned that you had a court appearance today. Thought I would spell you."

Kat finished up the sale and turned to the older woman. "He said he can manage without me."

Gwen's eyes became more hooded than they already were. "But wouldn't you like to be present? Perhaps you will catch a glimpse of 'you know who'."

Kat grimaced. "I'd rather let him deal with it until he forces the guy to meet with me. Right now they're haggling over how to manage the exhumation. And my stepfather is raising a stink about it. I do not want to see Jack Turner *ever* again."

"With Forseti litigating I doubt your stepfather can stop it. I've never seen him lose a case."

"That's good to hear. He scares me sometimes."

Gwen smiled. "Looks like the devil incarnate?"

"When he frowns the angles of his face seem to narrow,

and his eyes—they kind of swirl, you know? Lucky his hair is light and not dark or he'd really remind me of some dark lord."

Gwen laughed before glancing around the store. "Everything looks good, Kat. You're doing a great job. The customers love you."

Kat thanked her but was glad to see her go. Something was going on under the surface that Gwen was not saying. Kat knew it like she knew her own name; since when had she become so intuitive?

Kat was walking home when she had a vision so clear it was as though it was happening right in front of her. A wide-shouldered man with amazing blue eyes and dark hair was arguing with Forseti, their raised voices rumbling like thunder. The two of them looked to be standing in the clouds, a white mist billowing around their legs as charcoal thunderheads rose up in the background.

"Who sent you, anyway?" the dark haired man asked, his cobalt eyes narrowing.

"Cerridwen invited me to help since no one is representing Katel. Why have you not yet met with her? Are you not on the same side of things?"

The other man let out a roar of annoyance. "That is none of your concern!" he shouted.

"If you keep up this stubbornness it will not end well," Forseti said darkly. "You know what I'm capable of."

"And my power will outstrip yours any day of the week."

Forseti roared with laughter. "You do know who I am?"

"So what if you're the god of justice? I'm the father god, the all-powerful god. And I've been around a lot longer than you have."

"I'm not sure what secret you're holding back, Dagda, but trust me, I will uncover it." The darker clouds moved close, obscuring them as the voices faded.

Kat swayed with dizziness, the scene around her slowly coming back into focus. People frowned and stared as they skirted around where she stood. She moved forward into the throng and tried to calm her fast beating heart. Gods? They were gods? She began to run, hoping to outstrip the crazy thoughts bombarding her. She had to be losing her mind.

When she reached the apartment building she ran straight into Bran, nearly knocking him down.

"Whoa!" he said, grabbing her arms. "What's going on?"

"I…" She broke down, the tears she'd been holding back welling over.

Bran held her, his soothing voice feeling somehow right. That is until he began to massage her shoulders. She pulled away and reached for her key.

"Kat, I…I…"

She shook her head and walked past him into the building. Enough weird stuff had happened today without this. When she pushed the key into the lock she felt him behind her. "What are you doing—stalking me? Go away."

Bran's face seemed to pale. "I'm not stalking you—I live here."

"Not here you don't," she muttered, swinging the door

open and slamming it closed once she was inside. She threw the deadbolt across, feeling secure for a moment. But as soon as she reached the kitchen, everything returned full force. The crazy vision and then Bran, who she'd hoped to trust, taking it one step too far.

Her dark thoughts brought on a massive headache and a second later she was surrounded by a forest of gnarled trees that moved and twisted, alive with malevolence. She panicked and ran headlong into a thicket that pressed against her from all sides, thorns pricking her arms and hands as she tried to disentangle herself. She screamed and fought, trying to get free, but nothing seemed to help.

An urgent meow was what finally brought her back, green eyes regarding her solemnly from where the cat stood next to his dish. The forest and thicket disappeared as reality returned. It was several minutes before she was able to catch her breath, her hands shaking as she opened a can of cat food and scooped it into his dish. *What just happened, Bran?* But the cat didn't answer, his focus on eating. When she glanced down at her hands they were covered with pinpricks of blood, scratches up and down her forearms.

When her cell phone rang a few seconds later she had an adrenaline rush, taking two deep breaths before she answered.

"They've begun," a male voice hissed.

"Who's begun what—who is this?"

"Your meddling has finally paid off. Steer clear of dark places." The call ended.

Kat stared down at the phone, noting the number. It was local but not any she had in her contacts. Jack Turner appeared in her mind, a sneer on his face. She punched in Forseti's number.

"What? I'm in the middle of something here."

"I'm pretty sure Jack Turner just threatened my life," Kat told him. "And he indicated that digging has begun—is that true?"

There was the sound of muffled voices before Forseti said, "Yes, we're at the graveyard."

"You and who else?"

"Your stepfather and the man you so want to meet, myself and Johansson."

"And why did you neglect to tell me it was happening today?"

"Because you don't need to be here, that's why. Do you really want to see the remains of your mother? The body will be taken to the coroner's office; after he examines her we will know more. Please just stay out of it until we have all the facts."

"I hope you can do something about Jack—if he's capable of killing my mom he's capable of killing me."

"He'll soon be behind bars, Katel."

"I hope so," she muttered before hitting end. Her thoughts careened from one thing to the next, anger flooding her before she burst into tears. She needed to see a therapist.

The next morning when Kat arrived at work, Gwen was already there, busy stacking new jars of merchandise on the shelves. She turned when Kat came in, a smile lighting up her eyes. "You've been selling so much I had to replenish. My daughter is hard at work making more product—she's thrilled!" Her smile faded as she peered at Kat. "What's happened? You look terrible."

Kat fought back tears. "I need to see somebody."

Gwen cocked her head. "You mean a therapist or a psychiatrist?"

Kat nodded.

"My dear girl. I don't know what has happened but I do know when someone's in trouble. I have a name if you'd like it. My daughter went to see her a few years back when she and her husband were having some issues." She moved to the desk and dug through the drawer. "Here it is," she said handing over a business card.

Kat took it, wondering whether to trust Gwen's judgment—but then again she *had* recommended Forseti, who was doing a good job. And then she remembered her conversation with him the day before. There had been no word since late afternoon yesterday. She glanced down at the card in her hand.

Corra Crane
All problems great and small

"They dug her up yesterday," she said in a small voice, putting the card in her bag.

Gwen came close and put an arm around her shoulders. "My poor dear. No wonder you're feeling like this. Were you there for it?"

"No. I happened to call because Jack Turner threatened me. They were all there, including Jack and the man who refuses to meet me. Forseti didn't even tell me beforehand."

"Well—it's for the best that you weren't there, dear. Now what did this Jack person say to you?"

"He told me to steer clear of dark places."

Gwen's hand went to her mouth. "Did you relay this to Forseti?"

Kat nodded. "He told me Jack would be in jail soon."

"Let's hope so—it has been over a year since your mother's death. If he used some poison or other substance to kill her it may have dissipated by now."

Kat's eyes welled and she wiped at them distractedly.

"Take the day off, Kat, and give this woman a call. You should be hearing about the results of the tests either later today or tomorrow, don't you think?"

Kat nodded and turned toward the door. "So many strange things have been happening," she mumbled.

"Well of course this would be disturbing—is there something else, dear?"

Kat glanced over her shoulder. "I had a vision yesterday of Forseti and some other man—they were arguing and seemed to be standing in the clouds somewhere. They were referring to each other as gods."

Gwen laughed. "Gods? Well, I guess lawyers and others who have unlimited power may feel like gods. Perhaps that's what they meant."

Kat nodded, turning back to the door. As soon as she was outside she pulled out the card and her phone and punched in the number for Corra Crane.

Kat was sitting on a velvet settee in an office that reminded her of a boudoir. Gold and red were the predominant colors, the space filled to overflowing with baroque furniture. Fanciful figurines of goddesses sat on every available surface, a few gilt covered books scattered here and there. Paintings of cranes filled up the wall space, all of them ornate and fantastical like the art of Henri Rousseau. The woman who sat in front of her was diminutive and wearing a feathery gray dress. Her eyes were as round as marbles and an odd orangish color. Gray feathers wafted around, landing in Kat's hair and in her lap. They were reminiscent of something, she thought, picking one up and studying it.

"Sorry about the feathers," Corra said in a bird-like warble. "This dress sheds. Now tell me why you have sought me out?"

"I..." she began, watching another feather come loose from the gray dress and make a beeline for her lap.

"Yes, go on," Corra encouraged, reaching for the errant feather.

"I've been having visions of gods, for one thing. And all of a sudden I can hear really well—and my sight..."

"Visions of gods?" Corra repeated, her round eyes blinking like a bird. "Tell me about that."

"I was walking down the street when I saw these two men up in the clouds—they were arguing, and one of them was my lawyer." Kat laughed nervously.

"Your lawyer?" Corra let out a tinkling laugh. "Lawyers always think of themselves as gods, you know."

"That may be so, but I'm telling you, they were really there."

"And what was the argument about?"

"I think it was about the case my lawyer's working on. My mother..."

"Yes, yes, I know all about your mother, my dear," Corra said, preening her feathery dress with her extremely long and tapered fingers.

"How do you know about that?"

"Cerridwen called to give me a bit of background information."

Kat thought about that for a moment, wondering if it was ethical. "Well," she continued, "the person who seems to be running things refuses to meet with me. And no one will tell me who he is."

"You will find out his identity in due time, my dear. He has his reasons for keeping it secret."

"How do *you* know?"

Her round eyes met Kat's. "Didn't Cerridwen tell you? I'm psychic—I can foretell the future." She let out a trill. "I am the goddess of prophecy."

Kat stared at her, wondering if this was another vision. "But…you aren't really a goddess, right?"

Corra moved her head from side to side, dislodging more feathers. "Do you not believe in such things?"

"I'm beginning to wonder," she said laughing, sure that the woman was making a joke.

"There is more to this world than what you might think, Katel. You must open yourself to possibilities. We all go though life with blinders on, hardly noticing what's all around us. There is magic hidden in the strangest of places."

Kat had a sudden desire to run from the room, but when she glanced at Corra she found herself unable to do anything but stare. Corra's pale hair was turning into feathers, her legs lengthening into the legs of a very tall bird.

A crown of red topped the bird's head, her eyes now fully orange. She let out a warble and lifted from where she sat, letting wide wings carry her to the ceiling before dropping back into the chair. A second later she was a woman again, her hands folded demurely in her lap.

"See what I mean?" she asked.

Kat was sure she'd imagined the entire thing, her certainty that she was crazy stronger than it had ever been. "I..." she muttered, unable to go on.

"I am the crane goddess of prophecy," Corra continued, her voice taking on a hypnotic quality. "I will tell you that your future lies with us, although it will take some time for you to understand and accept this. There is a god who loves you but you have spurned him and hurt him deeply. Your memories are buried and you will not fully know yourself until they are restored. Your mother's exhumation will reveal things that will shock you. All will be well in time." The woman rose and held out her hand to Kat, showing her to the door.

Kat let herself be led out and heard the door close behind her, but when she turned back there was nothing there but a brick wall. Her mind floated in a vast and endless sea, her legs moving of their own accord. She was nowhere and everywhere at once.

It was sometime later that she seemed to wake up, finding herself sitting in a coffee shop, a cup of coffee on the table in front of her. She could hear the din of conversation and feel the different moods of those having them. She tried to close them out, not wanting to hear about grandma's hip replacement or the cancer so and so died of. When she glanced out the window she noticed that the sun had come out. She reached into her purse, put some money on the table and left.

The sun's rays sparkled across the sidewalk, lighting up the crystals imbedded in the cement. She bent to look more closely at them until a person bumped into her from behind and yelled some obscenity. When she examined her surroundings she found that she was quite close to home. She set off in the direction of her apartment.

On the way she found herself distracted several times by scenes of beauty: a tiny exquisite magenta flower growing up through a crack, the purple petals delicate and translucent, a newly emerged leaf in the most amazing shade of green she'd ever seen and each tiny drop of water clinging to it, a kaleidoscope of color. The complicated call of a bird somewhere high in the branches of another tree, the long shadows cast by the lowering sun. She began to cry, overwhelmed by the world around her that she'd never really seen until this moment. By the time she reached her apartment she was thoroughly overcome, as though she'd taken some hallucinogenic drug that allowed her to see beyond everyday reality.

She was just about to go inside when Bran appeared, a self-conscious smile on his face. "I'm so sorry about…"

When she waved her hand in the air, rainbow ribbons seemed to flow from her fingers. She gazed at them, waving her fingers some more. "What is happening to me?" she whispered.

"Your eyes have been opened." Bran took the key out of her hand and led her down the hallway. He put the key in the lock, turned it and swung the door inward, ushering her inside.

When he turned to go she grabbed his arm. "What... who...?"

He hesitated in the doorway until she pulled him through and closed it. "I know you, don't I?"

"Yes, Kat. We know each other intimately."

"Intimately—you mean we've had sex?"

Bran nodded, looking down.

Feelings welled up, feelings she couldn't deny. "Do we love each other?"

Bran nodded again, his gaze rising to meet hers. His eyes were like shadowy forest pools, his sensuous mouth curling slightly at the corners as they stared at one another. A pulse of sensation moved through her, the need for him so acute that she let out a gasp. When she reached for him he pulled her close, his lips finding hers.

34

K at woke in the morning, her body languid and heavy. She sighed and stretched, glancing at Bran asleep beside her. He lay on his back, one leg bent at the knee, one arm flung along the bed toward her. His lashes lay dark against his pale skin, his full mouth relaxed in repose. The night came back in provocative detail, the feel of his lips, the sensations she'd never felt so intensely, the smell and taste of him. Her senses were alive with him now, every nerve ending poised to connect with him again. She lusted after him, her body wanting him now just as much as she had the night before. It was like being newborn—but luckily not as a baby.

When she reached over and placed her lips lightly on his, his arms came round her, pulling her tight against him. His mouth met hers in a kiss that went on and on…until she had to have more. When he entered her she felt like she might explode, her senses so acute that she could barely stand it. Her body had a mind of its own as she twisted and moved to pull him in even deeper.

"Gods," he moaned, holding onto her hips as she

arched against him. She was unable to control herself at all.

When it was over they lay entwined together. "I…didn't expect this," he murmured into her hair. "I thought it would be a long time before we…"

"I have never felt anything like this—not ever."

"Not even the first time we made love?"

"I don't remember another time. All I know is that my nerve endings seem to be on overdrive."

"It's the goddess part of you," he mumbled, his warm lips tracing along her neck.

"Goddess…what goddess?"

Bran pulled back to gaze at her. "I thought you knew—after everything you told me yesterday, and your experience with Corra…I…"

"Corra…oh yes, the bird woman. I imagined all that."

Bran pushed himself up to lean against the headboard. "You didn't imagine it, nor did you imagine the world the way you saw it, or what happened between us. I was sure your memories had come back."

"My memories…what about them?"

Bran let out a sigh and ran his fingers through his tangled hair. "I had to clear your memories, Kat. Dagda insisted."

"Dagda—oh yeah, the big dark-haired guy who was arguing with Forseti."

Bran rose from the rumpled bed. "I think we need coffee for this conversation," he muttered, padding naked toward the kitchen.

When he returned she was staring out the window, unable to think of anything but him. "Did you put some kind of spell on me?" she asked, reaching for the mug he held out.

Bran chuckled and climbed into bed beside her. "I could ask you the same thing."

"I mean it. What is wrong with me?"

He took a lazy sip, gazing at her. "Why do you think there's something wrong with you?"

She took a gulp of coffee and stared down. "I don't feel like myself. I never would have hopped into bed with a man I hardly know."

"Didn't we go over this last night? We *do* know each other and we've been lovers. We love each other."

"But...I don't remember that. All I know is how I feel now, which is pretty much insatiable." She placed her mug on the table.

Bran raised his eyebrows. "Hold that thought. But first I need to go over a few things with you. Do you remember what we talked about regarding your mom? You told me that she mentioned a man named Dag—your father. Does that ring any bells?"

Kat shook her head.

"Oh crap," Bran muttered.

"I do know that they exhumed her body yesterday and didn't even invite me to be there. And so far I haven't been alerted as to what they found."

"If anything."

Kat frowned. "My stepfather killed her, Bran. Have I told you about that?"

Bran nodded, glancing at her. "Not in this particular timeline, but in the last one. Forseti and Dagda—you said you saw them arguing— are they working on this together?"

"Dag." She stopped and stared into space. "Mom... Mom said his eyes were like sapphires."

Bran chuckled. "He does have nice eyes, I'll give you that."

"They don't like each other at all—this Forseti and Dagda. Forseti referred to himself as the god of justice."

"And so he is," Bran said, placing his empty coffee mug on the other side table. "The *Norse* god of justice."

"And Dagda claimed that he was the all father god or something, and told Forseti that he was older than him."

Bran laughed. "It's true—he's centuries older than Forseti."

"Oh my god. I can't deal with this!" When she turned to jump off the bed Bran leaned across and grabbed her arm.

"Look at me, Kat."

She turned her gaze to his.

"What do you see?"

"I see the most beautiful deep green mossy eyes I've ever seen in my life."

"What else?"

"I see you." A second later something shifted, her mind racing to catch up. "I can really *see* you—who you really are," she said surprised, as visions crowded her mind.

"Keep looking into my eyes. What else do you see there?"

Kat leaned close, gazing into shifting colors that abruptly lifted, revealing a meadow filled with wildflowers, a pond with cattails growing next to it, a stand of tall trees behind. "It's my dream."

"That's where we made love the first time."

215

She turned away, dizzy for a second. When she turned to look at him again he moved his hands in intricate patterns, his eyes focused on hers. "I just returned your memories."

A split second later Kat was bombarded with tangled thoughts, her pulse speeding up. Her hands went to the sides of her head as images crowded and shoved, flooding her mind. "You did this," she said a few seconds later. "You took away my life and…" Tears welled and spilled over as she examined the past that he'd taken from her. She saw the apartment with the tree, remembering Airmid, and the herbs and the creams they made together and sold. But then she remembered the argument and how Airmid treated Bran and the raven—coming back to find the apartment vacated and not a trace of Airmid or the life they'd shared.

"I had to. Dagda made me."

Kat barely heard him, images continuing to pile up, one on top of the other. "What happened to your amazing apartment? Where's Airmid? Last I remember…" She let out a gasp, her eyes going wide. "Dagda's my father! I remember the conversation we had before you…"

"Before I took your memories."

"If he's my father why does he refuse to meet with me?"

"He wants to protect you."

"No wonder my hearing and eyesight are so incredible. But why now— why is it happening now?"

"Didn't you just have your twenty-first birthday?"

Kat nodded slowly. "I…so this is the time when what I am manifests?"

Bran nodded, watching her warily.

"Now that I know about Dagda he'll be forced to meet with me."

"No one forces the Dagda to do anything. But ordering me to clear your memories was a bit hypocritical considering that he knew who you were."

"But if he knows who I am, why? You said he wants to protect me—from what?"

"It doesn't make a lot of sense to me—you'd think he'd want to meet his daughter and help her adjust to being a goddess."

"That's what *I* would think. And why did he make you clear my memories?"

"Dagda had a child with a human woman and is now lying to cover it up. It is forbidden to do such things. If you hadn't connected the dots that night we might never know."

"But eventually when I…I mean I can hear and see like I never have before, and the way it feels with you…it's unbelievable."

Bran grinned. "For me too and I'm aware of who I am."

"What do I do now?"

Bran pressed his lips together and gave a one-shoulder shrug. "I say confront him, but it won't be easy."

"Will you come with me?"

Bran nodded. "Anything you want, my love. But first we have to find him."

"Mom…" she muttered, suddenly remembering. "I wonder what they've found out." At that moment her cell phone rang, the muffled sound coming from inside her satchel hanging over a chair in the kitchen. She hopped out of bed and hurried to answer.

"It was poison," Johansson told her, "administered over a long period of time."

"What kind?"

"Arsenic."

"She never seemed sick."

"I think he waited until you left on your trip to step it up."

Kat let out a sob.

"I'm sorry for this news. But I know you'll be happy that Jack Turner is now behind bars. I have one more meeting with the coroner to get all the necessary paperwork. Unfortunately there is no DNA, and now that he's sold the house, no way to trace the arsenic, which means he has the right to a trial."

"Where are Forseti and Dagda?"

"You know his name. How did that come about?"

She glanced at Bran watching her from the bed. "A friend of mine told me."

"Dagda has claimed her remains."

"He can do that?"

"Apparently that man can do anything he wants to do."

"He can bring her back to life," Bran called from the bed.

Kat nearly dropped the phone. "What did you say?" she asked, holding a hand over the microphone.

"Dagda has the power to bring the dead back to life."

Kat could no longer concentrate, her mind completely blown. "I have to go now. Thanks for letting me know." She hit end before the detective had a chance to say goodbye.

When she stumbled toward the bed Bran ran to help

her. "Gods, Kat, I'm sorry." When she collapsed he picked her up and carried her to the bed and placed a pillow behind her.

"Do you…is it possible that…?" she glanced up at him hovering over her like a mother hen. "Would he actually consider doing that?"

"I guess it depends on how much he loved her. He's been at this thing for months now, avoiding his duties in Otherworld to fight the powers that be to dig her up. I suppose anything is possible."

Kat began to cry, a pain moving across her chest. When Bran pulled her close she rested her head on his shoulder and let the tears flow.

35

"Do not tell me what I can or cannot do!" Dagda roared. Birds scattered and trees bent away as the sound rippled across time and space. Clouds massed around the two gods, dark and menacing.

"I am only suggesting that bringing this woman, or should I say decomposed body, back to life, will confuse your daughter even more. Her mother is dead, Dagda, and she's grieved for over a year. This is a selfish act on your part."

"My daughter is half goddess and will understand."

"And have you alerted her to who she is or that you're her father? No, you have not."

"All the gods damn you, Forseti! My life is not for you to decide. It may be a selfish act, but I loved and watched over the two of them until that bastard killed Siobhan."

"And why didn't you intervene before he managed it?"

"I was distracted for a while."

"By the Morrighan, I presume? And speaking of the war goddess, how will she react to having you bring this woman back from the dead?"

Dagda frowned and ran his big hands through his dark curls. "I am not in love with Morrighan, Forseti. What I felt for Kat's mother is the closest I've ever come to such an emotion."

"And yet you left her alone with your child and went back to Otherworld. What the fuck, Dagda?"

Dagda hung his head. "I had to. I was needed at home. You remember those years, do you not? As I recall you and I were at war."

Forseti sighed. "The war that lasted for two decades? Yes, I remember. My wife was killed by one of your minions."

"Sorry for that, but it is the way of war. I am glad that you and I have reconciled."

"Is that what you call this uneasy peace between us?" Forseti shook his head. "There is no justice in what you are considering."

"Justice has nothing to do with love, Forseti."

"All I ask is that you make yourself known to this young woman who has suffered due to your stubbornness. She needs to know the truth."

36

"**S**iobhan Davies was definitely poisoned," the coroner said with finality, handing Detective Johansson the last of the paperwork. "It is all written here and here," he added, pointing to where he'd elaborated in cursive.

"Thank you, Simon," Johansson said. "I'm glad we had a reason to dig her up."

"Always helps," the man said, pulling off his gloves. "Handing the remains over to this man, Dagda, is not usually done, especially since he isn't a close relative, but without a reason not to, I see little justification for saying no."

"With the husband in jail the only close relative is the daughter. I will notify her and make sure she's in agreement before we proceed."

Simon nodded and waved Johansson out of the room so that he could get back to work.

It was still early morning and Johansson had not yet had his coffee. His mood was not the best at this time of day.

When he punched in the numbers he wondered what Kat would say. She'd been furious throughout the entire escapade, angry with everyone. Now that she knew the identity of this man, would she be more inclined to agree, or would she fly into another rage?

"I've set up a meeting for you and Dagda," he told her right off. "He wants to meet in the park close to your apartment."

"When?"

"Today at ten?"

"I'll be there."

Once he hung up Johansson stared at his phone. Was that all there was to it? He had a sinking sensation that there was definitely another shoe about to drop.

Kat placed the phone on the counter and took a sip of the coffee Bran had brewed. Time to plan out what she wanted to say to this man who had made her life a living hell. But then she thought of her mother and wondered if her plan to unload was such a good one. Her mom had loved him and they'd conceived a child together. Would her mom be happy if she treated him badly? No. She would want Kat to love him just as she had. Siobhan Davies had been a kind person, not given to anger or upset, despite Dagda abandoning her and the many times Jack had treated her badly. She left her phone where it was and went to take a shower.

"Are you ready?" Bran asked around nine-thirty.

Kat glanced into the mirror. "I think so. Do I look okay?"

Bran laughed. "Are you kidding? You look like a goddess."

"That isn't an answer."

"You look beautiful, Kat, just like you always do."

Kat fiddled with an errant lock of hair and pushed it behind her ear and picked up her satchel.

When Bran and Kat reached the park Forseti was waiting for them. "Dagda placed a barrier around the area to keep you from being disturbed."

Kat glanced at the shimmering wall in front of her, trying to stay focused and not wig out. "Where is he?"

Forseti pointed. "Just walk through and you'll find him."

Kat took in a deep breath and let it out slowly. When she glanced at Bran he nodded. "Don't let him bully you," he whispered.

Kat gave him one last look before stepping through, surprised by how easy it was. The first thing she saw was a giant dark haired man sitting on a bench throwing breadcrumbs to the pigeons clustered around him. She would have liked to observe him for another moment, or even two, but unfortunately he felt her presence and rose to face her. "Katel," he said, his gaze riveted on her.

He had to be six foot five or six, his shoulders wide and his body rugged and muscular. She had a vision of her mother secured inside those big arms, sadness working its way into her throat. His face was in shadow, glossy black hair tangled and hanging past his shoulders. But when a ray of sunlight pierced though the clouds and angled across his features, it lit up his eyes, revealing the azure blue. His gaze seemed to penetrate right through the armor she'd erected around herself. Instead of the arrogance she'd expected, his expression was one of pain and uncertainty.

She could tell he was waiting for her to make the first move but she felt rooted to the spot. It took several moments before she could get her legs to obey her, the rat-a-tat of her pulse loud in her ears as she moved a few steps closer. Instead of the planned speech she'd practiced, where she told him how much her mom had loved him, she blurted out, "Why did you leave us? Why didn't you come back?"

Dagda frowned deeply, running agitated fingers through his curls. His gaze went to the ground where the pigeons fought for the last crumbs. "I didn't want to leave her. I loved her. Siobhan was everything to me."

"But you did leave her and you also left me, a tiny baby. She told me you were the love of her life and that she always hoped you'd return. And then she met Jack and look what happened to her. This is all your fault."

Dagda stared at his hands. "I didn't know. If I had I would have come sooner."

"If you're really an all powerful god how could you let this happen?"

"I…I wish I could turn back the clock and be there for you." His wide face looked ravaged, a few tears sliding down his cheeks.

"You should have revealed yourself to me," she continued, trying not to feel the pity building in her chest. "I had to learn who you were from Bran. And on top of that you made him wipe my memories. How could you? We love each other."

Dagda wiped at his eyes distractedly and shook his

shaggy head. "I only wanted to protect you, Katel. You didn't know who you were."

"And Bran didn't know either. You made him clear my memories knowing full well that I was half goddess. You owe him an apology."

"I had a very good reason for what I did," he said, his narrow-eyed gaze meeting hers. "The past is over and I will not express regret for an act that was done in good faith."

Kat was quickly made aware of Dagda's strength of mind, his expression implacable as he stared at her.

"I am considering bringing your mother back," he said abruptly.

Kat let out a little cry, a terrible image rising up in her mind. "In what form? Would she be like she was when you knew her or would she be the mom I remember? What about her memories? Would she remember Jack and what he did to her? I think that would be terrible for her. And now that she isn't even whole, how could you reconstitute her body?"

Dagda's eyes turned dark with pain. "She knew Jack was poisoning her."

Kat couldn't speak for a moment, trying to wrap her mind around what he said. "And she allowed it?"

"Your mother was a unique person, Katel. Siobhan wanted him to stop but decided that to confront him would make things worse."

"So she just allowed him to kill her?"

"That's exactly right."

"Why didn't you come back and save her?"

Dagda's gaze went into the distance where the barrier shimmered. "Your mother believed in fate and karma. She felt that her destiny was to die at his hands. His was to suffer as a result of what he did."

"And what about me? Did she consider how I would function after her death?"

"I think she knew in her heart that I'd help."

"But she never knew you were a god, right?"

"I'm not so sure about that. She was very canny and intuitive. The way I was with her, and how I left, may have tipped her off."

"So she knew and yet she got together with a despicable man and let her daughter suffer as a result."

"She knew I'd have to come back to take care of my daughter."

"But if she lived I never would have known about you."

"That's true. I thought of returning, but I was afraid of what it might do to your life. And then when she got together with Jack…he was good to her at first and I didn't want to interfere. And as you know now, it is forbidden; I had already broken the rules."

Kat stared at the shimmering bubble around them, her thoughts wandering down strange and twisted paths. "And now you're considering breaking them again. Why?"

Dagda ran a hand across his face. "Because I've met you and I've allowed myself to feel what I felt so many years ago. I want her back."

"But if as you said, her destiny was to die at his hands, how will she feel if you resurrect her?"

"She won't know. Would you like to see her again?"

"Of course I would, but…it scares me and it seems ghoulish and I don't know if she would like it."

Dagda let out a roar of laughter, making Kat jump.

"Ghoulish? She will not be like the walking dead, Katel, she will be flesh and blood like…well, like your friend the detective or any other human being. As far as liking it, I will make it so she does."

Kat tried to imagine her mother standing in front of her, but no image presented itself. "And would you be with her this time?"

"As much as I am able."

"I don't know how I feel about it. It doesn't seem right."

Dagda let out a heavy sigh. "Can we speak about this again? I am due in Otherworld, but I will be back in what you recognize as the day after tomorrow. I will come to your apartment."

"And in the meantime her remains grow more and more desiccated."

"It is her consciousness that's most important. And that is tucked away in a safe place."

Kat tried to get him to say more but he refused. Before they parted she broke down and gave him a hug, tears falling when she felt the protection of his strong arms around her.

"You take after me," he said, peering at her from under his heavy eyebrows.

Kat studied the jut of his chin, the shape of his eyes, the dark color of his hair. She nodded.

"What do I tell him when he comes back?" Kat asked Bran later.

He straightened from where he was stroking his

namesake. "If it were up to me me I'd probably agree to resurrect her, but it's not my decision to make."

"I miss her so much, but the other thing I worry about is Jack. He murdered her and hopefully will be going to jail, probably for life. In that scenario she can't be alive."

Bran made a face. "I'm sure Dagda has some way around that. Let it percolate in the back of your mind until you see him again."

Kat nodded, thinking about Dagda. She had wanted to hate him, had tried to hate him, but there was something compelling about the man. The vulnerability she'd seen in his eyes had disarmed her completely.

37

"**W**here is he?" Morrighan shouted, glaring at Rhiannon and Arianrhod. "And where is Airmid?"

Rhiannon twisted one shoulder in a gesture of dismissal. "You know how Dagda operates. Who knows where he is?"

"He's down there screwing around," Morrighan hissed, her dark eyes turning even darker as she stared over the balcony into a heavy gray fog. "He has now made earth impossible to *see*."

"From what I've heard he's dealing with our charge," Arianrhod said, trying to smooth Morrighan's ruffled feathers.

"And yet we have all been banned from earth? Has anyone seen Airmid, or Bran lately?"

The other two goddesses shook their heads.

"Don't you think that's odd? I swear this is turning into quite the clusterfuck."

"What language!" Arianrhod hissed. "Where did you even hear that term?"

Morrighan let out a nasty laugh. "Dagda uses it."

"He'll be back soon," Rhiannon assured her. "He has to clean up the mess we made down there."

"*Our* mess? Can either of you assure me that Bran and Airmid are not down there right now? Bran is in lust, and Airmid…not sure what is going on with her, but…"

"If they are, Dagda will take care of it," Arianrhod said primly. "Best for you to mind your business here."

"That's just it—my business is with the Dagda! How can he ignore me like this?"

"You do not trust him?" Arianrhod asked innocently.

Morrighan pressed her lips together and frowned. "No, I do not. If he's cheating he *will* regret it."

38

Kat could not get enough of Bran. Making love with him was like an addiction, her heightened sensitivity taking her places she'd never dreamed were possible. He didn't seem to mind, acquiescing every time she dragged him off to bed. But she was also aware that she was using him to forget the decision she had to make. Why not fly away on the wings of desire rather than think about resurrecting her mother from the dead? Even thinking in those terms gave her an odd feeling in the pit of her stomach.

The morning of the day her father was due back Bran stopped her for the first time. "Not right now, Kat," he said, taking hold of her wandering hands. "Dagda will be here at some point and I don't want to be in the throes of passion when he arrives."

Kat snorted. "I guess you're right."

He shifted on the bed, pulling himself up to sitting. "Have you made up your mind?"

Kat reached for her robe. "I have no idea what would be best."

"It's not about what would be best. This is about what you want. As I said before, don't let him talk you into anything."

"I have the sense that he'll do it no matter what I say." Kat's gaze slipped into the distance. "I have several questions to ask before I can make any kind of an informed decision."

She tied her robe and padded toward the kitchen. The mere idea of seeing Dagda again terrified her. He was a larger than life god whose mere existence was intimidating and difficult for her to fathom. Would she ever get used to the reality of being his daughter? *I sure wish you were here, Mom,* she thought to herself. *You'd know what to do.* She laughed at the irony.

It was just after noon when she heard the knock on the front door. Her heart leapt into her throat. "Go answer it," Bran said with a shooing motion. "I'll make myself scarce."

Kat straightened her shirt and ran her fingers through her hair, turning just in time to see Bran opening the window. A second later he was a raven and was exiting the apartment on wide wings. She hurried toward the door.

When she swung it open Dagda filled the entryway, his shoulders so wide that he had to turn sideways to enter the apartment. Should she offer him tea, a beer, coffee?

He took immediate control, moving past her to pace the apartment before settling on the loveseat she'd purchased at a garage sale. "Where is Bran?"

"He decided that we needed to be alone."

He nodded. "Smart thinking. Now tell me, Katel," he continued, his piercing sapphire eyes meeting hers. "What have you decided?"

Since his bulk nearly filled the entire loveseat she pulled a chair in from the kitchen table. "I haven't come to any conclusions," she muttered, settling on it. "I need to ask a few more questions."

He watched her expectantly.

"If she comes back what happens to Jack? He's in jail for murder and awaiting his trial. If she's alive it will negate it all, and I hate that man with a passion."

Dagda shifted, leaning forward with his big hands on his knees. "There are an infinite number of ways around this. Jack can never exist in her life, or Jack can be a man she was with for a while, and isn't now, or..."

"Okay, I get it. You can create whatever reality you want. But what about her memories, or mine, for that matter?"

"It's what you want it to be—you can remember everything that's happened or you can have the same memories your mother will have."

Kat frowned and looked toward the window where rain lashed against the glass. It seemed like the rain and cold had been going on forever.

Dagda nodded, as though he'd heard her thoughts. "The winter has been long, but soon wildflowers will appear, and all of a sudden birds will be singing and the sun will warm your back."

Kat gazed at him. "So poetic, but this is the city—yes, there will be birds, but flowers? Maybe a few."

"There are always flowers no matter how dreary the place where you live. Now please, can you bring your thoughts back to the matter at hand?"

"You said you'd be here some of the time. What does

that mean in real terms?"

"I have duties in Otherworld, Katel. But that does not mean I won't spend time with your mother. She will not be lonely."

When his eyes shifted and changed, turning soft with love, Kat knew he was desperate to be with Siobhan again. "If you loved her so much why did you leave?"

"Didn't I answer that already?"

"Not to my satisfaction."

Dagda leaned back and ran the fingers of both hands through his thick curls. "Soon after your birth I was caught up in a war—a conflict that took all my time and energy. Once it was over your mother had moved on."

"Jack Turner."

Dagda nodded. "I saw her only once after that, and what she told me convinced me to stay away. She said that Jack needed her more than I did, that Jack was a troubled soul who required her help."

"When was that? I thought she didn't get together with him until the year I turned thirteen."

"She met him earlier, but they didn't get married until a few years later."

Kat tried to remember the years *before Jack*, but they had slipped away as neatly as if they'd been cut free with a sharp knife. "She's fading," Kat murmured, her eyes filling.

"And she will be gone forever if we don't do something soon."

Kat stared at him. "But you told me that…"

"I know what I said. I was not lying when I said it, but as each day goes by I can feel her slipping further away. She is in between worlds right now."

"And if I say yes to resurrecting her—will you take away all my memories?"

"Do you want to keep what you know intact or do you want to be blissfully ignorant of all that has transpired this past year?"

"When Bran took my memories I always felt that something was lurking in the background of my mind, as though I'd forgotten something important. I don't like that feeling."

He scoffed. "I am better than Bran at clearing your mind, Katel. There are certain details I can leave and others I can take away, depending on what you want."

"And my heritage?"

"You will know me as your father, nothing more."

"And my relationship with Bran?"

Dagda shook his head.

"But I'm half goddess—why would you do that? We love each other and there is no reason we have to stay apart."

"I never said I would do anything. I am just allowing you to weigh your options."

"I want to keep all my memories," she said decisively.

Dagda nodded, his gaze opaque.

Kat woke more tired than she'd ever felt in her life. Every muscle ached, her head pounding.

"Are you awake?" she heard someone ask, turning to see a strange man in her bed staring at her. She let out a shriek and pulled the sheet up over her naked body. "Who are you?"

The man frowned. "Kat? You don't remember me?"

She shook her head and jumped out of the bed, backing away and trying very hard not to focus on his well proportioned unclothed body.

"Gods and dogs!" he roared, rising to pull on his jeans. "I knew he was messing around with shit, but how, after everything we've gone through, could he do this to you— or to me?"

"Who is *he,* and what things are you talking about?" she asked, moving toward the closet to dress. She shut herself inside, waiting for his response as she hurriedly pulled on a pair of jeans and a shirt.

"Kat...gods, I don't even know where to begin. That fucker is going to pay for this," he muttered darkly.

Kat heard him pulling on his boots and then the heavy clomp as he marched across the floorboards. A second later the door slammed.

Kat emerged from the closet and stared at the rumpled bed, puzzling over why he'd been here and what in hell was going on. Her body felt as though she'd had sex, but she had absolutely no memory of it. *Maybe Mom will know,* she thought, grabbing her phone off the table and punching in her number.

"No, sweetie, I have no idea what you're talking about. Would you like to stay here for a few days?"

"Is Dad around?"

"He's out of town for a week or so, but he'd love to see you too. Will you consider it?"

"I have to go to work but I'll come by later, if that's okay."

"It is absolutely okay."

Kat walked to her clerk's job at the bookstore, hoping the warm spring air would take away the strange feelings in the pit of her stomach. Waking to a stranger in her bed had definitely freaked her out. At least he'd left gracefully and not forced her into anything. Her mind twisted with flashes and visions that didn't seem part of this reality. Had she only dreamed the guy in her bed? He was certainly good-looking and his body was...*don't go there,* her inner voice warned. Something was seriously off.

39

irmid peered at Bran, noting his distress. His abrupt arrival out of the ether had taken everyone at the homeless camp by surprise. Hopefully they would chalk it up to alcohol poisoning. "He did what?" she whispered, not believing her own ears.

"Kat told me he was planning to bring her mother back to life but that he promised to keep Kat's memories intact. He lied to her and now she doesn't have a clue who I am. She's half goddess. Doesn't that count for anything?"

Airmid shook her head, anger spreading across her normally calm features. "It should. And also, I doubt Kat can be bewitched like this—she'll come out it of it sooner or later."

"And in the meantime what am I supposed to do?"

"I say this requires a special meeting. We might have to call upon the Moira."

The Fates? But they are not of our world…"

"They are not Celtic or even Norse, but it is Clotho, Lachesis and Atropis who decide life and death across all worlds. They will come if we require their assistance. All the gods must abide by their rule."

"Why didn't anyone complain when we discovered what Dagda intended to do?"

"Who knew besides the few of us? He gets away with it because of who he is."

"And yet he has broken our rules more than once."

Airmid nodded. "He does what he wants when he wants and is sure that no one will stop him."

Bran snorted. "Except Morrighan, who will have his head."

"Or some other necessary part of his anatomy."

Bran let out a laugh before his eyebrows pulled together. "If Kat's mother is now alive Kat will be devastated if we take her away again."

"Kat has no memory of anything but the present, the one that Dagda has just created. Once things are set back to the way they're supposed to be, she will know it's the right thing. It is what we must do unless the Fates decide differently." Airmid glanced toward the homeless camp where a fire burned brightly, the buzz of conversation moving across the expanse of rocks and dirt to where she and Bran stood. "We'd best get on with it before the entire scenario becomes so entrenched there is no way out."

"And he took away the cat I gave her. Bran is gone."

Airmid smiled sadly. "The cat was your way of keeping your memory alive?"

"Yes, but it didn't make her less attached to the creature. And now I'll have to start all over again."

"No, Bran, you won't. As soon as we fix this, her memories will be just as they were before Dagda decided to behave like a selfish lying tyrant." She grabbed his arm, tugging him toward the trees. "We're going to the castle."

Bran glanced back, noting that a mist had fallen all around them, obscuring the homeless camp from view. A second later they were in the ether.

Morrighan's mouth dropped open, her eyes narrowing and turning the color of red-hot embers. "You are telling me that Dadga, *my* Dagda, has resurrected a *human* woman that he had a child with twenty-one years ago?" Her fury echoed across the thick clouds, shredding them.

Airmid took a step back from the energy pouring from the goddess of war. "Most importantly he has lied to his daughter and swept away any memories she has of the past."

But Morrighan didn't hear her as she gathered her cloak around herself and disappeared in a swirl of black mist.

"I would hate to be in Dagda's shoes right now," Bran whispered.

Airmid turned to the other gods and goddesses gathered in the castle. "Shall we vote on whether to call on the fates?" She barely had the words out when nearly every god and goddess in the hall lifted their hands.

"We are decided then. The Dagda shall be called in front of a tribunal for crimes committed against Otherworld covenants."

Cernunnos, the horned god of the forest, stood up, his size and the stag horns erupting from his shaggy head adding to his stature. "And if he refuses to appear?"

"We will send out a search party and bring him

forward," the sun god, Lugh, replied, golden hair falling in waves to his shoulders. His bare chest was covered in tattoos of knotted Celtic symbols, his arms encircled with bands of the same. "He is not above our laws no matter what he thinks."

"This is true," Bran said, looking around the assembled group. "And as you all know by now, this young woman is half goddess and has pledged herself to me. What Dagda has done is a direct affront to all I stand for."

"Was this a purposeful act?" Cernunnos asked.

"I cannot say for sure, but the woman in question is his daughter, so it seems that he may have other suitors in mind."

"He does not consider you good enough for his daughter?" the warrior magician, Gwydion asked.

"Apparently not," Bran answered, his eyes turning as dark as coal dust.

There was a murmur of annoyance before Airmid clapped her hands. "Be that as it may, Dagda *will* appear in front of this court and explain himself. I will call on the fates and let everyone know when the next meeting will take place."

K at finished out her shift and got on a bus to go to her mom's house. Although the day was spring-like and warm, Kat's mood was as gloomy as the past winter months. Work had been uneventful, aside from the book she'd come across when she was shelving that related to gods and goddesses. It had caught her attention, and if hadn't been for an irate customer waiting for her at the counter, she would have taken it to read later.

The view outside the bus revealed trees leafing out and the bright yellow and purple contrast of daffodils and crocus poking up through the soil. It was spring, her favorite time of year, and yet she couldn't appreciate it. It was as though she'd woken up on the wrong side of bed, but this time it wasn't just bed, it was her entire reality.

The incident with the man still plagued her, her mind playing tricks whenever she thought back on it. She saw him smiling down on her, the pendant around his neck swinging and flashing in the sunlight. Her fingers went to her own pendant, feeling as she always did the hum of energy. Had he really had a nearly identical one around his neck? Her mind whirled away, taken to some completely different reality in which she and this man were comparing pendants.

She pressed her hands to her temples. *Please make it stop,* she whispered.

"Hi sweetie!" her mom greeted her when she arrived. "I hope work was okay for you today. Do you still like working there?"

Kat shrugged. "I don't know. Right now nothing much seems interesting. Where's Dad?"

"I told you he was gone for a few days. He has to work you know."

"What does he do, exactly?"

Siobhan let out a mirthless laugh. "Darned if I know. He never talks about work."

Kat noticed the lines of strain around her mother's mouth and the deep creases between her brows. Her mother wasn't happy either. "What's going on, Mom?"

Siobhan smiled. "Why, nothing dear, only missing your father."

"He's hardly ever here. I can't believe you don't know where he goes. He could be having an affair."

Siobhan pursed her lips and shook her head. "He wouldn't do that. He loves me."

"Love has nothing to do with it," Kat said darkly.

"But why would you even think that?"

Kat shrugged and let out a sigh. "It must be my bad mood. Something doesn't seem right today—maybe my stars are out of alignment."

Siobhan let out a tinkling laugh. "You and your stars. Pretty soon you'll be talking about gods and goddesses."

Kat stared at her mother in surprise. "I found a book today—it was all about gods and goddesses—Celtic, I think."

"Really?" Siobhan turned toward the carrots laid out on the butcher block and picked up a knife.

"You don't seem that interested."

Siobhan shrugged, the knife moving rhythmically.

"So when is he coming home?"

Siobhan stopped chopping to gaze at her daughter. "Well, to tell you the truth, I'm not really sure."

"This is unacceptable, Mom!" Kat shouted. "Dad can't just disappear for weeks and expect you to just wait for him. What are doing with yourself while he's gone?"

Siobhan stared into the distance. "Well, I cook, I clean, and I weed the garden. What else is there?"

"I thought you belonged to a book club and a gym."

"No, dear. Your father doesn't like me to be away in case he arrives home and I'm not here."

For a moment she had the strangest sensation that her mother wasn't real, just a robot that performed odd jobs around the house and serviced her father when he came home. Her head began to pound. "I think I need to go home now."

"Of course, dear. Whatever you think is best."

Her mom had practically begged her to come by and now she was just as happy to have her go? When she said goodbye her mother waved vaguely in her direction, all her concentration on the carrots in front of her.

Kat was in her apartment when she had another flash, this one stronger than the others. A very clear vision of the two of them, naked and entwined, came into her mind. And what they were doing was not something you did with a stranger. His body hovered over hers, the pendant around his neck swinging with his movements. She let out a gasp and put her hand over her mouth, trying to will the image of him away, but it stubbornly remained in her mind. And she was unable to stop the sudden feeling of arousal.

She sat on the loveseat and stared into space, fear settling into her as she tried to make sense of it. She had no memory of him, but her body did, the sensations unmistakable.

Kat was lost in a forest filled with gnarled trees. She was searching for something or someone, but couldn't find whatever it was. A pond came into view, dark but for the tendrils of moonlight cast across the water. In the distance she heard a man's desperate call, as though he was caught and either couldn't find her or was unable to get to her. Her heart went out to him but she knew she would never find him. He wasn't in this realm. She burst into tears.

In the morning Kat felt dragged out, as though she hadn't slept at all. She barely remembered the dream other than a feeling of loss. Her life felt robotic, as though both she and her mother had been assembled and sewn up by some creator playing with toys. She saw him as a puppet master, an evil grin on his face as he pulled the strings to make her dance.

When she left for work the world outside appeared hand made, the edges of it beginning to fray. Shimmering light hung in the far distance, making it seem as though that's where the world ended. If she walked far enough would she just fall off?

The people who came into the store didn't seem real to her either, their smiles pasted on, their clothes too perfect. When she gazed into the mirror her eyes had a glazed look, her hair not as she remembered it. *I must be losing my mind,* she thought. But something tugged at her consciousness, asking her to look deeper.

The rest of the day went by in a kind of haze as she shelved, did inventory and checked customers out. But it was the last customer who came in who stopped her in her tracks. "You!" she hissed, when he came to the counter holding the book on gods and goddesses.

"Sorry. I had to see you."

She glared at him, trying to find words after having the disturbing vision of the two of them. "What do you want?"

He smiled. "I want to buy this book."

She yanked it out of his hands and scanned it. "I thought it seemed interesting," she allowed, before telling him the price.

"It's about us—you and me," he said, glancing around to make sure no one was within earshot.

"Right. I'm a goddess and you're a god."

"I'm a god and you're half goddess," he corrected. "I'm Bran the blessed," he continued, opening the book to show her a picture of Bran.

She glanced at it, surprised by the uncanny resemblance, even down to the scruffy beard. "A lot of men look like that."

"Are they all the god of ravens and protection?"

A vision of a raven flew through Kat's mind just before she remembered seeing the same man who was standing in front of her climb up into a window, shape shift and fly away. She let out a cry, her hand going to her mouth.

"You believe me now?"

"No. I just had a weird vision."

He grinned and handed over the cash for the book. "We'll be together soon," he said, turning to head out the door. "Dagda's on trial."

Who in hell was Dagda? Kat wanted to run after him and grab his arm and make him tell her the rest of the story, but her boss arrived, his stern expression making her think twice.

"Are you closing up?" he asked.

"I...I didn't realize it was so late."

He must have noticed the confusion on her face because his expression softened. "Get out of here—I'll do the rest of it."

On the walk home Kat couldn't stop her thoughts from dwelling on Bran. He had a way about him, an assuredness that she admired. He was handsome and she was very attracted to him. Could it be because of the vision? It wasn't every day that she saw herself rolling around in bed with a man. When she noticed the raven hanging in the air about ten feet above her head she ducked and ran. But she wasn't really afraid of him.

When her cell phone rang she dragged it out of her bag and answered. "Just wanted to let you know that your father is back," her mother's lilting tone announced. "But Dag has told me that his next trip will be a long one.

Perhaps you'd like to come by before he has to leave again?"

"Not tonight, Mom. I'm too tired."

"Well, you'd better come soon. Dad leaves in two days."

"I'll see what I can manage."

The robot feeling was back and with it came the puppet master image. And this time it was her father pulling the strings. For some reason she was furious with him, black rage consuming her as she saw him in her mind's eye. If he was in front of her right now she wasn't sure what she would do. Tears threatened as she thought of her mother waiting for him endlessly. That was no way to live a life.

When the raven let out a screech and suddenly dropped out of the sky Kat took off running, sudden terror leaving her barely able to breathe. She hadn't minded it before, but this time the bird seemed dangerous and out of control. When she reached the apartment and glanced back, there was no sign of the enormous dark bird. Instead of being relieved she was left with an unsettled feeling, as though the bird represented some missing part of herself. *Stop it!* she told herself sternly, pushing the key into the lock.

"Hello, Kat!" Dag's voice boomed when she walked into her parent's house the next evening. He pulled her into his arms, nearly crushing the breath out of her.

"Dad, please!" she said, pulling away. "I'm not a little baby."

"I didn't say you were—you are a beautiful young woman with a wonderful life ahead of her—isn't she, Siobhan?"

"Yes, dear," Siobhan answered with her back to the two of them. She continued kneading dough, the rhythmic sounds hypnotic.

Dag marched over to her and drew her away from the butcher block. "You love me, don't you?"

She held her dough-covered hands out in front of her, her eyes unfocused. "Of course I do, dear."

"Siobhan—say it—say you love me."

"I love you, Dag."

"That doesn't sound at all convincing." Dag glanced at Kat. "Did it sound convincing to you?"

"I don't know, Dad. She did what you asked."

Dag's eyes turned dark, his eyebrows pulling together. "I made the perfect...the perfect place for you. I have populated...I mean, made everything exactly the way it should be. Why are you unhappy?"

Kat's mother stood stock still in the middle of the kitchen, her gaze on nothing. "But I am happy," she finally said.

"Gods and dogs!" he roared, his anger filling the room. "I want...I want you to be..."

"Dad, what is wrong with you?" Kat shouted. "Mom just told you she's happy."

He shook his head. "Lies—all lies. I did it wrong. I made a mistake. She isn't real—you're not real!" He pointed at Kat.

"What in hell are you...?"

"Do not swear! It is forbidden!"

"Dag, don't be mean to your daughter," Siobhan said, placing a restraining hand on his arm and leaving bits of dough. "Do you want me to wait for you in the bedroom?"

He threw her hand off and stomped toward the door, his eyes ablaze with a fire not normally seen in humans. "I fucked it all up," he muttered, opening the front door. A second later he was gone.

Kat stayed with her mom, hoping her father would come back. But finally she had to leave. There was only one more bus for the night. "Will you be okay?" she asked before she left.

Siobhan just stared into space without expression. "Of course I will, dear," she answered.

That night Kat had the same dream again, but this time she followed the calling voice across a meadow and through another forest until she came to a colorless void. 'Where are you?' she shouted. Mist swirled around her feet, obscuring her view, but when it cleared there was nothing but an empty blackness. She let out a gasp and stepped back from the gaping maw. She called again, her shrill voice sucked away into the darkness. There was no answer.

When she woke up she had the strangest feeling that her entire life was a dream. Like the movie she remembered seeing about the guy who lived inside a dome and didn't know it. *The Truman Show.*

41

The magnificent ceremonial hall of white marble and golden pillars was filled to capacity, the din of agitated conversations ringing out as gods and goddesses milled about discussing the upcoming event.

"Be seated!" a male voice called, clapping his hands.

Seats appeared in rows, those present finding their places among them.

On the dais the three fates wizened faces staring out expressionless over the assembled throng. On the stage with them sat Forsetti and Tyr, both Norse gods of justice who had been called upon to preside over the gathering.

When Morrighan swept in, a whirlwind came with her, leaves blowing across those already seated. She gathered her red cloak close, dark hair swirling around her face as she searched for a seat. When she found one next to Airmid, she leaned close. "That bastard has not dared to show his face to me since this fiasco began," she hissed. "I cannot wait to see him humiliated."

"That won't be all they do to him," Airmid whispered.

But the fates were standing and all whispering ceased.

They spoke as one, their voices melodic. "We are Clotho, who spins the thread of life, Lachsis, who measures the allotted time, and Atropis, who cuts life off with shears when the time is up."

Once they finished introducing themselves Forseti and Tyr stood. "We are here as the gods of justice who will decide the fate of the god accused today. The Dagda will be heard and his words weighed according to the laws of Otherworld and the realms of the gods. Who will bring this man forward?" Forseti boomed.

Cernunnos stood and motioned to the man sitting next to him. There was a collective gasp as the assembly got their first look at the current state of the Dagda. His clothes were torn, his hair filled with sticks, his face streaked with dirt and scratches.

"Cernunnos must have given chase," Morrighan whispered. "Did Dagda really think he could outrun him?"

Cernunnos led the father god forward and retraced his steps as Dagda settled in the chair set out for him. His face was haggard, his eyes bloodshot as he stared down at his feet.

"Poor baby," Morrighan hissed.

"Quiet," Airmid whispered.

"Who shall bring the charges against this man?" Forseti asked.

On the other side of Airmid, Bran stood up. "I will."

"And what have you to say against the all father god?"

Bran straightened and began to speak in a carrying voice. "Knowing full well that what he was doing was against our laws, the Dagda bedded a human woman and brought a child into the human world. And now he has resurrected the same woman from the dead so that she can once again be there for him. And to add to this offense he has taken the memories of his twenty-one year old daughter who is half goddess and just this year emerging into her power. All of this was done selfishly and with no regard for this woman's life or death, or the life of his daughter."

"And you have a vested interest in this!" Dagda shouted, his skin mottling with rage.

The fates let out a high-pitched trill that stopped his tirade.

"Kat and I had begun a relationship when the Dagda decided to strip her memories. He does not have the right to interfere in my life," Bran continued, "or in the lives of others. He has acted outside the bounds of our laws and shown himself to be self-serving tyrant who thinks nothing of others." The hall was silent as Bran finished and sat down.

"And you began this relationship before you knew her status!" Dagda shouted. "You should be up here on trial for your disobedience!"

Forseti raised a hand. "Please speak only when asked to speak," he said, glaring at Dagda before turning his gaze to the assembled throng. "Are there others who have a grievance to share?"

Morrighan stood, her eyes narrowed and dark. "Dagda has lied repeatedly to me and to all of us. He has spent time on earth with a human woman when we thought he was doing Otherworld business. He has brought an illegitimate child into the human world, and instead of introducing her to her heritage he has used his power to strip her status as a goddess. Katel is one of us and yet he has bound her to her human side. This must be resolved." Morrighan glared at Dagda before she flung her cloak dramatically and sat down.

"And who will stand up for this man?" Forseti called out.

"I will," a female voice called out from the back of the room. Rhiannon stood and faced the court. "The Dagda has broken rules, yes, but he has also done many good things. He has led us in battle, he has listened to our grievances and decided in a fair and just manner. He is the all father, the one we go to in times of need. This man made the mistake of falling in love with a human woman and having a child with her. Who among us can claim to be blame free when it comes to affairs of the heart? Can we not have sympathy when it comes to love or shall we condemn him for being true to himself? As far as his daughter is concerned, perhaps it is better for her to live her life out on earth and not know the pain of being a goddess."

"Sure has changed her tune," Bran whispered.

"Remember her life, Bran—she married a human and gave birth to his child. And she always takes the side of the downtrodden."

"Dagda isn't downtrodden—he's…"

Airmid put her hand on his arm when Forseti began to speak.

"Is there another who would care to offer a word in the Dagda's defense?" A moment ticked by and when no one spoke he turned to the accused. "Do you, Dagda, have something to say in your own defense?"

"I do," he said, standing. "Decades ago I fell in love with a human woman and we had a child together. I left her because I knew it was wrong. But when she recently died I was taken over by emotions I could not ignore. I had to do something, not only for her, but also for my grown daughter. I admit it was poor judgment on my part, but I cannot say that what I did was only for myself. My daughter…"

"Your daughter is now without her memories!" Bran shouted, standing.

"You are a selfish bastard who lied to her!"

Airmid tugged him down. "Don't give him reason to hurt you," she whispered.

"He can't hurt me now. He's in the wrong and he knows it."

The fates trilled again, their melodic voices echoing like birds.

"No more interruptions!" Forseti shouted. "Continue."

"I do not wish my daughter to be saddled with a lesser god," Dagda went on, "until she fully understands who she is."

"A lesser god?" Bran hissed, turning to Airmid.

"And I want her to be introduced to her power as a half goddess slowly, not all at once as some would have it," Dagda added, glaring at Bran. "She is not ready to place her life in the hands of one man or one god. She must find herself before she gives herself to another."

"You do not have the right to make that decision for her!" Bran yelled. "Kat *is* half goddess and needs to understand what that means!"

Forseti held up his hand. "If you interrupt this court again you will be removed. We will now hear from the fates."

The fates stood, the women who had been bent with age now young and beautiful, their eyes clear as they spoke as one. "There is no deviation from the laws of life," they called out. "The web of life was spun, the allotted time is gone, and the life has been cut with shears. This is how it is and how it always will be. This man has broken the sacred rule that governs life on earth and so he shall exact his fate."

Dagda paled as they finished speaking, his hands cradling his head.

"Tor will speak now regarding Katel."

Tor stood, a severe expression on his hiselled features. "Katel's memories are her own, as well as her relationships. Discovering her heritage is a natural progression that should not be halted. Protection is not an excuse for what the Dagda has done. I was inclined to be lenient about the other matter, considering the love he has professed for the deceased, but this act of cruelty against his daughter is not to be condoned." He glanced at Dagda before taking his seat.

"We will now discuss punishment and deliver our verdict," Forseti announced, turning to confer with Tyr and the fates.

The crowd grew restive as the moments went by, whispered conversations growing louder as arguments regarding Dagda's fate broke out. Finally Forseti called for quiet.

"We have come to a decision. Dagda, you will rise to hear the judgment." He waited a moment while the Dagda pushed himself to standing, the father god's features drawn.

"You will reverse what you have done, not only to

Siobhan Davies but also to Katel, your daughter. Siobhan will be as she was, dead and buried, and your daughter will know her life for what it is. You will have nothing more to do with the human realm. Once those tasks are completed you will be stripped of your powers for a period of not less than twenty years."

Bran shook his head. "Not stringent enough," he whispered.

"You want to kill him?" Airmid whispered back. "He is a god, you know. Can you imagine how he will feel without his power? It's beyond humiliating."

"Shush, you two," Morrighan hissed, leaning forward to hear.

"May I have time to say goodbye?" Dagda asked querulously.

"You may say goodbye, but then you must reverse the spell to the time when Siobhan's remains were still with the coroner."

"*Before* I met with Katel?"

"That is correct. There is to be no interaction between you and your daughter."

"But…who will instruct her…who will…?"

"That is the final judgment of this court!" Forsetti boomed out. "Once you return to Otherworld your powers will be stripped."

Dagda stared at the floor.

When Forseti, Tyr and the fates stood to signal the end of the meeting the crowd began to disperse, conversations regarding the verdict whispered as the gods and goddesses shuffled toward the entrance. "Not punishment enough," one god said, shaking his head. Another goddess had tears in her eyes. No one seemed particularly happy with the outcome, including the man accused who still sat at the front of the room with his head in his hands.

Morrighan pulled her cloak closed and headed toward Dagda. "You got what you deserved," she hissed, her eyes narrowing. "How could you do this to me? You are the most selfish and…"

Dagda grabbed her arm and held it in a vice grip. "What I did has nothing to do with you."

"It has everything to do with me. You cheated twenty-one years ago and you just cheated again. You've been lying all this time."

Dagda shook his head. "We could have gone on the way we were, Morrighan. Now it's all ruined."

Morrighan jerked out of his grasp. "You must be kidding. I never want to see you again." She stalked away without looking back, joining Bran and Airmid outside the entrance. "He actually seemed to think we could resume our affair."

Airmid let out a snort and Bran shook his head, his mouth in a thin line.

42

Kat shifted on the bed and opened her eyes. The world looked different this morning, as though some magician had sprinkled fairy dust all over everything. But a second later she remembered the exhumation and the mystery man who refused to reveal himself. She had to call Johansson and find out what had happened in the past couple of days while she'd been busy with Cerridwen's Cosmetic Cauldron.

She stretched and glanced at her phone. It was late, but today was a much-needed day off. She had a zillion things to do. Her phone rang while she was making coffee, Johansson's name appearing on the screen. She slid her finger across, hit speaker and then pushed the plunger down in her French press. "What's happening?" she asked, pouring coffee into a mug.

"I have some disturbing news," he answered. "Your mother's remains have been stolen."

"What? How is that even possible? Who would do such a thing?"

"I'm looking into it."

"Could Mr. Anonymous be that crazy?"

There was silence during which she heard muffled voices. A second later Johansson told her he had to go. "I'll call you later this afternoon."

At least Jack was in jail. The idea of stealing a desiccated body sounded macabre and ghoulish. An image of her mother in her spacious kitchen wearing a yellow dress with an apron over it appeared in her mind. Siobhan's hands were covered in dough and there was a large man hovering over her. Was that a dress her mom had worn in the past? If so she didn't recognize it. And who was the man? He didn't seem familiar. She sighed and shook it away, attempting to find something to eat for breakfast.

She was walking to the local grocery store an hour later when a man came up behind her and put his hands on her shoulders, scaring her half to death. When she pulled away and stared at him, the smile left his face.

"Kat?"

Kat backed away. "How do you know my name?"

His eyes darkened and narrowed. "That fucking bastard did it again." He waved his hands in the air, watching her intently for several moments before yelling, "Fucker!!!" at the top of his lungs.

Kat turned and hurried away. When she looked back the man was still standing in the middle of the sidewalk staring into space. Homeless, she figured, with his torn T-shirt and ripped jeans—and apparently crazy to boot.

She was home again by the time Johansson called back, his clipped tone giving her a bad feeling. "Haven't been able to pick up any clues from the coroner's office, and Simon tells me the place was locked up tight. There was no broken window or any other way to get in. I'm about fed up with this entire case. The important point is that we have the murderer in jail and he's about to be tried. Unless you care enough to pursue this latest curve ball, I say leave it. If some crazy idiot wants a skeleton let them have it."

"That doesn't sound like you," Kat said, surprised. "And I was hoping to rebury her."

"Are you religious?"

"No, but it seems the proper thing to do."

There was a heavy sigh. "There is no soul in those desiccated remains. Your mother is long gone. I can continue the investigation into the theft, but so far I haven't turned up one shred of evidence. This is taxpayers money we're using."

"What does Forseti say?"

"Who the hell is Forseti?"

"He...he's the...I'm not sure who he is," she finally admitted, her memories of him dissipating in a cloud of smoke.

"Well, if you remember let me know."

Kat spent the next half hour puzzling over Forseti and where the name had even come from. When she thought about it now it seemed like a made up name of a character in a book. But why would she have thought of it in the first place?

When she arrived at work the next morning Gwen was already there and going over the books. She looked up as

Kat walked in, the smile on her lined face making her seem ten years younger. "Such a lovely spring morning," she enthused, glancing out the window.

"It is nice outside today, but I...I..."

"What is it, dearie?"

Kat glanced at Cerridwen, wondering whether to share her latest turmoil. "Mom's remains were stolen," she finally said. "And Johansson is backing off the case—says it's not important enough to pursue."

Cerridwen's expression darkened. "The remains are gone?"

Kat nodded. "Do you remember a man named Forseti involved in the case? Johansson doesn't recall him and I...well, yesterday he seemed real enough, but now..."

Cerridwen looked startled for a moment before she frowned and looked away. A minute later she said, "Forseti doesn't ring any bells." She closed the drawer that held the receipts and turned the key in the lock. "Would you mind watching the shop while I run an errand?" she asked, tucking the key into her pocket.

"Not at all—take your time."

43

"I'm telling you he has broken the rules once again!" Airmid stared at Cerridwen before turning to Arianrhod, Bran and Morrighan. They had come together at the castle to talk over the events of the past few days. Corra and Rhiannon had both declined to meet again, stating firmly that they had no interest in discussing Dagda's fate.

"Did any of you hear anything more about his sentencing?" Airmid asked.

Bran shook his head. "But I did discover that Kat has no memory of me. I figured he did that to thwart me before he was stripped of his powers."

"What is his issue with you?" Arianrhod asked.

Bran shrugged. "We've never gotten along that well, possibly because I'm a protection god and he considers protection his domain. But this thing with Kat doesn't make any sense to me at all. He seems bound and determined to keep us apart."

Morrighan made a sound indicating her displeasure, her eyes turning a color somewhere between red and black. "I would like to strangle him," she muttered.

"We all would," Bran said.

Airmid gazed into space. "We'd better have a talk with Forseti and find out what happened."

Forseti was easy to find, his time in Otherworld including visiting with old friends and generally amusing himself. They discovered him at the hall, using it for his own personal meeting place. He knew nothing of what had happened, his expression registering anger when they shared their stories.

"I was giving him the benefit of a doubt, allowing him more time to say good-bye. You're saying that he's stolen Siobhan's remains and cut Bran off from Kat again? He has balls of steel."

"What if he's taken Siobhan and disappeared with her somewhere on earth?" Bran asked.

Forseti ran a hand across his face and stared into the far distance. "If that's what he's done it won't be easy to track him down. His powers are still intact and he's as clever as they come."

"Did you seriously expect him to submit that easily to having his powers stripped?" Morrighan shouted. "You should have known better than that. You have basically unleashed a powerful god on an unsuspecting earth. Who knows what havoc he could wreak?"

"And he's probably redone the resurrection spell he placed on Siobhan—made it better," Airmid added.

"Can you at least bring Kat's memory of me back? I tried to undo the spell, but he's woven it too strong."

Forseti looked from one to the other. "I'm not an effing

wizard. But I can try to undo some of the damage he's done."

"I'd like to find him and kill him," Morrighan muttered darkly. "And I wouldn't be kind in how I did it, either."

"I suppose I need to call back Tyr and the fates."

"Will we have another meeting?" Arianrhod asked.

Forseti glanced up from where he was staring at the marble floor. "We'll need to decide as a group how to handle this—so, yes."

The meeting was convened for the next day, the gods and goddesses shuffling in as though they had no interest in being there. Many were missing. The fates had declined to come, stating flatly that they had done their jobs. It was up to the counsel elders and the rest of them to decide their next moves.

Forseti paced back and forth rubbing his hand over his face as Tyr sat quietly behind him. When Tyr began to speak the assembly grew suddenly still, listening carefully to what he had to say.

"This is an unusual circumstance," he began, his deep voice resonating. "We have made a judgment in this case and that judgment has been ignored. From my perspective I say it behooves us to find the Dagda and punish him— this time more severely. We are setting a bad example if we do not pursue this to the best of our ability."

"Who among us will volunteer to find this man and bring him back to justice?" Forseti asked.

Cernunnos stood, as well as Flidais, the goddess of the

woodland. A moment later another god stood, an enormous shaggy dog standing next to him. "I am Nodens. My dog and I will track Dagda and we will find him, no matter how far and wide he travels."

Forseti nodded. "Once the meeting is concluded you three will approach the dais for further instruction."

Once the meeting was over Bran turned to Airmid and Morrighan, his brows furrowed. "With his magic intact Dagda may be able to elude his hunters for a very long time. In the meantime Kat doesn't know me. If he was in front of me right now I would kill him."

Morrighan made a face. "I may just go after him myself even it I'm not on the list. He owes me."

"I hope Forseti can do something about Kat's memories," Airmid said, turning to Bran. "What are the chances?"

"Slim to none?" Bran said. "I may have to start over again."

"That could prove difficult," Cerridwen said, joining them. "She now thinks you're some crazy homeless person."

"And what's with Kat's powers? Did he bind them?" Bran asked.

"Apparently so," Cerridwen answered. "When she asked about Forseti I had to lie—I couldn't attempt to explain who he was if she had no memory of him."

"Will she come out of it? It's not possible for an elder god to bind a goddess's powers forever, is it?"

No one had an answer.

44

Kat's days seemed to drag, her nights even worse. Something nagged at her constantly, a thought that remained stubbornly just out of reach. On her way to work that morning she noticed the homeless man darting to hide behind cars and into alleys every time she glanced in his direction. She tried to ignore it, to tell herself he was harmless, but she wondered.

"Oh, don't worry about him," Cerridwen said later when she mentioned what had happened. "He's a fixture around here…no one pays him any mind."

But the worried expression in the older woman's eyes belied her statement. Something was wrong, not only about him, but also her general sense of the world around her. All she knew was that her mind seemed to have slipped a cog, her thoughts at times wild and scattered, featuring odd scenarios that had never happened.

The trial was going forward but so far she'd refused to be present for any of it. She had no desire to see Jack Turner, nor did she want to stand up in a courtroom and tell what she knew of him. The idea of bringing back that horror on top of everything else seemed over the top. If she wasn't careful she might have to seek out a therapist.

Unfortunately her wish to stay out of it was not to be. A few days later she was forced to be there, her testimony necessary after Jack's lawyer managed to wheedle out of a few of the charges. Johansson called her to tell her that despite having the physical evidence of poison, Jack insisted that he had nothing to do with it. His version of events was that she'd poisoned herself or someone else had, perhaps her daughter. "Katel is not right in the mind," he'd told the judge.

The morning Kat was due in court she rose from bed bleary and out of sorts; her sleep had been disrupted by the incessant cawing of a raven right outside her window. Even the earplugs she'd bought couldn't drown out his pathetic cries that went on and on. Why had he picked her window to peck at? He was still there, his beady eyes scaring her whenever she happened to glance that way.

Not only was she out of sorts and feeling half crazed from lack of sleep, but also the Uber driver was late. She barely made it to the courthouse in time to meet with the prosecuting attorney, a man named Forseti, who's name she vaguely recognized, although his appearance didn't seem familiar. He acted like he knew her, taking hold of her arm in a casual way to pull her into a secluded corner to give her tips on how to deal with the questions the lawyer for the defense would throw at her.

"Do not let him bait you," he warned. "His lawyer is

tricky, as you probably guessed from your deposition."

Kat nodded, remembering her stress and the questioning that seemed to twist her thoughts. As she continued to listen to Forseti she wondered why the room around her seemed to expand and contract with every breath she took. Lights flickered at the edge of her vision, a headache brewing. "I'm not feeling well," she told him.

"Nerves," he said, nodding. "This entire scenario is ridiculous. We have him dead to rights."

"Except we really don't," Kat muttered.

A few minutes later they walked into the courtroom, Kat's headache growing more intense with every step. Forseti smiled and gave her the thumbs up when she was called forward.

The defense attorney was relentless, trapping Kat in double binds and twisting her words to suit his purposes. "What motive would I have to kill her?" she finally shouted.

"Money. She was leaving it all to you until Mr. Turner convinced her to change her will."

"Objection!" Forseti shouted. "Documents not in evidence."

"Sustained," the judge said.

"Doesn't convincing her to change her will sound kind of suspect?" Kat asked, glaring at the judge.

The judge's narrow gaze met hers. "You will please limit your comments to the questions asked."

"Your mother died from arsenic poisoning? Is that correct?" the lawyer continued.

"Yes."

"Was the arsenic ever discovered?"

Kat looked toward Forseti, not sure how to answer. When he shook his head, she said, "No, I don't think so."

"So there is no DNA evidence to prove that Jack Turner did anything to hurt your mother. Is that correct?"

"There was evidence of the poison in her system and I think there was some DNA evidence of Jack there as well—I can't remember now," she said, one hand going to her head that hurt so much she felt like she might faint.

"So in truth you could have killed her just as easily as the innocent man on trial here," the lawyer said.

"Objection!" Forseti yelled. "The police arrested Jack Turner because they found physical evidence to connect him. This young woman was away at the time of her mother's death."

"Sustained," the judge said wearily.

Kat fell back against the chair, her breathing erratic.

By the time the defense attorney was finished with her Kat was seeing black spots in front of her eyes, her head splitting. When Forseti stood to cross-examine she hoped she had the wherewithal to keep it together.

"Were you aware of your mother's will?" he asked.

"No. She never mentioned it and I always thought she didn't have one."

"Perhaps this so-called will was fabricated."

"Objection!" the defense attorney shouted.

"Sustained," the judge said. "Please keep your questioning on track, Mr. Forseti."

In the meantime Kat had locked eyes with Jack Turner, the man's secret smile making her feel sick to her stomach. She knew without a doubt that Jack would get off, she could tell when she glanced at the dubious expressions on the jury members' faces. In her mind she saw the jury foreman rise and pronounce the verdict of 'not guilty'. Before Forseti could ask another question she lurched from the chair and stumbled down, nearly falling in her haste to be out of the courtroom.

Forseti caught up with her in the hall on her way toward the exit. "You can't leave, Katel. He's…"

She turned and stared straight into his ice blue eyes. "He's going to get off unless you make him produce that will. Mom never wrote a will and if he has one he forged it. You'd better do some magic, Mr. Forseti, or a guilty man will walk." She turned and stalked away, pushing the door open with her hip before raising her hand to call a taxi.

"You did well," Cerridwen told her later after plying her with herbs to take away her headache. "You cannot let him escape punishment for what he did, both to your mother and to you. I cannot believe they tried to implicate you in this."

"I thought it was a done deal," Kat said weakly, sitting on the stool behind the counter. "If that lawyer can't produce more evidence he *will* get off. I had a vision."

Gwen swiveled to stare at her. "A vision? What kind of vision?"

"Jack was free and he had this disgusting grin on his face."

Gwen watched her for a moment before turning to absentmindedly dust off a shelf. "Any other visions you can remember?" she asked, gazing down at the shelf of boxed creams.

Kat frowned. "I saw the jury foreman relay the verdict of not guilty, but that wasn't a vision, it was more like a premonition." She glanced at Gwen. "I used to have the most wonderful dreams and now I wake up feeling sad, like something is missing, but I don't know what it is."

"My poor girl," Gwen said, gazing at her. "I suggest meditation. It does wonders to calm the brain and allow the subconscious to arise. As to the trial, I think you should trust the prosecution to do their job."

Kat was in the back of the shop when she heard the door open and close. A moment later she caught bits of the conversation between Gwen, and of all people, Forseti. "You may have to employ your powers," she thought she heard Gwen say, "Kat had a vision of him getting off." And then Forseti's whispered reply, "I decided that two days ago. That murdering bastard is not getting away with this, no matter how clever his lawyer is."

"I thought you were the most clever of all."

Kat emerged from the back to see Forseti and Gwen standing close together with their hands clasped. "I didn't know you two knew each other," she said, surprised.

Gwen pulled her hands away and smiled sheepishly. "Is this the man representing you? I wish you had mentioned his name. Forseti and I go back a long way."

"I thought I did mention it. Did I hear you say something about powers or magic?"

Forseti laughed. "I've been known as 'the magician' in several cases I've worked on."

"Why don't you head home, dear," Gwen urged. "You look utterly done in."

"Thanks. I think I'll take you up on that." When she left the store they were still talking.

On her walk home Kat tried not to see the homeless man darting in and out of shadows, but when he peeked around a corner she couldn't take it anymore. "Leave me alone!" she shouted before hurrying on. But later when she was checking her phone for messages she accidentally hit the photo icon and brought up two selfies of the two of them together. In one his arm was around her neck and they both had idiotic smiles on their faces and in the other he was behind her, his chin resting on her shoulder. She stared at them for probably five straight minutes.

That night she meditated for the first time in her life, her thoughts floating away as she sat cross-legged with her hands on her knees. She'd seen enough videos to know the form and had read enough to know that she needed to breathe in and out of her nose. What she didn't expect was the vision of a life she didn't recognize. She let it float by and tried hard not to attach to what she was seeing, but when an image of the homeless man, naked and in her bed, appeared, her eyes flew open. She was suddenly acutely aware that she'd been there with him and they'd been going at it like rabbits. That coupled with the selfies had her reeling; what in holy hell was happening? Was there mental illness in the family? Now that her mother was gone there was no one to ask.

The next day she ditched work and went for a walk in the park. She needed quiet to analyze the vision and the photos and come to some reasonable conclusion about them—if there was one.

She was looking at the photos again when a very large man with piercing blue eyes appeared right in her path. She tried to skirt around him, but instead of moving out of the way he stood his ground, his gaze moving to her phone for a moment before focusing on her. She tried to back away, but it was like she was paralyzed, her feet rooted to the spot. When he moved his hands in some intricate dance in front of her face she squeezed her eyes shut, sure that he was about to accost her. But when she opened them again there was no one there. Her phone lay on the ground at her feet, and the photos she'd been examining were gone.

45

"Anything encouraging to tell me?" Airmid asked, glancing at Bran next to her. They were using the healing spring like a hot tub, soaking together.

He shook his head, running his fingers through his wet hair to get out the tangles. "She still has no memory of me, and as far as I can tell she has no powers at all. That bastard did a real number on her."

Airmid twisted sideways to grab a hazel branch to rub across her back. "You've given up?"

"I'm up here, aren't I? There's no point in stalking her. I was scaring the crap out of her."

"What does Cerridwen say?"

"She says that Kat had a few visions about me and also about the court case, but that now they've stopped. I thought maybe the goddess part of her was overriding what Dagda did, but I guess not."

"Maybe Dagda redid the spell."

Bran turned from where he was watching a dragonfly. "He'd have the nerve to appear to her?"

"She wouldn't recognize him."

Bran let out a sigh. "I hate this. I miss her so much and I can't do a fucking thing about it."

"There's been no hint of Dagda anywhere."

"Who said that?"

"Cernunnos and Flidais. The other Norse god with the dog hasn't been seen or heard of since the day he left."

"Nodens hates the Dagda as much as we do right now. I hope to hell he finds him. Where could a god hide out for this long without being detected?"

"Probably in plain sight."

"At least Forseti managed to put Kat's stepfather away for the murder. He resorted to his god powers, didn't he?"

Airmid nodded. "He thought that the defense attorney might have been a wizard."

"Wow. What the hell is going on down there?"

"Have you tried to bring her memories back?"

"Yes. And it did nothing. What I can't believe is how Dagda managed to bind her goddess power so completely."

"That's the reason I think he comes by periodically to do it again—maybe one of those times he'll get caught."

"By who? She won't remember him, and with the exception of Cerridwen, the rest of us are up here now. He's certainly smart enough to pick his moments. Is there any god or goddess who is powerful enough to undo this?"

Airmid handed him the hazel stick. "Maybe in the Norse realm. Odin could certainly manage it, but who's going to ask him?"

"If it meant getting Kat back I'd be willing to try."

Airmid's eyes widened. "Have you met him?"

"No, but how bad…?"

"Bad, Bran. Very bad."

46

Forseti subpoenaed the will, and despite Jack's protestations that there had never been a will, it was found and shown to be a forgery. With the motive clear and the incriminating information about the suspicious death of at least one other wife, the jury found him guilty and Jack was taken away to prison for first-degree murder.

Kat had been in the courtroom that day and knew that Forseti had done something illegal to prove Jack's guilt. But to her it didn't matter, a burden finally lifting when Jack was removed from the court in handcuffs.

Outside the courtroom she thanked Forseti profusely and tried to pay him, but he refused her money. He told her goodbye and strode away without a backward glance.

At work a few days later Kat spoke to Gwen about her recent meditation experience, the older woman laughing when she relayed the recurring vision having to do with the homeless man. "Perhaps you are attracted to him deep down," she said, smiling.

"I found a couple of photos of the two of us on my phone. How could that be? He's a bum and I don't know him!"

Gwen's smile faded. "Photos? Can you show me?"

Kat shook her head. "A man came by when I was in the park and I dropped my phone. They were gone after that."

"A man? What did he want?"

Kat shrugged. "He waved his hands around and I closed my eyes. When I opened them again he was gone."

Gwen stared at her. "Stay away from the park, Kat."

"But what about those weird photos? How did they get on my phone?"

Gwen sighed. "I don't know, dear. But as I've said before, the homeless one is harmless. Perhaps it was a premonition?"

"You mean I imagined them? And a premonition sounds like something will happen between us in the future. Is that what you mean?"

Gwen smiled. "If they aren't there now, what other explanation can there be? As far as the bum, as you call him, who knows what lurks beneath that rough exterior?"

Kat let out a derisive snort, but she felt unsettled, her mind back on the vision of the two of them rolling around in her bed like there was no tomorrow. And she was the one taking the initiative. A flush of heat rose into her cheeks. She had never been like that wild woman who seemed possessed and crazed in her pursuit of pleasure.

It was a week later that Kat realized that the homeless guy had disappeared. He was like a feral cat that she knew was okay as long as she saw him every day, but now that he was gone she worried that something terrible had happened to him. As to the photos, weirder things had happened.

Maybe Gwen had been right all along—there was a small part of her that was attracted to him. The visions in her meditation were proof of that.

As the weeks and months rolled by Kat forgot all about the homeless guy, her visions and her worry about them fading with his absence. Two men had expressed interest in her and she was sure that one of them would ask her out the next time she ran into them at the coffee shop They were both nice enough.

In the meantime she'd developed an interest in herbs, especially the ones used in the herbal skin cream formulas; it honestly felt like she'd had a past life in which she was proficient in herbal lore, knowing exactly what combinations would work for the different creams and even the right amounts to use.

Being in the woods felt like a dream she'd once had, her searches always taking her along narrow animal paths leading to tiny streams that murmured in a language all their own. Whenever she left the main trail, heading off into the underbrush, it was as though the entire ecosystem changed, a shimmery haze filling in under the trees and the sun coming out when before the day had been cloudy. It felt magical, as though fairies might be living under the leaves and rocks, her imagination taking flight as she saw glints and glimmers of something that wasn't really there.

Sometimes she even imagined she heard the tiny creatures whispering.

When she rested beneath the shade of a massive oak tree her fingers went automatically to her Celtic knot necklace. It seemed to hold some essence of the woods, a tingling coming from it that sent more fanciful images running through her mind. Her trips began to take on new meaning as she searched not only for the mint and other ingredients for the creams, but also for mushrooms, herbs, berries and nuts. She was startled at how much she seemed to know.

"You are so good at this," Gwen said one morning when Kat added another batch of ground up herb to the stash in the back. "My daughter is very appreciative of the help."

Despite Gwen's warnings she continued to walk in the park, sure that her one encounter with the strange man wouldn't happen again. She was wrong. Twice he'd appeared at dusk just as she was turning to head home, her attention suddenly riveted by his piercing blue eyes. When he was in front of her it was as though she couldn't move, fear ballooning inside her chest and making it hard to breathe. He always made the same odd movements with his hands and she always either turned away or closed her eyes, reopening them to discover there was no one there.

She began to wonder about him and about how she felt after these strange encounters, like something important had been stolen from her. Her body would go strangely limp, as though her energy had all been sucked away. And when she reached home all she wanted to do was sleep.

Gwen was very disturbed when Kat told her about it, her eyes widening in alarm. "I warned you the last time you mentioned this. How many times have you seen him?"

"Two or three? He doesn't hurt me, although it is kind of freaky and I feel weak afterwards."

"Kat, listen to me. You *must* stay away from the park. That man is extremely dangerous. If you see him again, run as fast as you can in the other direction, preferably toward people."

"Who is he?" Kat asked.

But Gwen had nothing more to say on the subject. When she spoke a few minutes later it was to encourage Kat to increase her meditations. "It is the most important thing a human being can do," she said, her intense gaze holding Kat's. "That is where the magic lies. Please heed my advice."

Kat tried not to worry, telling herself that Gwen was probably concerned about rape or murder, but it seemed as though she knew more than she was saying. As to the photos, she was pretty sure she hadn't imagined them. Her world seemed to be unravelling, and her mind with it.

When Cedar finally asked her out it was a nice diversion, his attentions taking her away from her morbid thoughts about being crazy. They went to dinner and afterward, when he asked her to his apartment for a nightcap, she said yes. He had a nice smile and so far she'd enjoyed their time together. He poured snifters of brandy and brought them to the couch where she sat, handing her one. "I've never had brandy before," she said, sniffing the amber liquid.

"It's good stuff. Swirl it around for a moment and then take a small sip."

She did what he suggested, her mouth and throat burning when she swallowed. "Whoa. That's strong."

He grinned and took the glass from her, placing it on the coffee table next to his. A second later he moved close, his arm going around her shoulder. Before she could say anything his lips were pressed against hers, his tongue inside her mouth. She jerked away and stared at him.

"What's the matter?" he asked, surprised.

"I…I'm not ready for that," she said.

He frowned. "When you agreed to a nightcap I figured…"

"That I was easy?"

He shrugged and picked up their glasses and took them to the sink. "We've been talking for a while now," he said with his back to her. "I thought we…"

She rose and went to stand beside him. "I don't know you well enough to jump into bed, Cedar. I'm not like that."

He turned. "Kissing isn't jumping into bed, Kat."

She stared into his brown eyes, a whisper of memory moving through her. She had the sudden sense she was betraying someone. "I have to go home," she told him, moving toward the door.

"I'll walk you," he said, grabbing his jacket off the back of a chair. "Sorry if I came on too strong."

Kat smiled. "No worries. But let's just take things slow, okay?"

47

"We have to do something to stop this!" Cerridwen's voice echoed, the trees around the castle shivering with her anger. "I've warned her not to go to the park, but he isn't stupid. Dagda will discover her no matter where she is."

Behind where she and the others had gathered the castle shimmered, moving in and out of focus. It took magic to keep it alive, magic that came and went with the gods and goddesses now that they no longer assembled there on a regular basis. Something was shifting in Otherworld, the absence of an elder god diminishing the realm's essential aura.

Airmid's expression darkened. "How do we stop an all-powerful god who is as stealthy as they come? Until he's found we won't be able to curtail what he's doing."

"Why hasn't Nodens found the bastard yet?" Morrighan hissed, a frown of fury on her features. "It's been months and months and Dagda is getting away with breaking every law there is!"

Cerridwen glanced at Bran, who hadn't said one word. "What do *you* think?"

"I agree with you. I can't stand this. I'm in love with her, and every time Dagda reworks the spell it signals more waiting time until we can be together."

"You're the god of protection, Bran. Think about it in those terms. We cannot allow Dagda to continue what he's doing. There has to be some way you can keep her safe."

Bran gazed into the distance, his brows furrowed in a frown of concentration. "I would have to glamour myself to do any good at all," he said hesitantly. "She knows me as the crazy man who stalked her."

Cerridwen gazed at him for a moment before her eyes brightened. "I have an idea, but I am not sure you'll like it."

hen Kat arrived at the shop, Gwen had already opened, her bright smile taking away some of Kat's depression; she hadn't slept much at all, what with the fractured bits of dream images scattering across her short sleep cycles and waking her up. She couldn't shake the wrongness of Cedar's overture, the strange sensation of betraying someone still with her.

Once she was inside the store the older woman's expression grew serious. "I have a problem and I'm wondering if you can help me with it."

Kat pulled off her light sweater and went into the back to hang it and her satchel on the coat rack. She ran her fingers through her wind tossed hair before returning to the front. "What's up?"

Gwen gazed out the open door where dried leaves swirled in patterns. "I have a friend who has fallen on hard times and is unable to care for her son," she said, turning to face Kat. "She doesn't want to place him in foster care because she's afraid that once things are better they will make her jump through too many hoops to get him back. Is there any chance you'd be willing to let him bunk with you? He's a sweet and helpful kiddo and would be no trouble. I know your place is small, but I can buy you a futon or whatever you might need. Also I told her that I'd give you a monthly stipend to cover your costs."

Kat just stared at her, trying to wrap her mind around such an undertaking. "How old is he—what about school?"

"Mary was home schooling him. You could continue that if you had any interest in it. He loves the woods and he's interested in nature. You could take him along when you gather herbs."

"You didn't say how old he is."

"He's twelve."

"And his name?"

"Brant."

Kat gazed into the street where traffic was piling up. Rush hour. "I don't know, Gwen. It sounds daunting."

"What about it seems difficult?"

"I know nothing about children. What if something happens to him? I'm not equipped to…"

"I will be at the other end of a phone call, Kat. I would take him myself but I'm getting too old for such things. As far as being responsible for his health, Mary has given me his shot records and all health records. And there's a pediatric clinic not two blocks from your apartment."

"You've thought this through, I see," Kat muttered.

When a customer entered the store Gwen picked up her cell phone and disappeared into the back, leaving Kat to help her.

Once the woman walked out Kat stared after her, still

caught up with Gwen's proposal. She heard bits and pieces of the conversation Gwen was having with someone, her mumbled words of, 'Yes, I think she'll do it,' and '…perfect solution to our dilemma….'keep her safe'. But when another customer came in she had to turn her attention to helping the woman find what she needed.

It was after lunch before Kat had a moment to revisit the topic of being a surrogate foster mother. She was twenty-two now, plenty old enough to have a toddler of her own. And although this child was twelve and not hers, perhaps it was time to get used to the idea of taking care of someone other than herself. "Did you consider anyone else for this foster mother gig?" she asked Gwen in between customers.

"You were my first pick, Kat."

"And what about my job here? I can't leave him alone at my apartment."

"You can bring him along and leave him in the back to study. I have all his workbooks from Mary. Perhaps you can teach him the ropes here? He's certainly capable of wrapping the products for customers."

"What if we don't get along? He may not like me, especially if he misses his real mom."

"You are a loving person with a good head on her shoulders. I'm certain that you and Brant will get along splendidly."

"I just started going out with a man named Cedar. Can I still date or do I need to be home all the time?"

"Brant is twelve years old. I'm sure he can manage on

his own for a few hours. But if you and this Cedar might want to, well, you know, there won't be much privacy."

Kat let out a snort. "We can go to his place if it comes to that, but I'm definitely not thinking in those terms right now."

Gwen nodded. "Probably need to be cautious now with HIV and the other venereal diseases running rampant."

Why was she talking about venereal diseases? Kat shook her head. "Condoms are a given, Gwen. When are you thinking about beginning this venture?"

"As soon as we get whatever you might need. I can call today and have a futon delivered."

"I have a couch he can sleep on. More furniture is not going to work—the apartment is too small. What about food?"

"He'll eat whatever you eat. He's not picky."

"What if things don't work out—can I back out?"

Gwen smiled. "Of course, Kat. Nothing is set in stone. But I have the sense that you will grow very fond of this young boy. Shall I bring him by tonight?"

"I guess so. I don't have any plans."

"Good then. We will arrive shortly after the dinner hour."

Kat tried to imagine another person living in her studio apartment, failing miserably. The bathroom was the only room with a door. Undressing and dressing could be a major issue, especially with a boy that age. "Is he modest?"

Gwen frowned. "Modest? You mean embarrassed about his body?"

Kat nodded.

"I doubt it seriously since he was mostly raised in the

woods and on the street. Why?"

"Well, the apartment doesn't have much privacy."

Gwen shrugged. "From what his mother has told me Brant ran around naked until a year or so ago. Unless you have a problem I doubt it will be an issue."

When she heard the knock Kat hurried to the door. When she opened it Gwen was standing there and next to her was a tall gangly boy with bright hair and the most beautiful moss green eyes she'd ever seen. He was wearing torn jeans, a Grateful Dead T-shirt and dirty tennis shoes, a grin lighting up his eyes. Reaching to take the small carpetbag out of his hands, she smiled and stepped aside. "Please come in."

Fin

If you enjoyed this book please leave a review on the site where you purchased. To visit the author, please visit her website at: www.nikkibroadwellauthor.com
Read the exciting beginning of *Dagda's Daughter*, the next book in the series!

1

Oagda gazed out the picture window that overlooked the city, admiring the view from thirty stories up. Skyscrapers dotted the view, their reflective walls mirroring the other buildings around them. Copper, silver and gold competed for prominence as cloud shadows raced across intermingling with the images. He smiled, his mind returning as it always did to his perfect situation. Being a CEO of a major corporation was what he'd been born to do. It had taken him all of five minutes to convince the ones in charge that he was the man for the job. Being a god living on earth definitely had its perks.

A soft knock brought him out of his reverie. "Come!" he bellowed, moving behind his desk.

"Sorry to disturb you, sir," the mousy, bespectacled woman murmured, moving into the room. "But we have a situation that requires your attention." She moved forward to place a sheaf of papers on his desk. "First quarter earnings are looking good, but there is one slight hitch."

"And what is that?" he asked, looking down at the papers.

"New competition, sir. We are no longer the only game in town."

"Well, in that case," he said, glancing up at her, "get hold of the team and set up a meeting for this afternoon."

"Yes, sir," she said, backing out and closing the door behind her.

Dagda pressed his lips together and shook his head. Humans were so quick to fear the worst. Luckily the men and women he'd handpicked for his team were a bunch of cutthroats who only cared about the bottom line. In this world corporations were where the power was solidified—power that could be used politically. He chuckled, thinking about the congress that now ate out of his hand. If he ran for president he would win hands down.

When the Celtic knot ring on his finger caught his eye he had a moment of misgiving, his thoughts going to his wife, Siobhan. She was heavy with his child, the second one he'd bestowed upon her. Siobhan no longer remembered the first life the two of them had shared together, or the girl baby she'd given birth to. In her mind the baby she carried was her first. And he'd made her young again, in her best childbearing years.

Despite being his creation she retained her earlier sweetness and sense of right and wrong. Thank goodness this try had worked—his first try at resurrection had failed miserably, causing problems he was still dealing with. He imagined her in his mind's eye, her belly swollen with new life, her beautiful hazel eyes and sweet smile; his heart contracted with love, the feelings for her overwhelming in their intensity. If she ever discovered the treachery he used to run his company she would be furious with him. Luckily she didn't know anything about what he really did, her innate trust giving him free rein to conduct his life as he saw fit.

From there his mind turned to Katel, his first child with Siobhan. He'd bound her goddess powers and taken away her memories of the man she loved. Bran was a god, but not one Dagda wanted as a son-in-law or the father of his grandchildren. Bran was too soft, too loving. Katel needed a stronger man, one who could navigate this world that was turning darker and more evil with each passing day; power was the name of the game and whoever Kat ended up with needed to be an expert at playing it. Certainly he could set her up with one of his team; he could think of at least two of them who were the right age and handsome and smart enough to fit the bill. *She will be better off,* he told himself, trying to rationalize what he'd done and was planning to do.

Although living in another city, he spied on her from time to time; he had to bind her powers more often now that she had turned twenty-two. She seemed happy enough, but why she had a preteen boy living with her was perplexing. How had that come about? He would have to investigate further and find out what was going on. He had noticed that she was more difficult to locate these days. And when he did find her he had to use stronger magic to constrain her strength. He chuckled, thinking about what a mighty goddess she would make once he decided to unbind her; his god genes were strong. But when that would be, he didn't know—perhaps never if his life here continued the way he hoped. Soon he would be a father again with another half-god child—a boy. And this time he would be around to raise him.

He still felt constriction around his chest whenever he thought about Katel, some remaining guilt always rising up in him until he slammed it back where it belonged. He let out a humorless chuckle. *Is Katel my conscience? I was nicer back then,* he thought, trying to let go of the shame that always accompanied his forays into the past. Luckily the team chose that moment to arrive, their entrance into his office bringing his attention back to the present. He breathed out a heavy sigh and turned to deal with the problem at hand.